Mrs. Laurence Edmondston

The Young Shetlander, or Shadow Over the Sunshine

Being Life and Letters of Thomas Edmondston

Mrs. Laurence Edmondston

The Young Shetlander, or Shadow Over the Sunshine
Being Life and Letters of Thomas Edmondston

ISBN/EAN: 9783337136727

Printed in Europe, USA, Canada, Australia, Japan

Cover: Foto ©Raphael Reischuk / pixelio.de

More available books at **www.hansebooks.com**

THE YOUNG SHETLANDER,

OR

Shadow over the Sunshine:

BEING

LIFE AND LETTERS

OF

THOMAS EDMONDSTON,

NATURALIST ON BOARD H.M.S. "HERALD."

EDITED BY

HIS MOTHER.

EDINBURGH:
MOULD & TOD.
1868.

Preface.

THE following record has been often asked for, by the many friends of a talented and greatly beloved young man. It is at length offered in the hope that it may prove instructive as well as interesting.

The locality where he was born and brought up is peculiar and little known, even in these days of incessant travelling. Thirty years ago it was in a much more primitive and isolated condition. Steam communication, penny postage, and cheap literature, were then in the first stages of existence, for which reason some of the episodes and descriptions that mingle with the biographical narrative are recorded, as displaying a phase of society now almost obsolete in Britain, and also as illustrative of their bearing on the formation of a powerful and attractive character.

The study of Natural History, to which the subject of this memoir was so enthusiastically devoted, and in which he was so successful, is in these days much more generally pursued than in his time, and seldom fails to prove interesting. Thomas Carlyle lately thus wrote of it—" For many years it has been one of my constant regrets that no schoolmaster of mine had a knowledge of Natural History, so far at least as to have taught me the little winged and wingless neighbours, that are continually meeting me with a salutation which I cannot answer, as things are! I love to prophesy that there will come a time when in all Scottish towns and villages the schoolmaster will be strictly required to possess such capabilities."

In perusing the Letters that follow, it will be seen how generous was the help afforded to the youthful student, first to last and in every possible way, by gentlemen of the highest reputation in Natural Science ; a help which his friends gratefully appreciated at the time, and shall never forget. To those who have preserved through so many changeful years, and have now lent their young correspondent's letters, here to be made use of, especial thanks are now offered.

Contents.

Introductory;

AND

In Memoriam.

IT was on a bright summer's day in 1863, in the city of Glasgow, that a gentleman there resident, 'happened to be looking into a print-seller's shop window, and observed a water-colour drawing which was entitled "The Lonely Grave." It represented a tropical scene on the banks of a beautiful bay. A British frigate lay at anchor on an unruffled sea, and some stately palms over-shadowed a mound on a slight eminence. At the head of the mound was a rude cross, and on looking closer the gentleman read the name engraven on the head-stone. It was one familiar to him, and in the course of the forenoon, scarcely deeming it more than a coincidence, he casually mentioned the circumstance to his brother, who had, about two years previously, married a young lady of the same name, in short, one of the sisters of the lonely sleeper in that tropical grave. With fraternal interest, the latter gentleman at once hastened to the print-shop, purchased the drawing, and obtained the artist's address. He, Lieut. Anderson, strange to say, had not only belonged to the expedition, but was the midshipman specially told off to attend Mr Edmondston on excursions, and was with him to the last.

Thus, in the kind mysterious course of Divine providence, a chain of association, sunk for well nigh twenty years, and over which grief had thrown a veil of silence, was recovered; and a family that had not ceased to deplore the loss of their " first and fairest," was brought into contact with those who had been his associates in the last and most interesting year of his short life. Supplied in this singular way with many materials, hitherto apparently beyond reach, it has been frequently suggested that a short Memoir of an accomplished youth, whose name is still as a talisman in many hearts should be prepared. While it is beyond a doubt that few indeed, of the very many to whom he was known, are ever likely to forget him and the early blighted promise of his career,—to his kindred and to their descendants, a few particulars of his life and character will be more especially valuable. The materials are culled from the recollections of his still surviving, still sorrowing parents, and from his letters and papers.

In the *Times* newspaper of the 13th June 1846, appeared the following paragraph :—

" MELANCHOLY CATASTROPHE.—Letters from some of the officers of the ' Herald,' and her tender, the ' Pandora,' have been received, dated April 24. The ' Herald,' Capt. Kellet, had been to the Gallapagos, and returned to the coast on the 22nd January. While off the mouth of the small river Sua, about five miles from Atacamas, an accident occurred which has deprived the expedition of one of its most valuable officers, just at the period when his services were beginning to be required. A party had been employed on shore, and on returning to the boats, a loaded rifle happened to be touched by one of them, when jumping into a boat after wading through the surf. It went off and the ball first struck the arm of the clerk, slightly wounding him, and then passed through the head of Mr Edmondston, the Naturalist of the expedition, killing him on the spot. His death was instantaneous. His loss will be greatly felt, as Mr Edmondston was an exceedingly amiable and talented young man, deservedly regarded by his messmates and all on board the ' Herald,' and, although but twenty years of age, had greatly distinguished himself in his profession. He had lately been elected Botanical Professor of the Andersonian University of Glasgow ; he was also the author of a botanical work, ‘ The Flora of Shetland.’ His remains were buried on shore on the following day with funeral honours."

In the " Voyage of the Herald," published after her return to Britain in 1853, by Mr Berthold Seemann, the author says :—" The piece of oak which was placed at the head of his grave may be searched for in vain ; but his brother Naturalists will meet on the shores of the ocean on which their talented colleague perished, an evergreen shrub, with dark red panicles. It is the *Edmondstonia pacifica,*—a monument to his memory by an ardent admirer of his talents."

" This plant is figured in plate xviii. of the ‘ Botany of H. M. S. Herald,’ and is so different from all known genera, that it will probably become the type of a new natural order."

Paragraph extracted from the late Professor Edward Forbes's " Literary Papers," under, Notice of the Surveying Expedition of H. M. S. Herald in 1846, (page 98).

" Captain Kellet was accompanied by a promising and talented Naturalist, Mr Thomas Edmondston, who, though but a youth, had already given good earnest of his powers, and love for science. We remember well the zeal and delight with which this young genius— for such he assuredly was—entered upon a mission so suitable to his talents and taste, and so likely to prove prolific in discovery. Alas! all these hopes and anticipations were fated to be destroyed. Mr Edmondston met with an early and awfully sudden death. He was shot by accident when returning from his work, whilst the ' Herald ' was anchored off the river Sua, in the Bay of Atacamas."

Copy of a letter, from J. O. Goodridge, Esq., R.N., Surgeon to the Expedition, addressed to A. J. Symington, Esq.

                             " January 19, 1864.

" It would give me much satisfaction could I give fuller information regarding the late Mr T. Edmondston ; but at this late date many circumstances have passed from my recollection. When he first joined the ship he was very young ; but, by his most estimable disposition, soon became esteemed and loved by all. Never, through the whole of my sea life, have I known any loss more deeply regretted, or one which so completely destroyed the very existence of an expedition."

Rear-Admiral Kellet thus writes to A. J. Symington, Esq., on 9th May 1864 :—

" So long as recollection is left me, time can never sweep away my admiration for poor young Edmondston's ability, or my *esteem* for his personal character. How well I recollect the loneliness of the ship, and the depression of all on board when the accident was reported. We buried him, poor fellow, in a lonely little spot, but surrounded by the most luxuriant foliage; a place that the poor fellow himself would have loved to ramble about. Captain Chimmo made a drawing of it."

Extract from a letter written by the Reverend Dr Gordon to Mrs Edmondston.

> " The Manse, Birnic, Elgin,
> " 17th October 1865.

" Your note brought back to my thoughts the many pleasing and instructive hours I spent with your valued son, while he was in this district for a few weeks, twenty year ago, and also revived the deep feelings of regret which his sudden decease caused to myself and to all his acquaintances. I know not an instance in which the early death of an individual so much blighted the well founded hopes of his advancing the interests of Natural Science generally, for he was well prepared in almost all its departments,   G. Gordon."

Acrostic on Thomas Edmondston, by Mr Whiffin, Purser of H. M. S. Herald.

" On the 18th October 1847.—We directed our

course to the Sua River. Most of us paid a visit to the grave of Thomas Edmondston. The luxuriant vegetation had spread a verdant mantle over the tomb, and surrounded it with brilliant flowers. It was to all a sad recollection ; many an expression of pity was uttered, and Mr J. G. Whiffin, who was present on the occurrence of the accident which deprived poor Edmondston of his life, penned the following acrostic :—*

" 'Twas from this beautiful and rock bound bay
  Heav'n deemed it right to call his soul away
  One moment's warning was to him denied ;
  'Midst life and youth, and health and hope, he died.
  Alas ! that boastful science could not save
  So apt a scholar from his early grave !
  Even those who knew not of his private worth
  Deplore his talents buried in the earth.
  'Mong flowers that gem the softly verdant ground,
  O'erspread with trees, his grave is to be found.
  No crowd his resting place shall ever view ;
  Still sad affection will induce a few
  To gaze, where plants, o'er which he lavish'd years,
  O'er him, now silent, shed their dewy tears,
  Nor seek to hide a grief denied to nobler biers !"
          " Voyage of the Herald," vol. i., p. 216.

----

* There is an error in the spelling of the name.

The following sketch of Thomas Edmondston's character was written to A. J. Symington, soon after he had obtained possession of the water-colour drawing called " The Lonely Grave," by Dr Edmondston, his father, who is in all respects thoroughly competent to appreciate and delineate it :—

" I have noticed with intense pleasure the lively and affectionate interest you have taken in what relates to your deceased brother-in-law. No one ever knew him from childhood up, who was not charmed with him. Not only were his intellectual faculties wonderful, but his fancy, his affection, his manner, were to the last degree captivating. A capacity for the severer sciences, united with the most ardent love for manly sports and gymnastics—the power of indefatigable application with the most playful imagination and humour—a boundless memory with a precocious and powerful judgment—a strongly developed power of philosophical generalization with a perspicuous and fluent style. Meek and gentle as a lamb, he ever showed the unflinching courage of a lion. He had no hot-bed forcing, —every thing came to him naturally, spontaneously, I may almost say intuitively. He was as extraordinary as a child as a stripling. Nature did almost all for him,— art, or what is called education, little, beyond what he derived from the society of his own family. His deportment was so affectionate and engaging that never in the course of his too short life—no, never!—can we recollect a frown or act of wilful disobedience. All this is saying little of what he was. No wonder we never recovered the blow of the separation. He was the darling of his shipmates. Captain Kellet wrote of him, that in all his experience he had never met one whose mental powers and information had so impressed him. Edward Forbes lamented him as a serious loss to science; and all this of a boy of twenty from the solitudes of Unst!"

CHAPTER I.

—

Early Childhood.

THOMAS EDMONDSTON was born at Buness, in the island of Unst, the most northerly of the Shetlandic group, on the 20th September 1825. He was the eldest son of Laurence Edmondston, M.D., well known to naturalists and others as one who has done good service in different departments of science. His mother is the eldest grand-child of the late venerable Dr John-ston, minister of North Leith, whose piety, benevolence, and exertions in founding the Blind Asylum of Edinburgh, are remembered by many.

We have much faith in the doctrine of hereditary excellencies. We think that those who have had ancestors remarkable for great or good qualities, have a right to " thank God and take courage," and that when we find a young person singularly lovable, and richly endowed intellectually, we may, without greatly erring, be led to the conclusion that he was fortunate in his forefathers.

The Shetland branch of the family of Edmondston has been resident there, and connected with most of the old Norse or Scandinavian families, ever since the reign of Queen Mary, when a non-juring clergyman found in those islands a safe retreat, and eventually a living as a parish minister. A son or grandson who succeeded him, is traditionally said to have been a very clever and accomplished man,—especially distinguished for his attainments in medicine and botany. His descendants—almost all of them—emigrated, as by far the greater proportion of the Shetland young men do to this day.

For thirty years there had not been a son born in the family, and for double that space of time, not one in the ancestral mansion, so that the birth of the young Thomas was lovingly welcomed. And this circumstance would perhaps account for the more than ordinary interest and attention bestowed upon him from the very beginning. He was born in the house of Buness, the residence of his uncle the late Thomas Edmondston Esq., where, five years before, the late eminent *savant* of the French Academy, Monsieur J. B. Biot, had resided for some weeks engaged in astronomical observations, to determine the exact amount of the depression of the earth at its poles.

For this purpose a station was necessary as far north as possible, and on the same degree of longitude as the points in France and Africa where similar measurements had been already effected. That favoured locality was Buness; and the accomplished Frenchman, with the assistance only of an intelligent boat carpenter, there succeeded in making a series of astronomical observations of great value to the scientific world. M. Biot was of a most amiable domestic character, and his memory is proudly cherished in the scene of his lonely sojourn. Soon after his return to Paris, he wrote for the French Academy an account of his visit to Unst, so eloquent, so touchingly truthful, that we imagine we cannot do better than give an extract here, in order to present some idea of life in the Shetland islands, which, little understood now, was much less so then. Indeed the scenery and domestic manners of that day, so graphically and lovingly portrayed, are, in the onward progress distinctive of our time, become things of the past, and therefore belong to history.

After detailing the nature, intention, and results of the trigonometrical observations, M. Biot goes on to mention the kindness and hospitality he experienced in the household at Buness, and the excellent opportunity he enjoyed of becoming familiar with the inner life as it were of these remote islanders. " Had it been otherwise," he says, " I could not have imagined what allurements were powerful enough to retain them in their stormy, foggy, country ; without roads—without a tree on hill or plain,—a climate of rain and of tempestuous winds, where the atmosphere is constantly impregnated with cold, saline moisture, the only alleviation of the severity of winter being the sad condition that there is no summer.   That which binds them to their country is the peace—the profound unwavering peace they enjoy,—the sweets of which they profoundly appreciate.   For twenty-five years, during which all Europe was laid waste by the demons of war, in Unst never—hardly even in Lerwick—was the roll of a drum heard.   For twenty-five years the door of the house I dwelt in had remained open, night as well as day.   In all that time no conscription or press-gang came near to trouble or afflict the poor but peaceful inhabitants of this little isle.   The numerous rocks that surround it, which render it accessible only in favourable weather, serve like a fleet to defend them from corsairs in war time.   And what would corsairs come here in search of ?   Here are received the news from Europe as if reading the history of the preceding century.   They recall no personal misfortune, they awaken no animosity, therefore, they have not that interest,—or rather that momentary enthusiasm which rouses the passions—and they can philosophize with calmness on events which seem to them to relate to another world.   If they had only trees and sun, no residence could be more delicious, but if they had trees and sun, all the world would wish to be there, and there would be tranquillity no longer.

" This calm habitual security gives to the social relations a charm elsewhere unknown. Every one here in the upper class is kinsman, or connection, or friend ; and friendships are the same as connections. But as in this world evil must always be mingled with the good, the happiness of living as if one large family, is sometimes dearly bought,— it causes to be felt most bitterly the loss of any of the individuals on which are centred the affections of the rest. The unhappiness of one family is affliction to all. It proves nearly an equal grief when brothers or some other friends leave their home seeking fortune elsewhere ; for it is too common an occurrence, that their island, or all the islands, do not furnish sufficient employment for the better class of the population. The parting is felt by those who remain as a death—and a death it is in truth too often,—as very probably those who thus take leave are seen here no more. Even the friendships which these kindly natives contract for strangers whom they thus favour, become for their poor hearts only subjects of grief or regret, which the distant voice of gratitude but faintly alleviates.

" This necessity of expâtriating themselves, with Shetlanders of the upper class, is caused by the limited extension of commerce and of agriculture, in consequence of want of capital, and the few opportunities for exportation of the products of the country. A small portion only of the lands of each proprietor is cultivated. The rest serves for pasturage to herds of half-wild sheep and horses, which wander during the whole year over the hills, without care and without restraint. The people clear out around their cottages a portion of ground only sufficient for their own individual subsistence, and that of their family ; and they pay rent for it from the profits of the perilous but attractive occupation of fishing. All the men follow this calling, and with a degree of hardihood almost without parallel. Six men who are good at the oar, and who have confidence in each other, associate themselves together as a crew for one boat, which is a slight skiff, entirely undecked. They carry with them a small quantity of water, some oat cake, and a compass, and in this frail vessel they advance into the ocean till they lose sight of land, a distance of fifteen or twenty leagues. There they cast their lines, and remain for a day and a night, or even more if weather be very favourable. Should fish be plentiful they each gain ten or twelve shillings on such a voyage.* If the sky becomes overcast and the sea

----

* It is to be remembered that the account of Shetland by the amiable and accomplished French philosopher was written well nigh half a century ago. As respects the fishermen's earnings, the extent of commerce, and improvements in agriculture, the islands have made very considerable advances, partaking in the onward march that distinguishes these days. *(Edr.* 1868.*)*

rises, they struggle in their tiny boat against its fury until they have secured their fishing lines and tackle, the loss of which would be ruin to them. Then they pull and sail in the direction of land, through waves that run mountain high. The most experienced among them, seated in the stern, holds the helm, and judging of the direction of each wave, avoids its direct shock, which would be sufficient to engulph them. At the same time he directs the movements of the sail—which his most skilful coadjutor has charge of—he orders it to be lowered at the moment the boat mounts on the crest of a billow, in order to moderate her descent, and to be raised whenever the skiff has descended into the space between the rising waves, in order that the wind may hasten it to the crest of the next. Sometimes enveloped in profound obscurity the unfortunate adventurers cannot see the mountain of water from which they fly, and can only judge of its approach by the sound of its roaring. Meanwhile the wives and children are on the sea beach, imploring the mercy of heaven—imagining they see the little bark that bears their only hopes—at times believing they can view it submerged in the rolling billows—or preparing to assist the husbands and fathers, should they come near enough for succour—and sometimes calling aloud on those who hear no more. But their lot is not always so unfortunate. By means of skill, immense toil, and cool courage, the boat comes forth conqueror in the fearful struggle,—the horn of the successful fishers is heard,—they arrive in safety. Kisses follow tears, and the joy of meeting is increased by the recital of the perils from which they have escaped. Yet for these poor people, even the harshness of their fatherland has its charms. They love these old rocks of which the outline is so familiar,—their rugged forms shew them the narrow passage through which their boat must pass, when returning home with a favourable wind it re-enters the sheltering bay, saluted by the wild cries of the sea birds. They love those deep and silent caves, into which they often venture their little skiffs, over the murmuring heaving swell, to surprise the sleeping seal in its wild retreat. I myself feeling calm and safe under those fishermen's guidance have contemplated with admiration the high precipitous cliffs of primitive rock—that frame work of the globe, the strata of which sloping towards the sea, and undermined at the base by the dashing waves, seem to menace the destruction of the frail bark that bounds along at its feet. At our approach clouds of sea birds issued by myriads from their retreats, surprised at being disturbed by human beings, and making the solitude re-echo with their confused cries ; some darting through the air, others plunging beneath the waves and re-appearing almost immediately with the prey which they had caught—while here and there a porpoise or a seal would elevate its head above the transparent water. Here life seems to abandon the *land*, cold and humid, and to take refuge in more varied and active forms in the water and the air. But when evening spreads its veil over these wild retreats, everything returns to peacefulness and silence. Sometimes a gentle south wind softens the air and permits the stars peeping from their clouds to shed their pure light on a scene of the most profound repose which is unbroken by the slightest noise, except, it may be, the distant murmur of the dying waves, or the sweet plaintive cry of a gull hasting, belated, to its nest.

"After a sojourn of two months I quitted these islands, carrying with me recollections for my life-time. An equinoctial gale conveyed me back to Edinburgh in fifty hours. This quick transit from solitude to the 'din of cities,'—from a patriarchal simplicity to the refinements and luxuries of civilization, is not without attractions. Colonel Elphinstone showed me, by the most flattering reception, that friendship and goodness had not all betaken themselves to the Shetland Islands.

."What I have said concerning the social virtues of Scotland and the Shetland isles, presents these places under an aspect so different from our Continental habitudes, that I should not be surprised if in France,— or even in England also,—many people should think that there is some exaggeration in the delineation ; and that I have involuntarily yielded to the partiality which a foreigner generally has for a new country where he has been received with hospitality. Nevertheless, let me assure any who so think, that I have only spoken the simple truth.   Perhaps I may be believed in what I have said concerning Scotland, but for Shetland, from whence shall I obtain witnesses?   Although the mere distance is not great, yet the difficulty of the navigation, the inclemency of the climate, and the lack of commercial enterprize, keep travellers far from these coasts ; and those who at intervals are led thither by necessity, hasten to depart as soon as their affairs permit.   Perhaps a sojourn of two months in an untrammelled and disinterested position has permitted me to view these islands more closely than do most of the Scotch who visit them.   Many persons even in Edinburgh have very erroneous ideas concerning them ; and in general it is a pleasure easily procurable from one end of Europe to the other, that of hearing each country slander its more northern neighbours.   In Italy the climate of France is considered rude and severe,—see what Alfieri says of it.   Here, in Paris, we think our country most beautiful, but England appears to us the land of fogs. At London people do not complain of their climate, but speak of Scotland as a country almost deprived of sunshine.   The Scotch think this opinion quite ridiculous,—but greatly pity the poor Shetlanders.   The latter in their turn assert that they suffer much less extreme cold than do the Scotch,—but they think that the inhabitants of the Faroe Islands and Iceland must be very unfortunate. I am persuaded that the Icelanders again feel disdain for Spitzbergen.

"The truth is, that in every climate in the world man may live with a degree of almost equal comfort and happiness if he carry with him the virtues of social life, and the resources of commerce and civilization."

Amidst the scenes thus eloquently described, and while the amiable and accomplished foreigner's character and undertakings were yet fresh in the hearts of the family circle at Buness, Thomas Edmondston spent his first seven years. M. Biot was the theme of many reminiscences, and it is easy to suppose that on a clever and singularly impressible boy they could not fail to have a deep influence, and even to evoke aspirations after the fame and worth thus presented to his admiration. Indeed, the boy's first alphabetical lore was culled from the inscription on a large stone on which the philosopher had erected his astronomical instruments ; and which remains on the lawn in memory of the circumstance. The child's first natural idea was that it was a tomb-stone, and that honoured dust lay there. But when he knew that M. Biot lived, that he might see him, hear him,—learn of him perhaps some day, to do so became his early dream and ambition. Circumstances forbade the realization of a personal interview, but several letters passed in future days between the venerable philosopher and the aspirant he kindly adopted as his "young coadjutor." Thus were

sown and nurtured the seeds of that *honourable ambition*,—ever onwards—a trait so well marked in this
young Shetlander's character.

Beautiful in form and fragile in constitution, while
singularly attractive and intelligent, the boy in those
infant years undoubtedly ran a great risk of being
spoiled by the indulgence of a small circle of relations,
to whom he was as a sunbeam in a cloudy and lonely
spot. But it soon became apparent that no amount
of attentions, or even of praise, and ill disguised
admiration, could injure a disposition naturally modest,
sweet, and pliable. The utmost result that his sharp
observation drew from the attentions he was in
the habit of attracting from all with whom he came
in contact, was a spirit of *self-reliance*, which became
another leading feature in his more matured character. With a wonderfully fine memory, at once
ready and retentive, and even from the first dawning
of intellect an intense thirst for knowledge, he united
great exuberance of spirits, and mirthful appreciation of all sorts of fun and humour. At sixteen
months old he knew all the letters of the alphabet
correctly, although he could pronounce but very few of
the consonants. Indeed, for years he spoke imperfectly,
the ideas flowing far too fast for the less pliant bodily
organs. So great also was the quickness of his observation, that nothing whatever coming before him seemed
above his attempts to define and understand. It

became, therefore, the main object of his friends to repress rather than to stimulate the impatient ever busy brain, to withold rather than gratify the craving for knowledge of the too fast unfolding intellect. Had this child lived in cities, or had his precocious propensities been stimulated and encouraged, he would most probably have shot up into undue proportions—have put forth the richest blossom and have withered prematurely, like too many similarly fragile hot-house plants. The strengthening of his constitution, and the care of his health then became to his parents a paramount consideration ; and constant exercise, the simplest country food, and the invigorating but not chilling sea breezes of his native isle, overcame the childish delicacy, so that he grew strong and healthful. The first intense joy of his childhood, as it has been to many another first-born, was a baby brother two years his junior. The earliest transports of gladsome lovingness and the succeeding proud guardianship and tutoring of the endeared companion are well remembered. A letter to a relative when he was just three years old says, "Tommy is very amusing with his wise old-fashioned remarks, and eager for his daily lesson in repeating texts and poetry. He has learned most of Mrs Barbauld's hymns with scarcely an effort. About the subjects they treat of he asks the most extraordinary questions, which we endeavour to repress as being far beyond his comprehension. He volunteered some extraordinary statements to his uncle two days ago about heaven, which, as it was the place where good boys go to, he wished greatly to see, but as it was so far away he could not possibly venture unless he had a good stout horse. If uncle would only give him that, he would certainly go at once, and would not be deterred by any statements as to the difficulties or even dangers of the way." Here peeped out the dauntless courage and love of enterprise he ever displayed. All strangers, and not a few used to visit Unst, thought him a wonderfully engaging child, and when the first modest bashfulness had been conquered by their attentions, his intelligent prattle so surprised them that they could hardly be persuaded of his extreme juvenility, even although his stature was the ordinary one for his age, and his complexion almost feminine in its fairness and delicacy.

In conducting the early education of this interesting and precocious boy, it is not to be inferrred that, although books, or what may be distinguished as school learning, was very sparingly admitted, he was not allowed to gather up new ideas, or imbibe knowledge in a mode much safer but probably quite as efficient. He was never shut up in a nursery, or left to the care of servants, but was always with his mother, and was presented to any friends or strangers who might be visiting at Buness. On his second birth-day (1827) Sir Edward Parry (then Captain) came in with his ship to Baltasound, on his return from his last voyage, the unsuccessful attempt to reach the North Pole. With wonder and delight Tommy examined the sword, the epaulets, &c., even the buttons with the anchor, as entire novelties to him, escaped not his notice, while to the amiable Parry, and his chief officers, who had been for five months beyond the limits of civilized life, the child was a novel and precious experience. It was about a year after this that another eminent man, although in a very different department—the late Dr Adam Clark—visited Balta-sound. He had a yacht for his tour, and a party of friends with him. He preached in the drawing-room of Buness to as many as could obtain standing room in it. It was an old fashioned well proportioned room, and was cleared out for the purpose of holding a religious service, that the neighbours might have the opportunity of hearing a preacher so justly esteemed. This was the first sermon at which Tommy was ever present. Sooth to say, he was a most restless auditor; and, eventually, had to be kept as still as possible in a small anti-room. Here again we have alighted on Biot's apartments and Tommy's birthplace. But when the small congregation united in singing, the child's delight was unbounded; and, as always when most pleased, he was entirely still, the flexible countenance plainly shewing all he felt, till the large blue eyes actually filled with tears on meeting those of his mother.

Such incidents as these were doubtless amongst the

influences tending to the formation of an extraordinary and powerful character, which, in other circumstances, or in a less peculiar locality, might or might not have been thus rich in its unfolding.

Although any strain on the precocious intellect was carefully avoided, there was no lack of pictures and nursery rhymes such as all children delight in, and from which many extract healthful mental food. Before he could speak, Thomas would point to the pictures by name with the most eager delight, and with hearty ringing laugh appreciated what was ludicrous or incongrous in the time-honoured rhymes; but to attempt to soothe him to rest by crooning what would soon send most children into slumber, was only to excite and interest his fancy, till perfect stillness and darkness was found the best recipe for his natural wakefulness, and an idiocyncrasy that craved for incessant activity,—as he used to say a year or two afterwards, when he was implored to be quiet, " I was never made for stillness mamma." It was a sort of prophetic key to his whole career.

One of the very first things most persons recollect of him, was a custom of making long harangues— whether to auditors or not, seemed to him a matter of indifference. These discourses consisted of dialogues or tales, chiefly from Dr Aiken and Mrs Barbauld's " Evenings at Home," or other poetry or prose he had learnt. While his pronunciation was so imperfect, that it could scarcely be understood, his graceful manner and energy were so remarkable, that the simple peasants or servants, who occasionally were admiring listeners, prophesied "*he certainly would be a minister some day*," the force of their appreciation " could no further go."

The mechanical process of learning to read was accomplished in a fashion of his own, and with the least possible trouble to himself or others. He used to get any person whose attention he could claim for a few minutes, to read over a sentence or sentences two or three times, which was sufficient to fix the matter correctly in his memory. Then he took the book, and by steadily observing the look of each word as he repeated it, he was able to recognise it again wherever he encountered it ; by this means avoiding all the drudgery of spelling by syllables. The second chapter of St Matthew's gospel was the first thing he mastered in this original way ; and the word *Jerusalem*, being distinct and remarkable, was the first he was enabled to recognise, in search of which he patiently turned every leaf of the New Testament, without overlooking any place where it was to be found. In fact that word *Jerusalem* became his *open sesame* to the first mystery of the art of reading. At four years of age he could read any part of the Bible fluently, and seemed captivated with its quaint but nervous phraseology, its sublime poetry, and its matchless narratives.

As soon as any decided taste developed itself, it was Ornithology he preferred to every other branch of knowledge, and "Bewick's British Birds" he loved above all his easier story books. He was, indeed, by inheritance an Ornithologist, and it is not surprising that the boy should soon learn to prefer what his father was so able and willing to teach. Birds,—in books, in his walks, as they flew, or twittered, or swam, or became his pets and playthings,—were his enthusiasm. One day, when his papa was absent, a lad brought in a small unknown bird found dead in a field, but the child, without a moment's hesitation, said, in his imperfect pronunciation, " It's the Golden Crested Wren to be sure," and he stroked the beautiful plumage with tears in his eyes. He had never seen one before, except in the pages of Bewick.

On another occasion a man brought a wild swan he had shot, one of a small flock that had been resting on an inland loch, weary with their journey through storms, on the way to Iceland for the breeding season. The splendid bird was laid on a table, after being duly admired and measured, and the boy was left alone with it. He immediately mounted a chair, and was observed to stroke the downy breast again and again, saying softly to himself the hymn from Mrs Hemans, " Death hath lowered thy crest and unplum'd thy wing," while large tears dropped on the dead bird's snowy vest.

In spring, 1831, Thomas took hooping cough, but got over it without injury to his constitution. He had, however, at this time his first sorrow in the death of a

baby sister, whose memory all through his life he cherished as something too lovely and sacred to be touched upon,—indeed he never could bear even a passing allusion to it, although, of his loving and beloved grandmother, who died in the same month, he delighted to talk constantly. Many proofs of his warmth of affection will hereafter appear, but the acute sensibility of a boy so young is rare as it is beautiful. Another short extract from a letter written at the time, will shew that it is not merely fond memory that draws the sketch :—
" Tommy is a noble generous boy, magnanimous, unselfish, and of intense sensibility,—almost infant as he is nothing less can be justly said of him. He is very fond of, and indulgent to his brother, and so intelligent that one may converse with him almost as a companion. He grows tall and stout—still very restless and volatile —mind and body constantly employed about something or other, and his faults are only those of forgetfulness from his extreme vivacity, for he is perfectly tractable, and no mischief or unamiable disposition is ever seen in him."

While recovering from hooping cough, and necessarily more sedentary than usual, he found a never failing amusement in learning to write,—by copying on a slate any word he could get written down for his imitation. In this way he never wrote what is called a round copy, his hand writing being from the first distinct and characteristic, and his spelling always perfectly correct. Indeed we think it no slight indication of the minute correctness of his observation, that from the very earliest efforts of his pen, there are no mis-spelt words ; which is, we have observed, a common fault, resulting from carelessness, even in well educated young people ; and this boy, be it remembered, never learned spelling in the ordinary way. His eye was prompt and exact, and he wrote as he had seen the words in print. He delighted to write from dictation,—in that way he felt he proved his own progress. When he could get no one to read to him, he used to write anything he had committed to memory, and then proceeded to compose letters to his parents and other relatives ; although, as those were the days of expensive postage, the epistles never went farther than the fireside of Buness. It was thus that what is often felt a drudgery—a necessity and a painful one—became to little Thomas a relaxation— a pride and a delight. It was soon after this that a young gentleman visiting Shetland in the pursuit of natural science—for which it affords a field so inviting, and at that time so entirely unexplored—was so surprised and delighted at the boy's attempts at drawing, himself being an accomplished draughtsman, that he presented Thomas with a book of drawing paper, and a few general instructions. The book was soon filled, besides numerous scraps of loose paper, with spirited copies of birds, fishes, and insects. Eye and hand seemed equally apt, for the objects were sketched and shaded with the utmost swiftness and precision, and this useful accomplishment he retained and practised with hardly any farther instruction. One other trait belongs to this early period of Thomas Edmondston's unfolding character. He was possessed, as we have before mentioned, of a spirit of heroic courage, nothing ever daunted him. He was never known to shrink from any task bodily or mental. On one occasion, when not quite two years old, he was seated near some friends he was visiting, but a little apart. A number of domestic fowls gathered round, with whom he was sharing his lunch of bread and butter, when a powerful fierce cock, perhaps in supposed defence of the rights of his harem, flew at the child, who attacked the bird with a slight stick he had by him, bravely defending himself without a cry or a complaint. It might have proved a serious matter, for the cock was infuriated, and struck at the boy's face with beak and spurs, had not the noise the animal made attracted attention, and the brave little man was rescued from his perilous encounter.

The self-same energy and conscious power prompted him on all occasions to obtain the technical name of every species of animal he was acquainted with. How few children are there—how few persons even more advanced in years—who have not stumbled at the outset over the nomenclature properly belonging to studies otherwise attractive to them. Not so young Thomas, who, for the purpose of assistance in the matter, never rested till he obtained from his father some well-worn books and slight directions for the study of Latin, and was soon equally at home in the scientific as in the English or vernacular names of all the birds and quadrupeds of which he had any knowledge from books or observation.

Eager above all things to imbibe knowledge, he now began to understand the use and value of books, and to read and pore over them. Scott's "Tales of a Grandfather" was a great favourite, yet imaginative as he was, which will soon appear, he had no taste for fairy lore, or for the wondrous Arabian Night's stories, even although a beautifully illustrated copy was within his reach. It was a practice in the family circle to read aloud during the long quiet winter evenings, and young Thomas was an eager listener. Scott's novels and poems were about this time frequently chosen as the books to be read, and the boy's imagination took fire at those matchless tales of chivalry and romance, which probably he believed to be real histories ; and to his brother, in their bed-room, he used to rehearse what he had heard. He even conceived the idea of himself composing a story, and at first narrating it in parts to his friends, he afterwards at intervals for years filled sheets upon sheets of paper with the strange fancies of his busy brain. The young author thus began his romance of the olden time :—

" Once, long ago, before Hector was killed at Troy, there was a country at the back of China named Cheshea.

It was inhabited by the good people. It was very flat, but fine crops grew in it. On the other side of the hills there was another country called Breschia, and it was inhabited by the bad people, who were always at war with the Chesheans. They were so very bad that they carried off cattle and sheep, and when they could they murdered the good people and burned their houses."

Then follows a more minute description of the two countries, and of the animals peculiar to each, which also were adversaries as well as the people. One bird peculiar to Cheshea was the "Vovis," a species of stork, possessed of the noblest qualities, gentle and brave. It had a peculiar gift which rendered it most valuable to the Chesheans. Its scent was so keen that it could tell if any Breschians were approaching although at a distance of twenty miles; and if they were coming on a marauding expedition, the bird uttered a peculiar cry, which was perfectly understood by the Chesheans, as a warning of approaching danger. On the other side of the mountains which intervened between these hostile countries, there lived a bird called the 'Sweyn Derrick,' a species of kite very powerful and furious, and the mortal enemy of the "Vovis," so that many were the encounters between these inveterate foes. The "Vovis," was unable to fly, but he had a powerful, long, and sharp beak, with which he often transfixed his enemy, when pounced upon. Still the Sweyn Derrick often overcame, and would have done so much more frequently had it not been for the help of a faithful ally, a sort of knight-errant of the bird kingdom. This was the Ziticus, a sort of hawk, not so large and powerful as the " Sweyn Derrick," but furnished with a formidable weapon in the shape of a turned up horn on the upper mandible : he was, besides, fearless and active, and when he heard the cry of the " Vovis " he rushed to the rescue and made short work of the murderous enemy. Some of these encounters were illustrated in a spirited manner. The " Vovis " was the sacred bird of Cheshea, and to kill one of them was punishable with death. Besides these useful sentinels the Chesheans were much beholden to the good offices of a herd of *tame whales,* which played an important part in their wars.· When setting forth on some expedition each warrior in full armour would take his seat on one of these accommodating leviathans, all the artillery and other material of war being likewise arranged on the ample backs of these monsters ; and thus an army would be transported across dangerous seas or estuaries, and enabled to surprise the enemy, or escape if in danger of being overpowered by numbers. Of course the story had a hero. This was the " Marquis of Fieldfare,"* a

---

* From this arose the soubriquet of " Marquis," by which Thomas was known for many years in the family, as well as by his own name. Indeed letters are extant addressed—" Marquis of Fieldfare," at Buness.

prodigy of strength and valour, always armed in *coat of-mail*, with sword, dagger, and double-barrelled pistols. The tale is chiefly composed of the adventures of this extraordinary man. He had a twin brother who was stolen away in infancy by the bad people, and as soon as the Marquis arrived at manhood he announced that he was resolved to search the world for his "long lost brother." No arguments or appeals could shake his purpose. Boldly he sallied forth from the strong castle of his ancestors in the disguise of a Swedish knight. Every page, as may be supposed, is full of stirring startling incident. Fifty ordinary men were no match for the redoubted marquis, who mowed down open or treacherous enemies like stubble. Often he was *mortally* wounded, but somehow he always recovered. Sometimes he was taken prisoner, but while his captors were preparing for him the most horrible tortures he managed to escape. He was often engaged in duels, and at least half-a-dozen times shot his deadly foe the chief of the Breschians "Earl Keen." One of these occasions is described in the following brief and matter of fact manner,—"The following evening the Marquis was walking in the garden. He saw a man skulking among the trees. He then called out—' who's there?'—no answer. The Marquis drew out a pistol and fired—the man fell—it was Keen, and he was killed. The Marquis returned to the castle, ate a hearty supper, and slept soundly as if nothing had happened."

A very short time after this the Marquis had another encounter with this same Keen who certainly had a charmed life, for nothing ever could put him *hors-de-combat.* There is a graphic enough account of a storm and shipwreck, the only person saved being the Marquis. On another occasion he had been taken prisoner by the Breschians, and was consigned to a desert island, where he was left to perish miserably by starvation. Sitting on a rock by the sea shore, hopeless, yet undaunted, he suddenly descried a great black object approaching, which his eagle eye soon recognised as one of the tame whales of his country! The monster at once answered his familiar whistle, and rescued the hero from his impending fate. After innumerable adventures, equally novel and surprising, the Marquis discovered his brother in a terrible dungeon in one of the strongest castles of Breschia, — with incredible hardihood he rescued the prisoner, and together they returned in triumph to their native land.

In the foregoing synopsis of the boy's romance we observe the natural ignorance of mere childhood, in the anachronism of supposing fire arms in use " *before Hector was killed at Troy.*" The early tastes peep out in making heroes of birds. The knight's disguise as a Swede was prompted no doubt by a thought of Linnæus in his wanderings ; and then the coining of the names, the glorification of noble resolve, and fearless adventure, and yet the absence of all supernatural element in the story, are distinctive traits in the imaginings of a boy between six and eight years of age.

He was a little past seven when his parents and their children removed to a house that had been built for them on a portion of the Buness property called Halligarth, just on the outskirts of the home demesne. There he uninterruptedly resided for the succeeding seven years. Hitherto he had had no regular lessons, or other instruction than that picked up *con amore* from his friends and his own observation. After this his parents assisted him more systematically, and during the years of 1834–5–6, he obtained all he ever had, or required to have, of *school* education.

CHAPTER II.

—

School Days.

1832-37.

IT has been said, we think by Dr Samuel Johnson, that "true genius is a mind of great general powers accidently determined in a particular direction," and Edward Forbes emphatically described his young friend Thomas Edmondston as "a genius." An explanation of the particular direction which his great natural powers took we may look for most especially in the peculiarities of his native place. Isolated for a great part of the year from all society, and for two or three summer months apt to be favoured by intimate association with the most accomplished and improving visitors—afar from libraries and shops, the treasures of art and the gauds of wealth, there remain to the Shetlander the objects of nature in all their grandeur, variety, and freedom of access. To Shetland various sciences have been indebted,—Trignometry, as we have seen, through Biot,—Geology through Professor Jamieson,—Ornithology through Drs. Macgillivray and Edmondston,—Muscology through Edward Forbes,—and more recently Conchology through Mr Jeffreys. In all these departments the islands have proved a rich and interesting field for discovery; so that it would seem a native genius there must perforce become a naturalist as Thomas Edmondston did. He himself thus writes on the subject, "These remote islands are highly interesting to the naturalist, for in the variety and frequently the rarity of their natural productions, they are not exceeded by any other district of the same extent in Britain." In Botany, however, the field was as yet unexplored. Thomas was in his ninth year when an intimate friend of the family suggested to her clever little favourite the study of botany, which soon became his passion. Dr Edmondston was engaged at the time in planting various forest trees in a large high walled garden for the purpose of disproving if possible the general impression that trees will not grow in Shetland. Each leaf, then, of above seventy species, became a study for the young tyro, and in a time almost incredibly short he could distinguish each by name. A few years afterwards he gave his opinion on the debatable subject of trees growing in Shetland thus,—"Trees in a wild state are entirely unknown here, and although several trials have been made, I do not think it probable that planting

will ever become a successful speculation in the islands.
The principal obstacle appears to me to be neither the
general hardships of the climate, nor, as is generally supposed, the prevalence of sea spray, which in winter is
often carried by the wind miles over the land, but rather,
I imagine, it is the shortness of the summer and the
early autumnal gales and frosts.   The trees, also, which
put out leaves early in spring are liable to be nipped
by frost, and few species have time to form their buds
before they are checked in September.   It is undeniable
that trees must have once existed extensively in Shetland, from the great abundance of peat which is principally formed of the debris of former forests.   The
time when these crowned with foliage the now barren
hills of *Thule* must have been very long ago, and we
can with no greater plausibility argue from that fact
that trees ought now to grow here than that the
ligneous ferns, and endogens which occur in the
quarries of Scotland should now flourish in the soil
beneath which their petrified remains are found
embedded."

Many of the trees in the garden at Halligarth have
however grown well, some of them are now from twelve
to sixteen feet in height, and are accounted a wonder
and an ornament.   Together with the interest of this
experiment in arboriculture, Thomas obtained from his
father " Wildenow's Introduction," and Macgillivray's
edition of " Withering's British Botany," and plunged

at once with the utmost zeal into the technical details
of the science. He became an admiring disciple of
Linnæus, and spent many happy healthful hours wandering over the hills and valleys of Unst, and gathering
its vegetable productions.

While on this subject it may not be uninteresting to
give an extract from the journal of an accomplished
tourist who sojourned a few days in Unst. The eldest
son of the late highly esteemed Sir William Hooker
was on his return from a naturalist's expedition to the
North Cape in a trading vessel, and on account of
stress of weather the ship ran for shelter to the bay
called Baltasound. Dr Hooker wrote thus :—" 3rd
Sept. 1836. Dr Edmondston brought his two sons on
board to see our remaining rein-deer. The eldest is a
particularly intelligent boy, passionately fond of natural
history, and his attempts at drawing are highly characteristic of the objects for which they were intended.
He has made a catalogue of the phænogamous plants of
those most northerly islands, the *Ultima Thule* of the
British group. Of this list it may be observed, imperfect
as it may be, it is the only thing like a commencement of a *Flora Shetlandica* which we have, and it is
the production of a boy of eleven years of age, who
possessed only two books on botany, and had no other
assistance whatever."

There are some leaves remaining of a sort of journal
kept by Thomas, an extract or two from which may be

amusing, but we shall premise a few sentences about his *coadjutor* and *countryman* the well known Shetland pony.

In no other part of Britain is the horse found in a state of such absolute savagism. Unstabled, ungroomed, very partially tamed or made useful, and that never for the first four or five years of their life, these diminutive horses are found roaming on the hills and commons at their own wild will ; not however without owners, as may be observed by certain marks, generally made on the ears, and of which a register is kept in each parish. Every family, whether in hall or cottage, is owner of one or two or many ponies. During spring and summer they are used with pack saddles for carrying manure or peats, and the gentry never think of walking even short distances, riding being considered the correct thing, as to most persons it is doubtless the most agreeable. All the ponies have proper names given them as soon as they have made any acquaintance with their owners. "Murphy" was called so because when a foal he had been saved from orphan starvation by being fed on potatoes. "Herman" got his name from his birthplace. Thomas had a very small steed of his own, and having just read in "Blackwood's Magazine" an article called "Christopher on Colonsay," with which he was much entertained, he named his horse "Colonsay," and, after some studies in Northern Antiquities, he called two others "Sigmund," and "Thora." They are never called " ponies," pony being only a comparative or diminutive expression where horses generally are so much larger. Dr Edmondston had an enclosure about a mile from the house, where, when grass began to fail at home, the riding horses were sent. It was an extensive pasture forming a promontory that projected into the sea. Here poor Colonsay met his death one day, and similar catastrophes often occur in Shetland. He had ventured too near the cliff in pursuit of some tempting looking pasturage, but lost his footing, and fell over. This enclosure is called Swinaness, and when the horses were in a rollicking mood, or perhaps averse to what they anticipated would be a dull wearisome journey, bearing the doctor to see his patients, they often gave great trouble to the servants, keeping them running after them for an hour or more—allowing them to approach close, and then starting off at the gallop, as if in triumph. It very often happens that these knowing animals will allow themselves to be caught and bridled by a child, when no other person, or several together, could by any means gain the object. Several of the horses belonging to the family knew the boys, and would even come at their call. One of them would never allow himself to be caught by any one except the young lady who was accustomed to ride him ; to her he would respond at half a mile's distance, and come bounding towards her. Nor was he at all a safe or a docile steed when any one but herself was the rider. As a rule, the whole race are free of vice, easily maintained, and patient of hardship, but in the degree of sagacity natural to each individual there are vast differences, some being essentially and obstinately *stupid*, while a few subjected to very similar training, or rather to no training at all properly so called, become affectionate, knowing, and very amusing. With this slight explanation we proceed to the journal.

Halligarth, 23rd Sept. 1835.

" On the 20th of this month I completed my tenth year, and I feel grateful to God for preserving me so long, and I pray Him that he will in future protect me.

" Mamma advises me to keep a journal of what occurs during each day especially relating to myself, and this is its commencement.

" I rose in the morning about eight, washed myself went down stairs and had breakfast ; went to Mary Park. Saw both my aunts there, and sat awhile with them. Came back, and wrote a few lines of an index to ' Chambers' Journal,' which, however, I must give up. Spent some time in keeping the crows away from the chickens—my tame crow attracts the wild ones. After dinner went to Swinaness with Herman, got a heavy shower when coming back ; saw a splendid rain-bow.

" *Thursday.*—Rose at eight, said my prayers, and went down to breakfast. Went an errand to Buness. Biot, little Mary, and me were bidden to dinner, and afterwards Uncle invited Biot and me to stay all night and have a rubber at whist. I won tolerably, and so did Biot.

"*Friday.*—Mamma says this last which I have written is very ill done, both in respect of writing and blots, and that I must try to do it better. I came from Buness after breakfast; went to Swinaness for Murphy, and, after dinner, read Natural History to Papa.

"*Saturday, Sunday, Monday, and Tuesday.*—I have forgot to write my journal. I hope I shall be more punctual in future. After dinner went to Buness with Biot, and Mary. . . . . .

Thursday omitted.

(No date).—"The Member of Parliament for Orkney and Shetland has been in Buness for these two days, and I have been there almost the whole time. After breakfast went to Swinaness with the two horses."

This diary was soon abandoned and was never punctually kept. At the date it begins, harvest was proceeding busily—and the school was shut, as is usual at that season. For, before this, Thomas and his brother Biot had been attending the parish schoolmaster, as private pupils in the evening, at his own house. He was a licentiate of the Church of Scotland, and an ex-excellent scholar. Like many of his class he was an intense student—books, of whatever kind, were his passion—and to a pupil whose desire it was to learn, he was one of the most useful and patient of teachers. But he was deficient in tact, was easy and careless with the idle, and had little idea of the discipline necessary for the disorderly and riotous. He was meek, gentle, and somewhat eccentric,—peace to his memory! he was a kind and efficient teacher to Thomas and his brother, and the affectionate regard between them all became cordial and unchanging. For about three years, but in a desultory way, Thomas attended this worthy man; first in the evenings, and apart from the general school, but when considered able to take care of himself and his brother, they went daily at the usual hours.*

In the Unst school there were from fifty to ninety scholars—male and female,—the schoolroom was low and dark—the floor was of earth. A huge fire place admitted, however, of a good fire, and each scholar daily carried with his books a large peat (which is an oblong piece of dried turf). When scholars were in full attendance, this made an excellent fire all the time of the

---

*The Parish Schools of Scotland are an institution peculiar to it. To every parish the schoolmaster is an official as necessary as the minister, and only second to his reverence in public estimation; his house and garden—his schoolroom and salary, belong to the landed proprietors, but, like the manses and glebes, are under the direction and surveillance of the presbyteries or church courts, and the protection of the civil law. A parochial schoolmaster cannot be removed or deprived of his emoluments, except through his own misconduct,—and all the children of the parish may attend, on payment of a very small fee. It is thus that the Scottish peasantry are almost all able at least to read and write. Thus did Robert Burns and the Ettrick Shepherd get all that education, of which they made a use so glorious.

lessons. But there were many days when only a few or perhaps no other pupils attended, when the largest number of boys and girls were necessarily employed at their homes, and schooling was not·to be thought of by them. These were the intervals when Thomas took full advantage of the master's greatest leisure, and he would sit for hours alone in the cold cheerless room, intent only on his books. In the most busy times of learning, on the other hand, the scholars were dismissed for about an hour in the middle of the day, ostensibly for the purpose of eating the bannock of oatmeal they generally brought with them; but besides that, they had a good game at foot-ball, or some other play. On these occasions Thomas invariably remained within, for then he could claim the master's exclusive attention, and his biscuit or his wheaten bread and butter were given to or shared with some poor child that had none. He was a very general favourite; the boys looked up to him, not because of his rank in life being superior to theirs, but because of his unselfishness—his obligingness,—his giving no offence. Only in punishment of wrong done to others, then he never hesitated to give battle to boys far his superiors in size. There was a girl who attended regularly; she was fatherless, very poor, and weak in mind; the other girls and boys used to teaze and sometimes ill-treat her. As soon as Thomas Edmondston was aware of this he set himself to put a stop to it; he constituted himself the poor girl's champion and defender, and gave some of her tyrants severe reproofs, and when these were insufficient, good pommellings, so that he himself not only gained respect, but screened her from all the annoyance she had previously borne in helpless weakness and distress.

We have said the attendance of Thomas at this parochial school, where a clergyman, although unbeneficed, was its teacher, was but desultory; it was so in consequence of an ordinary arrangement in such schools, certainly not the most favourable for the spread of education. The master we have been attempting to describe, seldom exacted fees from his pupils; he took what they liked to give, which was too often nothing; he had therefore only the small stipend allotted by law. But he had besides, a small bit of garden ground and pasture, and he rented an arable field or two. In spring and autumn, of course, therefore, he had his digging and sowing, his weeding and reaping to do, just in the way his cottar-pupils' families had, and so while the services of the youth were required at their homes, the master himself worked on his little farm. His stature and strength were almost gigantic, and those terms of school vacation were welcome and healthful, albeit not exactly conducive to the vigorous " shooting of the young idea." These labours appertaining to seed-time (vernacularly termed *the voar*,) and to harvest, required some weeks of a recess in April and September more or less; but eager as he was, young Thomas could not

task the time his master required for his own agricultural operations. But probably a day or two of very
unfavourable weather would intervene. Then the young
student would avail himself of the opportunity to snatch
instruction as it were, from one ever ready and proud
to impart it to him. During the summer, also, many
young persons who ought to be at school, are employed
in Unst bringing home the peats from the moors for
winter firing, or attending at the fishing stations, where
their help is required in the process of drying the
salted ling and tusk which the fishermen have taken at
the deep sea. The young Edmondstons, again, would
take advantage of the fine season, so short and precious
in that climate, to make excursions—visit friends—fish
and sail about—gathering up knowledge and experience
in other and probably as useful arts, certainly in much
more healthy circumstances than if they had spent the
long bright hours in a cheerless damp school-room. On
the whole, it was chiefly, if not exclusively, during
three or four months of the winter seasons, that Thomas
was anything like a regular attendant at the school,
where he studied Latin and Greek, Algebra and Mathematics. The choice was in some measure his own, and
he believed the ordinary branches of English education
quite beneath him as a *study.* Grammar, Elocution,
Geography, and History, he picked up by reading at
every odd moment, when he had nothing else to do.

But how did this bright clever boy fill up all those

weeks or months when his regular studies were from one cause or another interrupted? Was he merely what is called a "book worm"—reserved—contemplative—unadventurous? Altogether the reverse, as we shall see.

CHAPTER III.

—

Recreations in Shetland.

E have mentioned the bringing home of the winter stock of fuel by means of the ponies. The scenes connected with this annual business are quite unique and belong to Shetland life alone. Early in the month of May the able bodied men, before beginning the summer's fishing, *cut the peats* from the deep moss, situated generally miles from the dwellings where they are to be needed for dryness and warmth in the wet, cold, and stormy winter of Shetland. During some succeeding weeks the females of the households attend to the drying process, lifting the peats from the wet bog, turning over and raising them up, that air and sunshine may harden the oblong brick shaped masses and render them fit for fuel. When July arrives the ponies are in requisition; a hovel altogether of turf is also raised where the peats are ; the place is called the " peat hill," although it should in reality be a moor in a valley.   In those huts live a woman and a light active boy, the former to take care of horses, help to load them and generally look after her employers or parents' interest in the peats ; the boy drives the horses home ; the peats hang on pack saddles in light straw baskets called " *Keyshies ;*" slowly he walks behind a long string of the heavily laden, patient animals.   When unloaded he gets some refreshment and lets the horses have a little grass, then mounts one of the strongest, gallops them all to the hill again and again ; several times a day this occurs, so he is said to " ride the peats ;" he must be up and beginning the days labour as early as two in the morning, when the sun is appearing,—but, by seven in the evening, he is fast asleep on his turf bed, his horses made fast on some good pasture.   It becomes a great amusement to visit those primitive domiciles in " the peat hill," and a ride with the horses there, when the day's work was done, was a common custom with Thomas,—when he tried races with the peat boys, it must be said, without leave asked or given, as it was not a very safe sport for himself, nor quite proper for the tired little ponies.   " Boys will be boys, however, all the world over," has often been said and sung.

Living amongst an almost exclusively fisher or seafaring population, Thomas never cared much either for sailing or fishing. There is excellent trout fishing in a series of inland lochs and short streams, stretching eight miles from the extreme north to the south-west of Unst. But the taste of the angler was never his; he had nothing of the patience necessary for the lover of the "gentle craft." Nor had he any of the enthusiasm of his brother for sea fishing with rod or line; on the contrary, if Thomas were with a party on an expedition for fishing with the long lines, he was chiefly occupied in attempting to catch any floating star fish, or examining and securing, against all remonstrance of the boatmen, the sea urchins or any of the molluscæ brought from the deep by the fishing lines. Carrying home and studying and preserving these treasures was altogether to him a far greater gratification than catching fish, as he used to say, *only* to be sold or devoured.

On one occasion during boyish play there happened an alarming circumstance, which but for the interposition of a merciful Providence, might have proved fatal to three. In Unst, not far from Dr Edmondston's residence, is a quarry of the rare mineral called "chrome ore." It is found no where else in Britain, except in some of the Shetlands, and for many years has been a source of income to the lairds, besides giving employment to many men who work the quarries. The mineral is found in veins among the serpentine rocks, of which great part of the island is composed. Now Thomas had often seen how the quarrymen bored the rock, put in the blasting powder, and with a train exploded the mine, so as to get at the chromate.   He and his brother with a lad a little older than either, who was partly attendant, partly useful companion, fancied it would be a nice play to bore and blast some stones, chiefly that they might hear the grand report.   The lad Johnnie was sent to buy a pound of gunpowder with some pocket money the boys had got.   Having with great labour and a large nail bored a hole as deep as they could, they filled it with powder from the quart bottle in which their whole stock was kept.   Lighting the match paper they had themselves made and retiring a few feet, they found their mine did not explode, as it had done on previous occasions, and Thomas went forward to see what was the matter.   In an instant there was a fearful report, the three boys were flung to a distance of several feet in different directions, and not able to comprehend what had happened, only Thomas held in his hand the neck of the bottle, the rest of it with the powder was nowhere; and a blackening of his face and a slight scarification on the back of his hand, was all the damage.   Of course there was a great alarm in the house, but their father was absent, and they only received a lecture from their uncle.   In truth they had got a fright so serious that they needed no other warning against playing with gunpowder.

A favourite recreation of Thomas Edmondston in this second lustre of his age, as it had been of his father before him, was the taming and petting of wild birds of different kinds. Ravens, and the hoodie crows, are numerous, audacious, and destructive; but if taken from the nest ere fully fledged, they make sagacious and amusing pets. So does the shag, or cormorant; indeed, than this latter, none are more easily domesticated, or more affectionate to those who are kind to them. Thomas had a kestrel for some months, that lived in the garden, one wing being cropped. This bird knew the boy's footsteps and voice, and greeted him with a peculiar cry even at some distance. Various kinds of gulls having been rendered domestic by the children —when themselves too were babes—have frequented the yard and garden for as long as twenty years, daily returning and partaking with the poultry of their food. There has been a controversy among Ornithologists as to a peculiar variety in the plumage of one of the gull species (the *Larus Parasiticus*), and frequently did Thomas procure from the fishermen's lads two of these birds from the same nest, in order to try and set at rest the question, as to whether the white feathers on some of them was the result of age or sex. The problem is yet unsolved; this species will not live long in domestication, for they feed on the half digested food of another species, and are hence called *parasiticus*. Now, when the boys had pets like these to provide for, their wits had to be set agoing to procure fish for the water-fowl and flesh for the carnivorous, and to endeavour by degrees to accustom them to food more easily accessible, such as porridge, or curds, and the omni-present potato. One large and beautiful bird, very rarely found in Britain, except in Unst, the snowy owl, has been kept for some time on different occasions by one or other of the young Edmondstons.   Only one was ever sufficiently tamed to be allowed to walk about the yard, and it was banished at last for depredations among chickens and ducklings.   They are large, have powerful beak and talons, and are not to be trusted ; for as the nest of this splendid bird has never yet been found in the island, the individuals that were caught—only slightly injured by the shot—were too far advanced in life for the commencement of successful education.

That singular creature, the seal, has, in several instances, been completely domesticated in Unst.   There was a very interesting one in Buness when Thomas was a baby.   Once, having been left asleep in his cot for a few minutes, the seal made its way into the room, and was found gazing intently on the face of the sleeping child,—meaning no harm we are sure, but yet considering the size and immense power of the animal, which two men could not restrain, it was a sight to shake the firmest nerves ; yet, the gentle creature, when called, floundered and flopped away at once to its own region.

There was another very fine affectionate animal of this species, which had been many months a denizen of a comfortable out-house, but was so completely tamed, that he was allowed to go on the sea daily for recreation and food, returning at once to the land when called by the person who had the special charge of him. It was a severe and long felt grief to the boys, when this interesting creature lost its way in a sudden snow shower, and having strayed a few miles out in the bay, went ashore on a low beach, where, doubtless, expecting the welcome he had been accustomed to, and the draught of new milk he enjoyed after his bathe, he advanced confidently, but was instantly clubbed and killed.

There are many superstitions associated with the history and manners of the seal in Shetland. One is that those who injure them will not thrive. And it was verified in the case of the man who killed that pet " selkie." Their skins and fat or blubber are valuable, but, in general, they are carefully avoided by the peasantry, as " no canny." Indeed, the singularity of the animal, half fish, half dog, its immense strength, its unusual mournful cry, quite like that of a child, and, above all, the soft melancholy intelligence of its large and beautiful eyes, combine to make ordinary Shetlanders eschew their acquaintance.

Otters are also found on the shores of most of the islands, and are caught in traps, or shot. One of these animals was tamed by the family, whose pleasant pastime it ever was to study the dispositions and habits of all species. The otter seems a link between the seal and more decided land mammals. The one alluded to was accustomed to play with a sagacious, good tempered shepherd's dog, but, after some month's trial, was dismissed to liberty and the sea shore, for officiousness, and sometimes mischief.

The bay of Baltasound, on the shores of which were and are the residences of the Edmondston family, is situated on the east side of the island of Unst, and takes its name from the narrow channel or sound that separates the larger isle from the small uninhabited one called Balta. The bay is above two miles long, and three-quarters of a mile across. It is shut in by Balta from the rough surges of the North Sea, and forms the most northerly harbour in Britain where vessels may find safe access and refuge in time of need. It had been for many years the resort of French, Dutch, and Belgian fishing sloops, which were accustomed to run in for fresh water and other supplies, or for shelter in boisterous weather. Very frequently a corvette or sloop of war would be in attendance on the part of those governments, in order that the fishers might be protected and assisted in cases of necessity. It was the custom of Mr Edmondston of Buness to send his servant (of whom more hereafter), very often accompanied by his boy nephew, to offer the strangers any hospitality or help in his power. Not unfrequently it would happen that none of the foreign officers could speak English. Young Thomas then, although still ignorant of French, or any other modern language, would pick

up the surgeon, or even an intelligent midshipman not
beyond school days, and with the tyro Latin he had
acquired, would make amusing and, indeed, useful
companionship. The same with the good natured
Dutch skippers; a word or two once heard of their
lingua franca, interpersed with *broad Scotch*, and Latin,
and the meaning of everything was made clear. With
all this quickness of apprehension, there were mingled
the simplicity and frolic of the mere boy he was. His
manners were equally removed from assumption and
timidity. When the newspapers and periodicals arrived
in files as they did, because of the few post days in that
remote locality, Thomas used to skim everything with
avidity in a time so short, that it was hardly noted. Then
he would read the interesting parts to his uncle, and
argue the political situation with him, or amuse the circle
with imaginary personations of the chief public men of
the time; next minute he had disappeared, and would
be deep in algebraic calculations, or writing labels for
his herbarium. At this time, deprived by geographical
position, of the society of any companion of his own
rank, excepting only his brother, both boys were thrown
much into contact with the peasant and fisher lads,
their uncle's tenants or dependants; and this arose
not so much that these boys needed other society than
their own immediate circle of relatives, but, that at
school, they freely mingled with the other boys, and,
more especially, that the Shetland gentry, as a rule,

have far more intimate associations with the peasantry than is usual elsewhere. The lower class, again, are confidential with their superiors, polite, and perfectly respectful in their demeanour towards them. They never presume on familiarity, or seem betrayed into forgetfulness of the difference in rank. This is a favourable and well known trait. Both in sport and more serious occupations, it will readily be imagined, that Thomas became a leader, an oracle, an example to many far his seniors in years, but in mental culture, as in grade of life, as much beneath him. Brave, and even daring, he took part in such amusements and adventures as youth is so fond of, or as the locality would admit of. One dangerous sport alone was strictly prohibited, and he willingly gave his friends a promise, that he would never engage in it. This was " fowling," generally so called,—venturing on those rugged and lofty cliffs, where the wild fowl rest and nestle, where a single false step, or a piece of crumbling rock giving way, the adventurous climber is precipitated to a certain and horrible death. Many such 'accidents take place in Shetland, and yet they do not seem to have the warning voice one would expect. The youth, for the sake of a supper of wild fowl eggs, or a young bird or two, will run risks that makes the blood run cold to think of. Not the gain, but the enterprize, the danger, perhaps emulation of a comrade's hardihood stimulates the rash attempts. There is one man in Unst to whose exploits

Thomas often listened with a kindling eye and cheek, who surprised and captured a sea eagle on her nest on a frightful crag, inaccessible to any foot but his own. Of this daring feat Thomas wrote an account, which will be found in its place further on. His own brother very narrowly escaped the fowler's dreadful death, but it occurred from his only venturing too near the edge of a steep incline, when his foot slipped, and he rolled over several yards towards the brink of a sheer precipice. By a strong exercise of presence of mind he recollected his danger, and, as his body rolled over the edge of the cliff, he managed to turn and grasp the long grass and turf that grew there. Imagine the situation ! Hanging by the hands only over an abyss where, at the base, roared the sea over broken rocks 200 feet below. Should the frail hold give way ! There was only time for a mental prayer for help, and he very gradually drew himself up by the strength of arms and hands alone. He was at this time about seventeen, and had been accustomed to practise gymnastic exercises, to which circumstance alone, under Providence, he believed he owed his safety. Once the centre of gravity of his body was secure on the slope, it may easily be supposed he crawled cautiously, and with a wildly beating heart, to the level place above, where his cousin waited in speechless, motionless terror, and the moment when their hands met in the assisting welcoming grasp, was one never to be forgotten by either.

Thomas was both manly and cautious, and, it may be supposed that like most boys, he was eager to handle and to use a gun. It was under the auspices of his uncle's confidential servant that he early learnt to use the heavy fowling-piece, with which he became most expert at shooting birds and rabbits. The only game, if so it may be called, in Shetland is those burrowing creatures last named, and the numerous species of sea fowl. Thomas had been well accustomed to the gun before his relatives at all suspected it; for Peter kept the secret, afraid that the indulgence might be forbidden, and yet confident in his own and the boy's carefulness. In after days he ever smiled at the prowess of his young favourite, to whom he in turn was indebted for much general information, and many wonderful stories of other lands. It is with pleasing, yet melancholy satisfaction, that a few particulars are here added of this remarkable man, who died in the prime of manhood from hereditary lung disease.

Peter Sutherland was a fisherman's son, and intended for the same life occupation, but, when a mere boy, he was employed at one of the fishing stations of the Buness tenantry as a " beech " boy,—that is, one who attends to the spreading out, turning over, and gathering up again of the salted ling, tusk, and cod, as they are dried on a stony beach near the place where the boats arrive with their spoil from the " haff," or deep sea fishing grounds. Peter shewed in those early days so much intelligence, quiet industry, and bodily strength, that he was taken to Buness, and became a helper about the home farm; afterwards the chief hand in the master's pleasure boat, and finally his trusty *factotum* and overseer of all his possessions. Peter was a genuine Scandinavian in the fair hair and complexion and mild blue eyes; he was above six feet in height, and well proportioned, with prodigious bodily strength, and a wonderful versatility and ingenuity in the multiplicity of affairs that come under the notice of a country gentleman; and a keen sportsman in a locality so very remote, that hundreds of devices were required, often on the spur of the moment, to supplement the absence of all shops and tradesmen. Peter had no education, properly so called. He could understand what he read to himself, and was fond of books of travels or *theology*, and when the newspapers, magazines, or a new novel, were read aloud at Buness, Peter might almost always be descried in a dark corner of the low roofed old fashioned parlour, an eager and appreciating listener. His manners were naturally gentle and polite; he was brave, yet prudent; reserved, yet kindly. He was also well known as the strongest man in Shetland. The heavy burdens he could carry,—the pair of heavy oars he pulled without a visible effort,—the powerful animals he could fearlessly take hold of and keep fast, were physical qualities as useful as they were admired and even envied. Had such a one been a brawler, or of a tyrannical disposition, he must have been feared and avoided, but he was quite the reverse, modest, quiet, and placable.   On one Christmas morning, when some neighbours had been enjoying freely the usual " *Yule Dram*," two brothers, who had most unprovokedly nourished a jealous hostility against Peter, attacked him out of doors, challenging him to fight.   He replied that he would, but " one at a time."   However, they both rushed on him, and it was a sight to be remembered to see Peter, one hand wounded and bleeding with the first onslaught, yet stand firm, holding both the men at arm's length, one in each hand, until bystanders took them off.   His temper was not even ruffled.

It was with this man, careful, trustworthy, and intelligent, that his master's nephew made most of his earliest excursions.   Being in the house when the child was born, the strong willing arm was the first to teach the brave but fragile little one to ride the diminutive pony, and to hold the tiny fishing rod over a small pond in " make-believe " angling.   It was Peter who manufactured or mended the toy tools and armoury, and, in years more advanced, was his guide and assistant in many expeditions, with mutual satisfaction, and, who shall not say, mutual benefit.

CHAPTER IV.

—

Boyish Studies.

1835–38.

HAVING thus shortly sketched the chief recreations available in Shetland life, and they may not appear altogether idle, uninstructive pastimes, let us see a few of the mental exercises which, to Thomas, were, indeed, quite as attractive.

Natural history was his passion, his work, his study, and his play, yet how varied were the subjects that engaged his boyish attention, may be gathered from the contents of a " common place book," with which his father presented him on his eleventh birth-day, advising him to note down any extracts or observations he might consider useful or interesting. It was commenced forthwith, and is closely filled, clearly, and very correctly written. A list of the subjects, with a few extracts *verbatim*, will suffice to point out the untutored and nearly unprompted workings of a noble boy's mind and heart. The first pages are of birds. This is the account of a pet kestrel he had lately had.

" Kestrel *(Falco Tinnunculus).*—This beautiful and interesting bird is very easily tamed when young. I got a nest of kestrels from Burra-firth, consisting of four birds, two of which I gave away in presents; the third escaped, and found its way to the place where it was brought out. The fourth I reserved for myself. It was about the size of a starling *(Sturnus Vulgaris),* barred on the back with dark chocolate colour, of a dirty yellowish white below, with black streaks or spots; head rather large; neck short; cere and bill yellow. The latter, in the individual before me, was not much hooked; and, also, a little (accidentally) to one side. It was quite tame, and allowed any body to handle and examine it. It loved a warm roosting place at night, and when whole birds were given as its food, it first plucked them carefully, and laid the feathers in a heap in order to sit on them at night. It knew my step, and followed me, and came to my call. After a few months this interesting bird died from picking up something from the floor."

After this there follows a series of notes on the different species of gulls, verifying, from his own observation what he ever delighted to do, the discoveries his father had made in Ornithology. The following, on *Insects,* succeeds :—

" What is called in Shetland the midge, is probably the May-fly *(Ephemera Vulgata)*, and not the *Culex Pulicarius* as is supposed. It may be argued that the *Ephemera Vulgata* has four membranous wings, and, therefore, belongs to the order *Neuroptera*, while the other is a *Dipterous*, but I have seen individuals of the May-fly with only two wings, and there are others of the same genus with only two wings, as the *Ephemera Diptera* and *Marginata*. Mr E. Stewart, in his ' Annals of Natural History,' says, ' In the evenings, in the month of June, it assembles in vast numbers above and near running streams, and seems to divert itself for hours together, ascending and descending in the air as if dancing,' (page 225.) This corresponds exactly with the habits of the Shetland midge, commonly called *Culex Pulicarius.*

" The ' Horn clock ' of Shetland is likely the cockchaffer, *Scarabæus Melolontha Vulgaris.*

" The *Musca Vomitaria* is the Shetland fish-fly."

The next entry is a complete list of the Linnæan system of classification, commencing with plants, then the mammalia, and birds.

Following this are,—

Some quotations from Shakespeare.

An extract, in Danish and English, from " The Frithjoff Saga."

The legendary letter of Publius Lentullus to the Senate of Rome, concerning Jesus Christ.

Theories of the Earth, according to several celebrated men.

The prayer of Charles XII. of Sweden to St Nicholas, his patron Saint, against the Muscovites.

An account of the equipment of Linnæus when setting out on his botanical tour to Lapland.

A memorandum of the localities in Britain where grows the Linnæa Borealis.   And

Some extracts from an old " common place book ;" decidedly metaphysical and speculative, especially on the question, " Is there any future state for the animal creation ?"   This last was a subject Thomas delighted to advocate, and, perhaps, no one who has not investigated the point, can imagine how much authority and ingenuity may be brought to bear upon it.

Other notes of his own occur interspersedly : here are one or two :—

" A young sailor (Andrew Spence), who has been in Brazil, has brought home with him a parrot.   I have seen and made a drawing of it.   It was scarcely fledged when the lad got it.   Its head and neck are grey ; its wing feathers bluish green.   It has a pretty long tail, &c.

" A great cause of the scarcity in Shetland is owing to the ground being worn out by forcing up potatoes with manure, instead of turning them out of beer or oat root, which, also, invariably produces the best potatoes.

" *Phoca Barbata* (Greater Seal).—Cause of the strong smell of coal tar proceeding from the skin. Coal tar is known to consist in a great measure of carbon, as does the air which proceeds from the lungs. When the animal in question is under water, where it retains respiration for a long time, the air proceeds from the skin under the form of carburetted hydrogen, of which last the air in the lungs contains a great quantity."— *3rd January* 1837.

			WILD PLANTS.
" In Southern Georgia grow	.	.	2
„ Spitzbergen .	—	.	. 30
„ Lapland .	—	.	. 534
„ Iceland .	—	.	. 553
„ Sweden .	—	.	. 1289
„ Brandenburg	—	.	. 2000
„ Piedmont .	—	.	. 2800
„ Coromandel .	—	.	. 4000
„ Jamaica .	—	.	. 4000
„ Madagascar .	—	.	. 5000

" A Stork *(Ardea Ciconia)* was lately killed at Dunrossness, and is now in the possession of Mr W. M. Cameron, Gardie. It is, I believe, the only instance of a stork being found in Shetland.—*4th June* 1837.

" Mr Cross, the ingenious Englishman, has produced a very singular result by the action of electricity on powdered flint. On bringing the voltaic battery to bear on powdered flints, he was greatly surprised to see living insects come out. It is accounted for in this way, viz., that the ova of insects being in the flint, by the action of the electric battery they were hatched. The insect is of a different species from any now recognised. Other gentleman have tried the same experiment, and produced the same result.

"*5th November* 1837.—I have this day seen a cuckoo in the field at Halligarth."

It will be sufficient merely to say, that the rest of the entries are chiefly lists on subjects of Natural History, copied from books, to which he had not always access, as,—

> " Ray's Animated Nature."
> " Tournefort's System of Plants."
> " Linnæus Systemæ Naturæ."
> " Hooker's Flora," &c.

There are also copies of some of Sir Walter Scott's songs in the " The Pirate," which he had read at this time with intense interest,—the date, 18th May 1837.

The nomenclature of plants was very early a favourite branch of study, so that there was working in the boy's mind, the idea he afterwards began to follow out, viz., that of founding a new and more perspicuous system. It was this idea that stimulated him so early to learn Greek, which is the key to so much of Botanical nomenclature. In the note book there appear some elaborate remarks on the system of naming species and

genera,—whether copied or original does not appear.
The last entry is a catalogue of the plants composing
the *Materia Medica* of London and Edinburgh Colleges.
And about this time it is remembered he said with the
utmost enthusiasm, " I must be a doctor, it is the noblest
profession in the world."

Immediately succeeding the common place book, of
which the contents have been mentioned, there follows
another, which has appended to it rather a curious
history.   On the fly leaf is written,—

" Presented to Thomas Edmondston, junior, by W.
Auld, Esq., Edinburgh, 27th July 1837. This book
belonged to a Sergeant-major in the French army during
the retreat from Moscow in 1812–13."

The book is an octavo, bound in vellum, and was blank,
a few leaves of the Frenchman's memorandum having
been obviously torn out. Perhaps the owner lay in
his last sleep on a bloody or a frozen bed when it was
taken from his person. Its new possessor soon filled it
with pen and ink sketches of birds, plants, and their
several organs, and also catalogues. A few leaves contain plain and popular refutations of the chief dogmas
of Popery,—transubstantiation, Mariolatry, purgatory,
auricular confession, and indulgences.

There are several other larger books, and numerous
scraps of loose paper, full of drawings, chiefly in pencil.
The sketches are wonderfully correct copies from
" Bewick's British Birds," with fishes, and many plants

from nature. There are, also, fanciful birds and other animals, the like of which never existed, and imaginary persons, regarding whom he wrote and talked romances. But he never, so far as is known, indulged in the unkindly and dangerous habit of caricature.

The following, written on the torn out fly leaf of a book, carelessly scrawled and corrected, is interesting, and is believed to be original :—

"Thomas Edmondston, junior,
" *20th March* 1837.

" A PRAYER FOR SUNDAY EVENING.

" O Lord, I bow before Thee in the dust, on this the close of another Sabbath. I acknowledge Thy wisdom and goodness in ordaining Thee one day in the seven, for Thy everlasting glory and praise. O God, for the sake of Thy dear Son, teach me to remember the Sabbath. This was the day when Thy beloved Son rose triumphant over death and the grave. Hell conspired all their forces to keep him in, but he broke their chains, and now lives triumphant at Thy right hand, a merciful mediator and intercessor for us fallen and depraved sinners. I thank Thee, O my Lord, for all the blessings Thou hast bestowed on my unworthy head. Pour the sanctification of Thy Holy Spirit on me, and let all the world see how unworthily and sinfully they behave towards Thee ; yet Thy loving mercies are not restrained. O, well may we say with the sweet

Psalmist of Israel, ' Thy goodness endureth for aye.'
Keep, O Lord, and protect me during the night, when
all nature is hushed, and raise me up on another day with
all my faculties alive to praise and laud the Maker and
Giver of all good ; but, if Thou choose me not to enter
upon another day in this world of sin and tribulation,
O, prepare me for the next, and, whenever it happens,
prepare me to endure it, and trust in Christ as my only
rock and salvation. *Amen.*"

" Our Father," &c.

Within the leaves of one of the note books was a
loose slip of paper, apparently the fly leaf torn out of
an old book. It contained the Lord's Prayer in old
Shetland dialect, in the handwriting of Thomas Edmondston, and was probably taken down from the mouth
of one of the two aged men, who still, in those days,
recollected a few words or phrases of what is now totally
extinct. On lately submitting this specimen to His
Imperial Highness Prince Lucien Bonaparte, who is
acknowledged to be the best authority as to the various
dialects of the languages of Europe, he gives it as his
opinion that " the old Norse or Norse, was a distinct
dialect, not only of the Icelandic, but of the Faröese,
and that it was spoken in two varieties, very similar in
Orkney and in Shetland," and this, as a specimen of
the Shetlandic form, His Highness considers most
interesting, and worth preserving. For which reason
a copy is here given, only remarking, that it is supposed

there may be slight inaccuracies, hardly to be avoided in writing from oral sounds a language totally unknown; but yet, from its resemblance to the Orkney form of the same words,* it is, on the whole, wonderfully correct.

THE LORD'S PRAYER IN OLD SHETLANDIC

Fy vor o er i chimeri, Haagt vara Nam det; La Koningdom din cumma; La villin vera guerde i vrildin sin dacre chimeri; Gav wis dagh ur dought brau; Forgivie sindor wasa sin vi forgiva dem as sindor wasa wus; Lea wus ki o vera tempa, at delivra wus fra adla idluor; For du er koningdom ri puri o glori.

---

* In Barry's History of Orkney; 2nd. Edition.

CHAPTER V.

—

Botanical Tours.

1838–39.

THE gradually progressive preference for Botany over the other branches of Natural History is obvious in Thomas Edmondston's note books and drawings, and in this study his zeal and diligence received great encouragement and reward by a visit to Unst of Dr Gilbert M'Nab, (son of the late Mr Jas. M'Nab of the Edinburgh Botanic Garden). On looking over the herbarium Thomas had acquired, consisting of Unst plants only, Dr M'Nab expressed the utmost surprise and satisfaction at the accuracy with which the young collector had scientifically named the specimens. Of one or two only he expressed himself doubtfully, and sought information. One of these turned out to be a plant altogether new to the British Flora. There was much that was touching and ennobling, and long to be

remembered in the flush of astonishment and delight
that suffused his ingenuous countenance when the
experienced botanist told the boy he had found a new
plant,—he, who had never been out of his native island,
never had seen a plant from any other. He soon took
Dr M'Nab to the place where still grows, and grows only
there, the *Arenaria Norvegica*, to which various refer-
ences will be found in the succeeding correspondence.

The boy's delight and enthusiasm in the study of
botany were farther to be encouraged by an excursion
to the neighbouring island of Fetlar with his father,
where, in two busy days, he possessed himself of
specimens of all its vegetable treasures. The following
season, Mr Goodsir (late Professsor of Edinburgh University), and the late lamented Edward Forbes, visited
Dr Edmondston, and with them Thomas was permitted
to examine for a few days some of the immediately
contiguous islands, and soon afterwards he obtained the
anxiously desired leave to make a botanical tour of
Shetland. It was rather a perilous undertaking for a
boy under fourteen ; but he accomplished it alone and
with great success, although the weather during the
whole time was most unpropitious. He went first to
Lerwick by the small sailing packet that weekly
traverses the 60 miles of angry water lying between
Unst and the Shetland *metropolis*. Lest we should be
misunderstood, we may explain it is the *only* town in
the archipelago, and contains about 3000 inhabitants,

but it is the emporium of trade, the seat of law executive, and the *terminus* of the steam traffic for mails and tourists from the south. Thomas was there only two days, and then began his progress to Sumburgh, the extreme south of the land. Anon, by the west side to some of the islands there, and then home through Yell. He was always hospitably received, and entertained as long as he chose to remain at the manses, or residences of the gentry or tacksmen. Indeed, the wayfaring traveller need never be at a loss for shelter and refreshment, albeit there are no hotels or places of public entertainment. That there are none is doubtless a drawback in the way of parties of tourists, but a single pedestrian like Thomas, or even two, will rarely have to complain that the proverbial Scottish hospitality has waxed cold in the extreme north.

It was in the course of this three week's tour that our young Botanist obtained from personal observation the principal materials for a short account of the islands appended to his Shetland Flora, published a few years afterwards, from which the following is extracted :—

" The Shetland Islands are a group lying between 59° 5′ and 60° 50′ N. Latitude, about 70 miles from the extreme north of Orkney, and 130 from Cape Wrath. The islands exceed 100 in number ; of these, however, not above 30 are inhabited, the remainder being islets (vernacularly called *Holms*), and *Skerries*, which are appropriated to the grazing of sheep or abandoned to the sovereignty of the sea fowl.

" Shetland is peculiarly interesting to the geologist, as it is one of the best examples in Britain of the formation called *primitive*, from its being considered the oldest deposit of rocks. Almost every part of the islands is composed of this formation, and all the rocks belonging to it are found here. From the dissimilarity between Orkney on the one hand and Faröe on the other, it appears evident that Shetland belongs to the series termed *oceanic* islands, for it is as dissimilar in geological structure to the sandstone nearly universal in Orkney, as to the trap and basalt of Faröe.

" The principal island of the group is Mainland, about 60 miles long from south-east to north-west. Its southern extremity, Sumburgh Head, with its fearful tide or roost, is immortalized by Sir Walter Scott in ' The Pirate.' A little north-west from Sumburgh is a still higher cape, Fitful Head, also rendered classic ground by the same magician's pencil, as the rather stormy residence of the pythoness ' Norna.' On the eastern shore of this southern district, called the parish of Dunrossness, is the low island of Moosa, on which is to seen the most perfect ' Pictish Burgh ' in the country. These curious old buildings have excited great speculation among antiquaries ; some considering them once fortified citadels ; others, because they occur pretty regularly along the coast, suppose that they were intended for watch towers, from which, by means of beacons, an alarm might be communicated in case of sudden invasion. Another hypothesis is, that they were used as store houses. But the extreme antiquity of these remarkable erections prevents any certainty as to their objects and uses being now attained. They are numerous in Shetland, but are generally much dilapidated.

" Lerwick, in Mainland, is irregularly built, and picturesquely situated on a rising ground close to the sea, on the south side of the expansive and beautiful harbour of Bressay Sound, and facing the island of Bressay. The small island of Noss lies eastward of Bressay ; close to it is an islet called the Holm of Noss, and across the fearful chasm that separates them is slung the cradle of Noss. This very original vehicle of transit has often been described by travellers, as most of them, should they only remain a day, make a point of visiting it, and, should the state of their nervous system allow, they may even make an aerial trip into the Holm. The cradle is just a strong wooden box slung upon two ropes stretched across the chasm between Noss island and the Holm. In this the adventurer deposits himself, and, by aid of the ropes, pulls himself across. The strong posts to which the ropes are fixed, were first placed in the Holm by a daring cragsman, who scaled the mural precipice from below. Tradition adds, that refusing to take advantage of the cradle in his return, but attempting to descend the cliff, he lost his life.

" The highest land in Shetland is Roness Hill, a large roundish mass of granite, about 1500 feet in altitude, and it is the only place where Alpine plants occur.

" Unst, the most northerly island, is also one of the most picturesque, and the most interesting to the naturalist. It is about twelve miles long, and may average three-and-a-half in breadth. The geological formation is varied, the rocks being gneiss, mica slate, quartz, euphotide, and serpentine. Several plants of great interest occur also in Unst. On the serpentine hill near Baltasound grows *Arenaria Norvegica* and *Cerastium Nigrescens*, neither of which has been hitherto observed in any other part of Britain. In a sandy bank at Burra-firth grows the rare *Lathyrus Maritimus*, not elsewhere found in Scotland. The northern extremity of Unst is Hermaness, and is one of the few remaining breeding places of the Great Skua *(Lestris Catarractes.)* On a high rock or stack named the *Outsta* (or out-stack), which is the most northerly British land, grows profusely *Cochlearia Officinalis*,—the plant therefore that penetrates furthest north, thus displaying its adventurous character.

"The climate of these islands is by no means so severe as might be inferred from its high latitude. The temperature even in severe seasons is seldom very low for any considerable length of time, and snow ; generally speaking, does not lie long. The insular situation, constantly exposed to the sea breeze, furnishes a ready solution of this phenomenon. In summer most visitors concur in considering it very agreeable, the heat being much less intense than in most parts of Scotland. The prevalence of moisture is characteristic of all insular climates, and of this likewise. Even the summer's smile is often obscured by damp fogs ; and in winter, snow and thaw alternate with a rapidity and perseverance less healthy than the long tracts of clear frosty weather with which continental countries are favoured.

" The Shetland Islands, taking them as a whole, have much tameness in the scenery. The hills are low, and woods are absent. These circumstances combined with the prevalence of peat-moss, and the small proportion of cultivated land, give a dull and sombre appearance to a great part of the country, especially if contrasted with the fertile valleys of the Lothians, or with the majestic scenery of the Scottish highlands ; so that in some degree the poet is justified who applied to them the epithet of ' Melancholy Thule.' Yet these unfavourable appearances are not without redeeming points, and few who have beheld a Shetland scene on a fine summer's day are likely soon to forget it. The numerous land-locked creeks and bays wrapped in profound repose and looking more like inland lakes than arms of the great Atlantic, while the humble cottages and crofts of the fishermen skirting the shore, and their light and graceful skiffs speckling the waters, impart to many a spot an aspect of peaceful retirement and primitive simplicity most pleasing to contemplate. But the most striking features must certainly be sought for among the maritime rocks and cliffs. Though the elevation of these is not so great as in Faröe and some other places, yet, I hesitate not to say, in variety and sublimity they are not to be surpassed. The overhanging precipices, gloomy caverns, and giant-like isolated rocks, of the most weird-like fantastic forms, peopled too by myriads of sea-fowl, while the surges of the northern ocean roll and boil and whirl in a ceaseless thundering roar, form a scene of grandeur and beauty which the lover of majestic nature will heartily appreciate."

Ever since Professor Edward Forbes' visit to Dr Edmondston, Thomas kept up a correspondence with him. To that generous and talented friend the youthful naturalist was deeply indebted for advice and assistance in those points on which they were so congenial. The letters Thomas sent to him are irrecoverably lost, but a few extracts from those of Forbes may be interesting.

"To Thomas Edmondston, Jun.

"Edinburgh, April 1840.

"My Dear Friend,—Circumstances have so fallen out that I have not been able to answer your most interesting letter before this. - - - - I regret much that Mr

Goodsir and I did not take the route in Shetland we first intended, the more so as the specimens you mention would have been invaluable treasures, as I am busily occupied with the lower classes of invertebrate animals. Among those tribes there is a grand field in Shetland. I know no place which would more certainly reward the investigator with a rich harvest, - - - - - I am sadly puzzled what elementary books to select for you. There are much better books in French than in English, and introductions to Botany are more numerous and better than similar works on Zoology. I enclose you a paper of mine on the star fishes. When my book on that tribe is out I shall send it you number after number by post. I should be very glad if you can give me any information on the Medusa's head star-fish, said to be called 'Argus' in Shetland, or on the sea-urchin with very long spines called 'Piper,' and any fancies of the fishermen concerning them. Mr Campbell tells me you have sent some notes to the Botanical Society. The plants you mention are good and most acceptable to the Society, and you may exchange them for foreign or other British ones."

"26th May 1840.

- - - - - - - - "Permit me to thank you for your notice of the 'Piper' and the 'Argus.' At the present moment they are most valuable. If by any chance you obtain a specimen of Euryalid send it, either dry or in spirits to Mr Goodsir. As to preserving starfishes soak them in fresh water for an hour, then boil in fresh water for ten minutes, and dry in a current of air. The medusæ cannot be preserved—make drawings of them. To extract a univalve mollusc, let the creature die in fresh water and remain there till it come out easily. - - - - - - Wishing you every success in your studies, I remain, ever sincerely yours,

"EDWARD FORBES."

CHAPTER VI.

—

Seeing the World.

1840.

IT may be imagined that how much soever Thomas Edmondston may have loved his home, making the most of the opportunities for improvement which it afforded, he would yet gladly hail the prospect of seeing a little more of the world, when it was purposed that he should accompany his mother and uncle to Edinburgh in the summer of 1840. On one of the last days of June, the voyage commenced in a six-oared boat. It was a most beautiful afternoon and the sea was still as an inland lake. There came on no darkness. The sun just hid himself in the north west for a short time, leaving a dim delicious twilight, while the boatmen rowed softly, and now and then a solitary sea-bird skimmed along, us

if, with eager wing and cry, it was hastening to its
nestlings. Then majestically uprose the god of day
again, and still the expanse of ocean slept calmly on.
Lerwick was reached before eight in the morning, and
the same evening the travellers embarked in the steamer
for Leith. They first called at Kirkwall, in Orkney,
then at Wick, then at Aberdeen, finally reaching Leith
on the afternoon of the 3rd July, and throughout those
two days and nights the weather continued perfectly
fine. The several stoppages on this northern passage
enliven and break the monotony of the sea voyage most
agreeably, and the youthful tourist enjoyed it excessively. Examining all parts of the vessel, and the wondrous mechanism of the steam engine, attending to the
comforts of some rare birds he was carrying to a naturalist
friend, and going ashore for an hour when the steamer
called at the places mentioned, Thomas was fully
occupied. Or he paced the deck, drinking in the balmy
ocean air that carries with it such a sense of boundless
freedom, and looking forth afar into the glorious future
on which he believed he was now entering. Whenever the vessel neared the land, with a telescope he
was looking out for trees. Ending the voyage in the
steamer at the populous sea-port of Leith, was not at
all favourable for his enthusiasm in that particular ;
but as he and his friends drove on to Edinburgh, the
shrubberies, with lilacs and laburnums in full flower,
afforded him unqualified delight. Transported at once

from Unst to the heart of Mid Lothian, his longings—
his sensibilities, all aroused and gratified—we may
perhaps slightly, but not wholly understand his feelings. The streets, the traffic, the buildings, were
entirely novel, almost unimagined, and yet not these,
or even the stately castle, and the noble hills round the
city, were in his thoughts, or they were as nothing in
comparison. It was "Oh, for the woods,—oh, just to
get to the plants on Arthur's Seat!"

In Edinburgh, Glasgow, and other places they visited,
Thomas saw many of his maternal relatives. Some of
the other persons and things he made personal acquaintance with, will appear in a few quotations from his
letters.

"Edinburgh, 4th July 1840.

"My dear Papa,—Here we are, safe and sound in
body and mind, domiciliated in the *domus* of Uncle D.
We arrived about tea-time. - - - - - Uncle and
I have been over half the town to-day. We have seen
Dickson's Nursery Grounds, and half a dozen monu-
ments. - - - -"

"7th July

"- - - - The chief thing I have to tell you is that
I am acknowledged the sole discoverer of *Arenaria
Norvegica* and *Lathyrus Maritimus.* I drank tea last
night with Dr Graham,* and took some of my specimens

---

* Professor of Botany in the University.

with me. He received me very kindly, and shewed me many specimens, and as I wished it, we looked over them all, comparing them with mine. . . . He has read a paper to the Botanical Society on the subject. Dr Hooker has published a new edition of his Flora, and therein mentions these two plants as found by me, so that it is all settled now. Dr Graham bids me always apply for any plants I wish for from the Botanic Garden. He is extremely urgent for me to come with him and a party of students for a week on a botanical excursion to Clova, by far the richest place in Great Britain, for variety and rarity of plants. But of course I can say nothing without hearing from you. I got an order from Dr Balfour to see the Museum of the College of Surgeons. It is a magnificent place. I saw Mr Mac Gillivray* there; he was remarkably kind —shewed me all over the Museum, and invited me to dine with him to day. He desired me to give you his very best thanks for the notes you sent him. I then went to the College, and gave your letter to Mr Small.† He took me all over the library, and told me to come whenever I wanted books. I met Professor Jamieson as he was going to his class-room ; he also was extremely kind. He was in a hurry then, but told me to come back, and he would give me an order to be in the

---

* Afterwards Professor of Natural History in Aberdeen.
† The Librarian.

Museum every day. . . . . . After leaving the College, we got an order to see the Regalia in the Castle ; went to Holyrood, and then I botanized some time with Ashby on Salisbury Crags. - - - -"

"Thursday, 2 P.M.

"I have been very busy all this day. I dined at Mac Gillivray's yesterday. He showed me all his most beautiful collections, &c., and gave me the new volume of his work (British Birds) for you. You will see yourself quoted all through the book, and in the preface he calls you 'his old and dear friend, and how you came to him with sympathy and relief, &c.' I go again to-night to my kind friend Dr Balfour's."

"11th July.

"I was at Roslin on Saturday botanizing with Dr Balfour and his class. We had a fatiguing walk of upwards of thirty miles, but I am not in the least the worse for it, though some of the students are. It is a most beautiful part of the country, and we got a number of fine plants. I found *Polymonium Cœrulium*, (in a hedge) which had not been seen in that part of the country before. We intend to leave for Glasgow to-morrow, and I have just been making a few calls. I called first on Dr Graham, who has mentioned me in the handsomest manner to his class as the discoverer of those two plants. He took me up and presented me to

Mr Goodsir, whom I was never able to find before.   I gave him your letter, and he told me to come and see him again when I returned to Edinburgh.   I then went to Dr Neill's office.   He has given me a letter to the curator of the Glasgow Botanic Garden.   I could not, unfortunately, see the printing process going on, as it was the people's dinner hour, but I will see it when I come back. - - - - - - Tell Biot I have got some arrows and shall send them by next opportunity."

"Glasgow, 15th July 1840.

"My Dear Papa,—We arrived here last evening by the canal boat, as it was the least fatiguing for mamma. It rained a good deal, and the boat was so full I had to sit outside, yet I enjoyed it very much notwithstanding. There was a very delightful English gentleman, (with a son in bad health wearing a respirator, poor fellow,) and we had much pleasant conversation.   He tried me with the names of all the plants on the banks of the canal as we passed.   But I don't know whether he could tell if I was right or not. - - - - - - The crops are more backward than I expected.   - - - - We saw the great preparations for the intended railway between Edinburgh and Glasgow. - - - - - I have been seeing the cathedral to-day, a most magnificent old building, and the citizens have subscribed £30,000 for its repair.   Afterwards I went to Sir William Hooker's.   He asked in the warmest manner for you. - - - - - He is a most delightful man. - - - - - - My kindest love to aunt Mary, Biot, and all the bairns, and I remain, your very affectionate son.

"Thos. Edmondston, Jr."

During the few days stay in Glasgow, Thomas was fully and delightfully occupied in the Botanic Garden, in Sir William Hooker's study, and in wandering in search of plants in the districts round the city. Sir William zealously interested himself in the welfare of his young friend—recommended a medical education and degree, as a matter of status, and note of general recommendation, and placed before the boy's sparkling eyes the example of his own son, then on the great Antartic expedition as naturalist, and how a similar appointment might one day be easily attainable for him. For months afterwards this idea recurred to the young student's mind. The suggestion became a prophecy, unexpectedly fulfilled,—how sadly to terminate !

Two of his little experiences in Glasgow may just be mentioned. In a wood near the city he first found growing the *Linnæa borealis*, which, after the great man he so much admired, he desired to have for his especial cognizance, and whenever possible wore a sprig of it in his cap. The other gratification was his obtaining as a present from a youthful aunt a botanical lens—a much coveted treasure. This aunt first saw him before breakfast on her arrival, bending over a book. Coming from polished Dublin society where young sprigs of his age were dandified and conventionally graceful, she fancied her new found nephew a little *countrified*,—to put it mildly. During breakfast she marked the sparkle, the intelligence of his full blue eye, and afterwards when he slung his botanical box on his shoulder and announced his intention of going to Sir William for a guide in a ramble, the young lady changed her opinion and afterwards was proud to have his escort in some cousinly visits.

From Glasgow Thomas and his mother went to visit some relations at Bothwell. Hardly a quarter of an hour after his arrival he disappeared for some hours, oblivious of tea or anything but the loveliness of the vale of Clyde. And before sleeping he wrote as follows—

"Bothwell, 17th July 1840.

"My Dear Papa,—I wrote you from Glasgow the day before yesterday, but I fear the *important* matters therein recited would prove neither 'edifying nor diverting.' This is a most lovely place,—I only wish you were here. - - - - - We are within a few minutes walk of the famous Bothwell Bridge, and the Clyde, overhung with willows, alders, spruce, silver firs, &c. It is beyond all description. I have been over a gentleman's grounds near at hand to which we have access. They are extensive and laid out with the greatest taste, which, with the natural beauties of the place, make it one of the sweetest residences possible. - - - - - It seems you have fine weather in Shetland. It is more than we have had. There have hardly been two really fine days since we came to Scotland. However, if it is good in Shetland I don't care. - - - We are very comfortable here, and as mamma is better and we have good accounts from home, I am very happy and 'spirity.' Many thanks to you my dear papa for giving me this treat.

"There is nothing doing in the political world just now, I believe. I have not looked into a newspaper for ever so long. I have so much to occupy my mind, I have neither time nor inclination for newspapers."

"21st July.

" - - - - - I have had some good botanizing and have found some plants that are rather rare. All the plants hereabout are new to me as they are chiefly wood plants, but I find no difficulty in making them out. - - - - - Tell Biot, with my love, I am very glad he has got the skuas.* The day before I left Edinburgh I saw one of the porters of the Zoological garden and enquired as to the health of their skua, the man said he was well, but I shall see him myself and report when I got back. They will be happy of any thing we can send them. Dr Neill and Dr Graham

---

* Skua Gull.—*Lestris Cataractes.*

were most happy over the growing *arenarias* I brought
them for the gardens. The Horticultural garden also
got some. How is *Colonsay* getting on, and *Murphy*,
and all the equine species at Halligarth? I hope poor
dear old *Charley* and *Ninsy* are in a favourable condition and behaving well. As we are to be at Kilsyth,
mamma bids me ask if you will give me a letter to Sir
Archibald Edmonstone.—Kindest love, dear papa, your
very affectionate son,

"Thos. Edmondston, Jr"

It became necessary that Thomas and his mother
should temporarily return to Edinburgh, partly on account of medical treatment for the latter, and partly to
meet some relatives from a distance.

"Edinburgh, 29th July 1840.

"My Dear Papa,—I wrote you a few days ago of our
return here, but the steamer has broken her paddles
and returned to Aberdeen. I enclose a copy of the
note I sent by Sir William's advice to Mr Sowerby with
a specimen of the *Arenaria* from which to make a plate.
Mr S. conducts the supplement to Sir J. E. Smith's
"English Botany." He gets all the new discoveries and
publishes them monthly. You will see I have not expressed my opinions too boldly, but have only said
enough to let botanists determine if I am right or not.
I saw Professor Jameson yesterday at the college. He
told the porter of the museum (a grey headed old

fellow,) that I was to be admitted whenever I chose ?·
You may be sure I walked in at once, and straight to
the lower gallery, where in proud pre-eminence, above
the petrified fragments of which (say geologists) our
globe is composed, stood the well known face and figure
of *Strix Nyctea*,* your very fine specimen. It is more
mottled than any other I ever saw, being very regularly
spotted with brown, on almost every feather. What
a splendid museum it is. It would take a life time to
master its contents, and in such fine preservation too !
but a great number are not labelled. The Professor
invited me to his closing lecture. It was on volcanoes
and other branches of meteorology. He is rather a dry
lecturer, and hesitates a good deal, but is clear and most
instructive nevertheless.

"We are going to Kilsyth on Saturday. I hope I
shall have an opportunity of presenting your letter to
our chieftain Sir Archibald. I am also very glad of
your letters to Mr Lawson and Professor Thomson."

"3rd August.

- - - - - "Every thing is dead here now. All
my botanical friends are out of town. Uncle came
from London yesterday. I suppose he is going home
soon. - - - - - I drank tea with Dr Neill one
evening. I was highly amused and delighted at the
way he treats his animal confederates. They all know

---

* Owl.

him, and I do think they understand what he says to them as well as I do. His old skua is failing fast, I fear. He has some gannets, shags, penelopes, parrots, tortoises, and a splendid golden eagle, and king vulture. The plants I gave him are thriving beautifully. - - - The Botanic Gardens and the College Museum almost divide my time out of doors. I called for John Edmonstone* the bird-stuffer to day. He is a fine good natured old chap, and I had a long talk with him about Waterton and Demerara. He is a good practical ornithologist, and remembered you immediately. I saw all his birds—they are beautifully preserved. He uses no wire. He told me his method which he learnt from Waterton, and which is quite easy. I have been reading Linnæus's Flora and Lochern's *Lapponica* and *Philosophia botanica* as you desired me. Tell me what books you particularly wish me to read—not the *sort*, but the *individuals*.

"Mamma though not strong and unable to walk, is pretty well. Poor little Isabella will be missing her I fear."

"11th August.

- - - - - - - "I am employing every moment of leisure in drawing. Mr Small is remarkably kind to me, he is indeed a worthy old soul. I have nothing to

---

* He was a Negro and took his surname according to sambo fashion, from that of his late master, Charles Edmondstone, Esq., father-in-law of Charles Waterton the naturalist.

do but to go to the College Library and ask him for any book I wish to see. Then there is a little room off the outer hall with writing desk, &c., which he calls mine, where I go and sit as long as I like. I have been engaged for two or three days on Donovan's British Shells, in copying the figures. It is a capital work, the best on the subject I believe, and I am studying it very hard ; also other works on various subjects especially mathematics, and different branches of Natural History ; but botany continues, and I think will to the end of the chapter, to be my favourite. - - - - I have seen most of the *great men* here, professors, ministers, &c. I saw Monroe and Dr Hope to-day. Dr Alison I have seen here several times when he was seeing Mamma,— Your very affectionate son, T. E."

The racy freshness—the boyish humour and the brotherly sympathies of the following, will commend it, we doubt not, to many readers.

"Edinburgh, 13th August, 1840.

" My Dear 'Felix.'*—I received your very acceptable letter two days ago. I have been very busy and not able to write you so often as I would have wished. But really what with all one's uncles and aunts,— grandfathers and cousins—and I dont know how many friends besides, all mamma's old acquaintances that had

---

* A soubriquet.

to be seen, I have been fully occupied, and then my own friends whom I have made since I came south, all most kind and attentive. I have little to tell that would interest you, whereas you have so much to say that I should be glad to hear.

" Are you attending to our garden? I shall send a hoe by first opportunity, but do not let it run over with weeds at least.

" When do you commence school? Give my best respects to Mr Robertson. What is poor Ninsy doing and our foals, and Charley and Bernard, and all the rest of the animal creation that inhabit our domains? The weather is awfully hot, so that I feel it quite oppressive in the middle of the day. Have you got any peats home yet? I suppose they are needed by this time !

" I think I told you I had got some capital arrows. Take good care of the bows ; we shall have some fine shooting at the Linties* with the good arrows, if I am spared to return. I have also got some slate pencils of a capital sort, also a good stock of black lead ones, and pens, and a knife for you, which I shall send with the other things by ' the Norna.' I hope you are taking care of my school and other books ; don't take them

---

* *Fringilla Montana,* which does great damage sometimes to the new sown turnip crop, requiring the field to be watched, and the depredators destroyed.

from the shelves, or let the bairns touch them. There are some beautiful botanizing places in this neighbour-hood, and lovely woods in which you might wander for a twelvemonth without getting out, and winding rivers where you might fish for trout and salmon for twenty years and not empty the place. That's a paradise—is it not? endless woods and rivers!—the one for botany, the other for ichthyology—which is the science for knowing, discriminating, catching, cooking and eating, fish—from two Greek words, signifying 'fish,' and a 'discourse.' I wish you were here, were it but to see the museum ! of all the sights it would interest and delight you the most; except the Botanic Garden, it did me. Gallery upon gallery of splendid birds set up in the attitudes of life, and enclosed in glass cases, &c.—Believe me, my dear brother, very affectionately yours, Signed, Thos. Edmondston, Jr."

"P.S. never fear my having a long coat,—spare your sneers on that point—I sport cap and jacket as in Shetland."

"Bothwell, 27th August 1840.

" My Dear Papa,—It is a while now since I gave you any thing like a full journalizing account of our pro-ceedings.

" We left ' Auld Reekie' by the canal boat on Saturday week, and arrived at the manse of Kilsyth, which is about 12 miles from Glasgow, at 6 P.M., and received a very hearty welcome. Uncle D. came to

Kilsyth on Monday, and took us by coach to Glasgow. Sir Archibald was in England, and the weather was too rainy for me to do much in botanizing. Mr Burns was making up an account of his parish for the new 'Statistical Account,' and he wished me to make an abstract of the botany, with a notice of any rare plants that might be in it. This I did, and sent it on from Glasgow, but I offered to go back again for a day or two if he chose and make out a proper list. Kilsyth is rather a pretty place, though it looks most so at a distance. It is rich in coal and freestone. Trap is the general formation. The coal pits there are the first I have seen. They are near the canal, and, therefore, the coal may be conveniently conveyed to Glasgow or Edinburgh. - - - - - - Well, we came to Glasgow, and put up at the Argyle Hotel for the night, and looked about a little, the next day coming here by coach at eight P.M. It is about nine miles from Glasgow. The following day, uncle D. having some business near Lanark, proposed that I should go with him to see the far famed Falls of Clyde. We left Bothwell on the outside of the seven o'clock morning coach. A gentleman who happened to be beside me, seeing by my tin case on my shoulder that I was a botanist, immediately began to converse with me. When he found I came from Shetland, and knew Mr Hamilton of Bressay, he told me he was his cousin-german, and we became well acquainted. He was on his way to Douglas to fish, but he gave me a letter to a Mr Patrick who had published a Flora of Lanarkshire, noticed by Hooker in the highest terms. Uncle D. and I went on from Lanark about three miles, in search of the residence of the gentleman he was going to see, but we wandered about three hours up one road and down another, and when we found the place, the gentleman was absent from home. We had another long walk before we found the Falls, but they, not to mention the plants I found, amply repaid us. The river was full of water, and the sun shining on the Falls made a splendid sight I can never forget; and yet, I must confess, even when standing on the nearest point to Corra Linn, I should have preferred to be at the Holse Hellyer.* By dint of fast walking we caught the latest coach back to Bothwell. Next day I went to Hamilton, which is half way between this and Lanark, to present my letter to Mr Patrick. He was very kind, and took me to some of the best places for plants in the vicinity, and gave me his ' Flora.' The first book that caught my eye in his house was the volume of the ' Wernerian Society's Transactions,' in which is your paper on the seals. This was a curious coincidence, and he was delighted when he knew I was your son. He knows all your discoveries and scientific papers as well as I do. He is an excellent geologist as well as a general naturalist.

---

* A very fine cave in the north of Unst.

" The day following I went to Bothwell Castle, the seat of Lord Douglas, and got capital botanizing, but had not time for the gardens and conservatories.

" Yesterday I went with Mr Hamilton to Wood-house, the seat of Campbell of Islay. The gardener there was very kind, and gave me as many specimens of Cape heaths and other greenhouse plants as I could carry. The day was too wet for much out of door botanizing.

" Mamma is much improved since we came here.

" Please tell aunty Mary that yesterday I ate apricots, grapes, and figs, from the trees !

" We have just heard that you and Biot have been paying a visit to Faröe. I hope you have had a pleasant voyage. If you have had as fine weather as we have been enjoying, I am sure you have been delighted.

" Post time approaches, and I must haste to sign myself with kindest love to every one.—Your affectionate son, Thos. Edmondston, Jr."

The little scene that took place on the evening referred to in the immediately preceding letter is very characteristic.

It was past nine P.M., quite dark, and pouring rain, when Thomas arrived from his day's excursion at Wood-house, &c. His clothes were completely soaked, but he carried in his arms the large bundle of exquisite exotics he had got, carefully wrapped in his overcoat, which he had taken off for the purpose. There happened to be a little evening party, chiefly of ladies, at his aunt's, amongst whom he entered with his treasures, all dripping as he was. The guests gathered round him as he spread the rich and beautiful flowers on the table, and the taste and eagerness with which he displayed and described them, soon caused every one to forget his own soiled and wet condition. With the tact for which he was remarkable, he soon discovered the blossoms that each young lady especially admired, and distributed the whole, to their great surprise and gratitude, saying, " These, though very rich and lovely and rare, are not the things I care for you know ; see here !" and in his botanical box they saw a few common looking, unlovely plants, which, ere he rested, he had carefully placed in drying paper, employing several hours of the night in the process.

Again returned to Edinburgh, on their way home, he wrote.

" Edinburgh, 17th Sept. 1840.

" My Dear Papa.—We were very happy over your letters this morning.

" The weather has been shockingly stormy, and some vessels turned back, so that we are not going this week, but positively the next—we are longing to be home.

" I have called on Mr Lawson with your letter, and he sent his foreman with me to the nurseries,—and to Dickson's,—Eagle and Henderson's, and the Princes

Street Gardens, and such places as I had not seen before, which was very instructive to me. I dined with Mr Lawson one day, and there was present an English nurseryman from Kent, from whom I got a great deal of information, which will be abundant matter for conversation when I get home. Mr Lawson is more of a theoretical agriculturist than a practical one, but his foreman, and his head botanist (a German named Killerman) are both excellent agriculturists and botanists. I was at the Botanic Gardens yesterday, and Mr M'Nab gave me a number of specimens, and much information about trees and plants. He, though an excellent arboriculturist, is also I think rather a *hot-house* and *evergreen* man. What I should like would be a conversation with a regular thorough-bred *forester*, which I have not yet had the luck to have. All those I have happened to fall in with, are gardeners, florists, horticulturists, or nursery-men, agriculturists, or botanists—all distinct *species* ! (I would almost say *genera !*) being truly and specifically distinct from your regular forester. But I have done all I could, and I have got as much instruction as possible, on every available point. I do hope it will be productive of some beneficial results to our little experiment with the trees at Halligarth.

"MacGillivray has been here for a long time to-day, and we have had some most interesting talk with him. *Lestris parasiticus* remains the same still, but it seems they have made out another species *Lestris Richard-sonii* differing in the length of the central tail feathers ! —humbug I opine.

"This time next week we shall be setting out. I hope your Faröese trip has done you good ; it also will be a conversational theme I am anxiously looking forward to ; and so "good bye" to correspondence, and "good day" to *talkee.*—Your most affectionate son,— Signed, Thos. Edmondston, Jr.

On the return from Bothwell to Edinburgh, Thomas had again spent a few days at Kilsyth manse, by the invitation of the venerable pastor, from whom after-wards he received a letter, of which the following is part :

To Mr Thos. Edmondston, Junr.

Manse of Kilsyth, 3rd Nov. 1840.

"My Dear Friend.—I have the pleasure of acknow-ledging the receipt of your botanical report of this parish, which I have sent to the Secretary of the Statistical Account. - - - - It was teazing that the weather was so unfavourable for botanical surveys, but I am not the less indebted to you for your kind services. I expect the M.S. to be returned soon for corrections or additions. The proof sheets are always, when possible, sent to the author, when so far advanced. - - - - - All join in kindest regards, and I am, my dear friend, yours most truly.—Signed, Wm. Burns."

CHAPTER VII.

—

Studies in Shetland.

1840-41.

THE return voyage in the end of September was by no means so enjoyable as that at midsummer. The North Sea affects short, jerky, angry waves, and there are many headlands and tideways to pass on the route. However, all was safely, if not agreeably, surmounted, as far as Lerwick, and by a fortunate chance the passage thence to Unst, in a trading sloop was a good one. Thomas was to reside in Buness during the winter, and his brother went to Edinburgh in October, for schooling there.

For some little time after his return, the volatile imaginative boy was very full of the drama, and got up little acts from Shakespeare and "Douglas," which caused great amusement in the domestic circle, especially as the supply of actors was so limited and unteachable, that they were perforce adopted as lay figures, while

Thomas did all the speeches. He even planned a tragedy, which he was to compose, but if it were ever commenced, nothing remains except the title page, thus—

LEON,

A TRAGEDY.

Dramatis Personæ—

LEON, - - - - Prince of Castile.
ALPHONSO, - - his servant.
ALEXIS, - - - a proud old Spanish noble.
ALICIA, - - - his daughter.
COUNT BRONCAUSI, an Italian, Alicia's suitor.

FIRST ACT.

LEON - - - - Solus.

"To Sir William Hooker.

" Baltasound, Shetland,

" 16th Oct. 1840.

" My Dear Sir William,—It is now nearly a month since we reached home, and I would long ere now have done myself the honour of writing you a few lines, if it had been but to offer my warmest acknowledgments for the great and unmerited kindness and hospitality I received from you, when I had the pleasure of seeing you in Glasgow, but I thought as you were intending to leave home for some time, my letter would have small chance of reaching you in Glasgow.

"Since I came down to Shetland, in autumn, I had the good fortune to pick up a few specimens of a very interesting plant, *Cynosurus echinatus*, in a situation where it has every appearance of being indigenous. I enclose a specimen, of which I beg your acceptance. It is, I believe, the first recorded instance of the plant having been found in Scotland.

"I am now busily engaged in studying the Cryptogamic plants, of which I have good reason to believe Shetland contains a great store. Books are our great *desiderata* in this out of the way place, and these are a great want. Any hints from you as to what plants are likely to be found, &c., &c., will be most valuable and most thankfully received.

" - - - - - The *habitat* of the enclosed plant is Bressay Island, about a mile inland, in a small sandy sheltered spot. - - - - -"   "T. E."

"From Sir William J. Hooker.

"Glasgow, 3rd Dec. 1840.

"My Dear Sir,—Your letter of October 16, has but this moment been brought by the post, and it finds me just on my return from Jersey, where I spent two months with my family, and where I have left Lady Hooker and my two invalid daughters for the winter. Certainly they are the better for the fine climate of that island, but I shall be very glad when they be permitted to return.

" I write to you at once, because I wish to say that I would not have you feel disappointed if your *Cynosurus echinatus* should prove not to be wild in the spot you find it in. How it came there it is perhaps hard to say, perhaps by some foreign vessel in ballast, or with seed of some other kind. Be that as it may, the plant is so completely a southern plant, that it never can be credited to be an aboriginal of the Shetland isles, unless it should make its appearance in an unsuspicious spot, and for a succession of years. Properly speaking, in Britain it is only found in the extreme south of England, where it was probably imported, and in Jersey where it *may* be wild. However, if it continues to appear in Shetland for a series of summers it will be worth recording, even though it be an imported plant. October cannot be the natural period of its flowering, which makes it the more probable that the seeds were not planted at nature's seed time. I wish you could have seen with me the very southern vegetation of Jersey, among which the *Cynosurus echinatus* grows. It is altogether of a southern aspect, and where there is a climate so fine that the famous *Agave Americana* is yet (end of November) flowering in the open air, in a garden in one of the streets of St Helier ; and I measured some Hydrangeas (the first imported from China), ten feet high and forty feet in the circumference of the branches.

" In studying the Cryptogamic plants, I would

strongly recommend you to take great pains in the collecting and preserving *good* specimens, neatly laid out, and properly pressed. They are then very beautiful and more easily determined than when carelessly preserved. It is a nice winter employment, when many of this tribe are in high perfection. I am just putting to press a valuable 'Manual of British Algæ,' by Mr Harvey, who has so deeply studied this tribe.

"It gives me pleasure to hear your mother is the better of her excursion to the south. Pray thank your father for me for his kind letter, which I received before I left Scotland in the autumn, and with best compliments both to him and Mrs Edmondston, believe me, my dear friend, faithfully yours,"

"W. J. Hooker."

"Mr Thos. Edmondston, Jun."

From Dr Balfour.

"Edinburgh, 19th Oct. 1840.

"My Dear Sir,—Many thanks for your kind letter, which I only received two or three days ago. It will always afford me much pleasure to keep up a correspondence with you, and to give you the botanical news of this part of the world. I was sorry you were not able to join our botanical party on the Saturday of your departure. We had a pleasant walk by Blackford and Braid-hills, Corstorphine, Craigleith, and Granton, and we picked up one or two good plants. We afterwards dined at Newhaven. - - - - Babington remained in Edinburgh for a fortnight, examining various *Herbaria*, and making observations to assist him in his ' British Flora,' which I have no doubt will be an excellent work. We had also a visit from several foreign botanists, more particularly Professor Link and Dr Klotzsch from Berlin, and Dr Vogel from Bonn. The latter talks of going in the expedition to the Niger.

"The only addition made to our Edinburgh Flora lately is *Myriophyllum alterniflorum*, which grows in quantity in Braid-hill marshes. You are still, I see, continuing to pick up good things. The plant you enclosed from Bressay is *Cynosurus echinatus*—a plant which has hitherto been found only in the extreme south of England. Be so good as to pick specimens of it next season (along with the *Arenaria*). Let me know, at your earliest convenience, the nature of the situation in which you found it, and whether or not any ballast has been deposited in the neighbourhood of it. I mean to notice it as your discovery at the first meeting of the Botanical Society, and I should like to have full particulars regarding it before that time. There are no news relative to the Glasgow chair. - - - - —I remain, my dear Sir, yours most sincerely,

" J. H. Balfour."

" Mr Thos. Edmondston, Jun.,

Baltasound, Shetland."

From Dr Graham, Professor of Botany.

Edinburgh, 14th Nov. 1840.

Dear Sir.—Your letters of 29th Oct. and 4th Novr. both reached me this morning. I might have got letters from New York in shorter time than from the date of the first.

I do not like to delay my thanks, and shall therefore write to-night, though already too late for post, and though I fear I must be very laconic.

Immediately upon receiving the grass from you, Dr Balfour brought it to show it to me, and I confirmed his suspicion that it was *Cynosurus echinatus*, and farther proved it to him by showing the specimens of this grass in my herbarium. I confess, however, that then, and even now, I cannot but think it has been accidentally introduced, and, I fear, it will not maintain its ground long with you. This is a very different thing from *Lathyrus maritimus*, which grows much farther north than you, and in very much colder climates. But *Cynosurus echinatus* is a native of the south of Europe, and does not, as far as I know, grow farther north than the south of England. I beg, however, you may be kind enough to watch it, and tell us what you see next summer. I understand there is no harbour in Bressay. Is it so? or do boats never pick up or lay down ballast on the island? I thank you very much for the specimens, and, I assure you, I shall always think my time well spent when employed in examining any of your Shetland plants, when you have the kindness to send them to me.   Do not be a bit afraid to send me things that are not *split and spang new*, or even which you may suspect are not very rare. I have very few Shetland things, and, therefore, almost anything down to *Cerastium viscosum* will be acceptable, even for my own herbarium, as establishing its geographical distribution in the British Islands; and, independent of this selfish reason, I shall always have real pleasure in helping you out of a doubt.

Pray be careful not to be too severe on *Arenaria norvegica.*   I should be very sorry to have it nearly eradicated even to supply my own wants.   I have not one specimen of *Primula Scotica* from Shetland.   I mention this because you ask specially regarding it.

I shall mention a few plants which you may probably yet discover in Shetland.   *When you find all these, I shall tell you of others.   Diapensia laponica ; Dryas integrefolia; Pedicularis*, one or two continental species; *Andromeda tetragona, Draba ;* one or two continental species ; *Saxifraga*, one or two arctic species.

" So much for your first letter, now for the second, containing the account of the Shetland dyes.   I have not had time to read this, but I thank you very much for it, and shall intimate to Campbell that I shall present it to the Botanical Society at next meeting, and read it in its turn.   The Society will hear it with much pleasure. With my best compliments to your father, and repeating my thanks to you, believe me, my dear friend, yours very sincerely, Robt. Graham."

P.S. I only now observe that you ask what quantity of *Arenaria norvegica* I should wish. I have many continental corresponents, every one of whom would like to have it, and many in this country would jump a mile for it, and, therefore, you see that numbers would not encumber me; but still I fear your being too free in gathering so scarce a plant.

Mr Thomas Edmondston, Junr.

From Professor Graham.

" Edinr., 30th Dec. 1840.

" My Dear Sir.—Your letter of the 14th inst., with greater rapidity than is consistent with the usual pace of your post, reached me this morning.

" I am much pleased to hear your report of the *habitat* of *Cynosurus echinatus.* It is strange enough that such a plant should be found in such a situation, but your reason for believing the plant really native of Bressay seems sufficiently good. Still, however, I shall be more thoroughly convinced if I find you observe the grass one or two continuous years in the same place. I am pleased to find you have such quantities of *Arenaria Norvegica* that you entertain no fear for its eradication. Be pleased, however, to recollect that the

deepest dish has still a bottom. - - - - - I beg
to be remembered to your father.—Yours most truly,

"Robt. Graham.

"Mr Thomas Edmondston, Junr.,

"Baltasound, Shetland."

By the kind courtesy of Professor Babington, a number
of letters, designated as "of much interest and ex-
cellence," have been recovered, addressed to him by the
young botanist he so generously patronized and assisted.
At the date of the first the writer was not much past
fifteen. A considerable proportion of the correspondence was entirely on scientific botany, the observations
and criticisms often doubtless crude, and probably
afterwards corrected when experience was added to his
early diligence and prompt powers of observation.

It will have been observed that the first friends
Thomas Edmondston acquired in the scientific world,
were through their previous acquaintance with his
father. So far the young student was favoured ; and
the interesting locality of his residence was, no doubt,
an inducement with them to continue their kind encouragement. It will soon be seen how he afterwards
gained for himself, and preserved the friendship of some
of the ablest naturalists of the day.

A slight explanation may be given of one of the
debated points in many of the letters to Professor
Babington. Near where grows the *Arenaria norvegica,*

there is found also a rare plant a *Cerastium.* There was a considerable difference of opinion for some time among botanists as to the species, or if it were not indeed a new species altogether. Young Edmondston was very modest about it; and though some great authorities thought it different from any species hitherto described, he deferred to the opinions of those who had most carefully studied the *Cerastia,* and the Shetland plant is now known as a variety of the *C. Latifolium Edmondstonii.*

" To Professor Babington, Cambridge.

" Buness, Shetland, 7th Jan. 1841.

" Dear Sir,—I trust you will excuse the liberty I now take in addressing myself to you, as I am personally a total stranger, although I have had the pleasure of knowing you intimately for some time by reputation, and being a very young botanist, I am extremely desirous of the honour of having as a correspondent one so distinguished in the annals of botany as yourself. I have heard of you from my friend, Mr Edward Forbes of the Isle of Man ; and Mr J. H. Pollexfen (now at Cambridge), informed me that you had some thoughts of visiting Shetland last summer on a botanical excursion, where, I assure you, I would have been most happy to see you. I was very unfortunate in leaving Edinburgh last year, just before you arrived

there, as I was promised the honour of a personal introduction to you.

" I have, for three or four years past, been employed
in surveying the botany of these islands. It presents
some interesting features, more especially with respect
to geographical distribution. I have also found a few
plants, extremely interesting in themselves, more especially *Arenaria norvegica, Pisum maritimum,* and *Cynosurus echinatus*—all new to Scotland. I am at present
directing my attention particularly to the Cryptogamic
tribes. If I can be of any service to you by furnishing
specimens, &c., I assure you it would give me the
greatest pleasure.

" As I am unacquainted with your address, I take
the liberty to enclose this to my friend, Dr J. H.
Balfour of Edinburgh, who, I hope, will be kind enough
to forward it to you, with a few lines, stating wherein
he thinks (from his knowledge of us both) I might be
of any service to you, and with best wishes, I remain,
with the utmost respect and esteem, dear Sir, your
most obedt. Servt."   " T. E."

" Buness, Shetland, 4th Feb. 1841.

" Dear Sir,—I yesterday had the pleasure to receive
your kind letter of the 24th ult., and beg leave to
return you my best thanks for the most valuable offer
of your correspondence. I am much flattered and obliged
by the expressions of esteem which you were kind

enough to make, and I shall do everthing in my power to merit that honour. I am most proud and happy to think myself competent to give you any information on the botany of *Ultima Thule.*

" Its more remarkable features are as follows :—

" 1st, Although some of our hills are of considerable elevation, they present few or none of those characteristics, in the nature of their botany, which are generally attendant on Alpine situations. The many very fine plants which abound on the mountains of Scotland (bear in mind that we Shetlanders do not consider ourselves as belonging to that ancient country) are, with few exceptions, unknown here. The highest land in Shetland (Rona's Hill) having an elevation of from 1500 to 2000 feet, has very much the same vegetation on its summit as at its base.

" 2nd. The very few Alpine plants which we *do* have, are chiefly met with on very low ground ; for example, *Arenaria norvegica, Cerastium latifolium, Arabis Petræa, Azalea procumbens, Ansurea* [?] *alpina, Lycopodium alpinum, Saxifraga appositifolia,* all occur on what may be considered the average *lowest* ground.

" As to varieties of plants, these are by no means frequent or peculiar. All the reproductive organs are, in general, greatly disproportioned in size, being much larger than the leaves and stem.

" I do not yet know the plan of your forthcoming work. It will, I have no doubt, be a most valuable one. Do you intend it to be in the form of a compendious manual, as 'Hooker's British Flora,' or in a more condensed form, or accompanied with figures? I believe it is to be arranged according to the "natural" method; and Dr Balfour tells me, what I am most happy to hear, that you are going to set our nomenclature on a proper basis.

"I have great pleasure in enclosing two specimens of *Cynosurus echinatus.* I am very happy to oblige Mr Borrer in this or in any other way. He is a gentleman with whom, like yourself, I am well acquainted by reputation, especially from his very able contributions to 'Hooker's British Flora.' The two plants I enclose are small, but I did not get any larger, with the exception of a single culm. I got only four specimens; the largest one which I allude to is a magnificent one, nearly two feet high, which I have retained for my own herbarium. I would send it now, but being so large, it could not be compressed into the compass of a letter without serious injury. If it could be of any use to you for making a description, figure, or otherwise, I beg you will consider it at your service. Meanwhile, I send the two lesser ones.

"From what I have said of our botany, you will perceive that it was more by accident than anything else I found what I did. The rarity and number of our plants are indeed very limited; but what we want in botany, I am inclined to think, may be abundantly made up in some of the lower branches of zoology. Our fishermen go a great way off from the land, and I have good evidence that many rare, interesting, and even new species of Mollusca, Corallines, &c., are often met with. I intend, in the ensuing summer, to devote much of my time to the investigation. My much valued, highly esteemed friend, Mr Forbes, has kindly promised his able assistance in this branch, in which, with many others, he is so completely at home. I am sure nothing could give myself and friends greater pleasure than to see you here, and I trust we may have that pleasure next summer.—I am," &c.

"Buness, 29th March 1841.

" Dear Sir,—I had the pleasure of your kind letter of the 6th inst. a few days ago. Our Shetland mails are not greatly to be depended on for regularity or despatch, especially in the winter time, but in a week or two we expect to have a steam packet running between Edinburgh and Lerwick, when I hope our letters will be conveyed more regularly.

" I am glad the specimens reached you in safety. The penny post is well formed for the conveyance of plants, yet I have several times had very fine specimens crushed by the Goth-like stamper of the post-office.

" I am just now extremely busy at the Cryptogamiæ. I have hitherto paid little or no attention to them, but Shetland seems to have a vast store of them, especially among Algæ, Hepaticæ, and Mosses. *Fungi* of any kind, from what I have yet been able to see, are extremely scarce. *Jungermanniu* and *Selyphophoi* seem to be abundant, but I am little *au-fait* among them. I trust your work will embrace the Cryptogamiæ.

" I sent to the Botanical Society of Edinburgh a list of the plants I have observed in Shetland. Perhaps a copy of it would give you some insight into our botany. If you wish it, I need not say it is at your command. Shall I send you a lot of *Arenaria norvegica* for yourself and friends? but I hope soon to have the pleasure of seeing you here to pick it for yourself. We have it in abundance, but only in one locality, not a quarter of a mile from where I am now sitting.

"I would take it as a great favour if, some leisure moment, you would be kind enough to investigate the claims of the *Cerastium latifolium* and *alpinum* to be considered distinct species from any specimens from the Highlands of Scotland and Wales. I confess I cannot see any good grounds for separating the two, and to all appearance they run into one in cultivation, whereas it seems that our Shetland *C. latifolium* (so called) is distinct from both. The Shetland plant is much more procumbent and spreading than the Scotch one. The leaves are roundly ovate, and covered with a small scattered white pubescence, scarcely discernible unless under the lens. The calyx is more funnel-shaped, and more closely pressed to the corolla. The latter is much more than twice as long as the calyx, campanulate, striped with green in the inside, and very handsome. The root is creeping, and the plant often scoloniferous. I am sorry I have not a good specimen to shew you, which would be much better than all I can say," &c., &c.

"Buness, 23rd April 1841.

"My dear Sir,—I had the pleasure, two days ago, to receive your kind letter of the 12th inst., for which I beg to return you my best thanks. It gives me great satisfaction to see that your views are similar to my own as regards the specific distinctions of the two alpine cerastiæ. I cannot conceive how they can have been ever separated; for every botanist must be aware, that among the *caryophyllæ* especially, scarcely two plants of the same species are found exactly alike. I cannot but think that the Shetland plant is distinct; it is more deserving of the name of *latifolium* than any other of the *genus* I know. But I suspect the chief distinction will be found to be in the great comparative length of the corolla, which is truly campanulate, and in conjunction with the dark green of the leaves, makes the plant, when growing, a truly handsome object.

"I enclose a specimen, but as it is but indifferently dried, this character will not appear in full force. Your experienced eye will, however, doubtless detect specific differences if such exist.

" As to the subject of my list of Shetland plants—in a late letter from Mr Campbell, the secretary, he says that the Council recommend that I shall go on with my survey of the islands this summer, also having the cryptogamia in view ; and at the end of the season the list will be published, with the addition of the *Acotyledones*, and such of the flowering plants as I shall observe in the course of a farther investigation. This they conceive will be more convenient than publishing it in detached portions. I will therefore devote myself, God willing, to this end through the summer. If, however, you would wish a copy of the list as it stands now, I shall have much pleasure in sending it to you.

" I am very much obliged by your kind offer of sending me some specimens. Anything in the *shape of a plant*, whether British or Foreign, will be most acceptable to so young a botanist as I am. I shall send a list, such as you recommend, in a day or two ; but, I repeat, that *nothing can come amiss to me*," &c., &c.

" Buness, 15th May 1841.

" My dear Sir,— . . . . . I am extremely happy to see that you are inclined to be of the same opinion with myself concerning the *cerastium*. It is certainly very probable that it is the true *C. Latifolium* of Linnæus, and has a better right to that name than any other *cerastium* that I know. I observe the characters you mention as probably distinguishing it from the others. The shape and size of the corolla are very striking. It is truly campanulate, and looks much like *Convolvolus sepium* in miniature. I shall be sure to procure you specimens *in fruit*, as I have never seen the Scotch plant in that state. I cannot say as to the comparative length of the capsule. The plant flowers in June, but individuals may be got in flower during the whole summer months. I have never seen it but in one situation, the same as that in which occurs the *Arenaria norvegica*. A reference to the Linnæan herbarium would probably settle all doubts on the subject. The pubescence will form a capital character.

I enclose a botanical list as you desired. I am sorry I have not one but what has been in use, as I am so far away that I cannot get them when I want. I have marked on the margin the plants *I have*. My *desiderata* left unmarked.

"I have put an S. after those I have observed in Shetland, so that you will also have a view of our flora. If there are any of these of which you would wish specimens, be kind enough to mention them as soon as possible, as I expect, in less than a month, to set out on my botanising through the islands. I expect to finish this summer the survey both of flowering and cryptogamic plants, and will communicate the result to the Edinburgh Botanical Society. I intend making a complete Shetland herbarium for it, and, if you choose, shall make another for you.

" I may mention, that though I have marked on the list the plants I have got, there is not one even of them but would be most acceptable as coming *from you.* Nothing—whether British or Foreign—flowering or cryptogamic—ligneous or herbaceous—terrestrial or aquatic—but would be interesting and acceptable to my collection. I have a good number of foreign plants in my herbarium, and am every bit as anxious to increase my knowledge of them as of the native ones. If you send any of these, please mark the Linnæan class and order on the label, as I have no book to trust to even for the classification. I mention this in case you may have any spare duplicates.

" When do you expect to publish your work? I suppose not for some time, as you mention having to be about collecting materials this summer.

" I hope you will altogether expunge some *genera* from the British Flora—as *doronicum, crocus,* &c.

" What do you think of Mr Borrer's arrangement of the willows, as given in Hooker's British Flora? I am but little acquainted with that difficult tribe, except through the medium of a few dried British and Foreign ones. But surely Koch's arrangement is more simple.

" Are you an advocate for the Jussieuan (or natural) system? I have always been a profound admirer of the simple and beautiful classification of the ' immortal Swede,' and I cannot but think that, with a little modification, the Linnæan would be the more preferable of the two,—for instance, the distribution of *Monœcia, diœcia,* and *polygamia* among the other classes. But, perhaps, Dr Candole's natural system is better than Hooker's. I really do think that nothing can be more *un*natural than some of the natural groups. In the very first order, *ranunculacea,* this strikes one very forcibly. What earthly affinity has *thaliotrum* with *caltha or aconitum?* Let me have the pleasure of hearing soon from you, and believe me," &c.

" 10th June 1841.

" My dear Sir,—I had yesterday the pleasure to receive your letter of 27th May. I particularly notice what you say of *Alchemilla alpina.* I have only observed it in one station in Shetland, viz., on the summit of Rona's hill, the highest land we have. I have carefully examined all my specimens. I cannot perceive the vestige of a junction at the base of the leaflets in any of them, nor can I see the slightest trace of difference between them and specimens from Clova. I enclose you a Shetland specimen, gathered in June 1839, on Rona's hill, North Mavine. I shall, if possible, observe it this summer more closely, and give you the result. I conceive that the mere circumstance of the leaflets being slightly coherent, unless combined with other distinguishing characters, would be scarcely in itself sufficient to form a specific distinction. This *archemilla* is, I think, one of the most beautiful of our many elegant Alpine plants, and is a great favourite of mine.   I enclose also a few specimens of *Arenaria norvegica*, and *Potamogeton natans*.   I shall send you specimens of the others the very first opportunity. You mention *vuca ciliaris* as one of the plants you would wish.   This very rare plant is, I am sorry to say, not a denizen of this corner of the world.   If it was marked as such in my list, it must have been through a mistake.   I have abundance of Cornish specimens, but never gathered it anywhere myself.   *Leontidon palustra* I think a very doubtful species ; but I shall send you what I consider to be the plant of Hooker in his British Flora.

"Pray try and ascertain the *cerastium*.   I enclose you a good specimen.   I have never seen the *cerastium nivalis*, but from description I think my plant agrees more with it than with *C. latifolium*.   If you have a duplicate you could send me I should be very happy. I should be particularly glad that this matter could be settled, as botanists may be here this summer who might anticipate us.   This you know much better than I can tell you.

"If you wish any more *arenarias*, tell me ; there is a very abundant crop of them this year.   Hoping soon to have the pleasure of hearing from you, &c., &c.

In the early summer of 1841 the brothers were re-united in Shetland.   Young Patrick Robertson, son of the late Lord Robertson, who had been much with Biot throughout the winter, accompanied him to the north, and the boys passed a happy summer together, in such healthful and yet improving pursuits as were suited to their age,—sailing, fishing, shooting, &c. The season was, moreover, signalized in the family by the visit of Chs. Edmondston, Esq. of Charleston, So. Carolina, with whom the boys partook of many excursions and fetes-champetres, it having been above forty years since the gray-haired uncle had left these scenes when only a boy like themselves.

It was on one of those excursions that a characteristic little incident took place. The scene was on the water under the cliffs at Burrafirth. Myriads of sea fowl were flying about, or resting on their nests, and the two elder boys earnestly besought that they might have a few shots—which was gratified. Peter Sutherland, as a precautionary matter, was entrusted with the charging of the light fowling pieces, the three elders—the brothers Edmondston—looking to have a little amusement. The young guest, Robertson, soon brought down birds, but Thomas was totally unsuccessful. Father and uncles, eagerly advising, pointing out fair, and then, easy shots. No ! was it the light motion of the boat in the sea ? Was it the too evident excitement of the young sportsman ? Was the piece he used out of order ? Again, and again Tom missed ; not a bird fell, while his young friend, and Peter, brought down several with the same gun. The tyro looked sorely mortified, and exchanged many glances with the faithful Peter, who knew so well this was not his first essay. At length there was a general laugh. They had tried the boy's sensitiveness and patience to the very utmost with joke, and what would now-a-days be called *chaffing*, and he had stood it, blushing and mortified indeed, but with the most unruffled temper. There are very few, perhaps, who would have come through such an ordeal with the same gentleness. The gun had, by private instructions to Peter, been charged only with powder, not shot ! The little *ruse* once disclosed, and due praise given to the unsuspicious boy for his patience, he began with renewed spirit, and soon astonished his friends by his remarkable skill.

To J. H. Balfour, Esq., M.D.,
      Edinburgh.

                      " Baltasound, Shetland,
                         " 28th August 1841.

" My Dear Sir.—It is now some time since I had this pleasure last, and although I have nothing of importance to communicate, yet I cannot resist the temptation of troubling you, to ascertain if anything of interest is going on in the botanical way among all you, the aristocrats of the vegetable-seeking world of Modern Athens. My botanical experience this season has been particularly disheartening. We have had an awfully bad season in every point of view, and my investigations have been often stopped from the sheer badness of weather. I have, however, in spite of that, gone through with my excursions, but have made nothing of them. A tolerable number of additions to my previous catalogue will certainly be forthcoming, but scarcely anything of interest or rarity. I am particularly vexed at not having been able again to find the *Cynosurus echinatus.* I am doing what I can with my dredge, &c., to collect *fuci*, and, I trust, I will have a considerable number to submit to the inspection of some more experienced cryptogamist than myself.

" Can you tell me if in *hypericum pulchrum* the flowers are sometimes found terminal and solitary? Almost all the Shetland specimens (and the plant is abundant) present that character, scarcely ever with the flowers in ' loose panicles,' as Hooker avers.

" I trust to see you in Edinburgh before your departure for Glasgow, as you say you will not leave till November,*—yours very faithfully, T. E."

The Phytologist was a popular Botanical Miscellany commenced in June 1841 by Mr Edward Newman, and edited by Mr George Luxford, A.L.G., F.B.S.E. As the preface to the first volume modestly states, " it

---

* Dr Balfour had been elected to succeed Sir W. Hooker in the Chair of Botany at Glasgow University.

owed its existence to the desire of recording and preserving *facts, observations,* and *opinions* relating to botany in general, but more especially to British Botany. Prior to its commencement these had no appropriate receptacle. There was no periodical to which they would be acceptable. For works of a general character they were esteemed too dull. For those of scientific pretensions they were supposed too trifling. By field botanists alone were they considered worth preserving. . . . . and these labourers in the delightful field of botanical enquiry, have freely availed themselves of its pages ; they have done all that was anticipated, and the Phytologist has become the medium of their communications with each other, and with the botanical public."

This journal was published monthly down to the end of 1847, and for three or four years Thos. Edmondston contributed many articles of interest to its pages, besides a pretty voluminous controversy with other botanists on the comparative merits of the Linnæan with other systems of botany. It was conducted with the utmost urbanity on both sides, and terminated in perfect amity, and, indeed, in one instance in a warm friendship. To other journals on Natural History he also frequently contributed. From among these articles the following is selected as likely to be the most generally interesting.

From the " Zoologist."

" ON THE CAPTURE OF A SEA EAGLE,

" *(Halliaetos albicilla.)*

" In these days the respective monarchs of the quadruped and bird kingdoms, the lion and the eagle, are not invested with the shadowy mantle of *super-animal* bravery and magnanimity with which the older naturalists, as well as poets, loved to clothe them. On the contrary, the courage of the African king of the desert has been more than once daringly and distinctly impugned, and even the eagle, whom we find gravely described in works of no very ancient date, as of much too noble a nature to fear even the ' human form divine,' and his having far too much respect for his dignity (or his stomach) to touch food which had not been slaughtered by his own royal self, is sunk into a place but little higher than the vultures, with whom, in fact, the great and discerning mind of the first of naturalists, Linnæus, associated him, and certainly with as much justice, as some more modern systemists, who have classed him with the falcons; so that he is found, not only to be glad to partake of a carrion banquet with the raven and the hoodie crow, but also to be endowed with no more of the faculty of courage, when pitted against his equals or superiors ' than those who regard ' discretion as the better part of valour.'

" The following incident may not be uninteresting,

as placing in a somewhat striking point of view the deficiency of courage displayed by this species, when placed in opposition to the ' majesty of man,' even in its own peculiar haunts.

The sea eagle or erne, is the only species, so far as I know, that breeds in these Shetland islands. The golden eagle and osprey are occasionally seen, but seem entitled to rank no higher than stragglers. The erne itself is scarce, and from its breeding in the highest cliffs, is very seldom procured from the nest, while its extreme wariness makes the shooting of it no easy matter. The Shetland cragsmen are probably among the most daring in the world; for unlike those of St Kilda, Faröe, &c., who scale the precipice by the regularly organised assistance of their companions, and with ropes and poles, the Shetlander fearlessly scrambles through the dizzy cliffs alone, and without other aid than is afforded him by the precarious holds he gets with his feet and hands. When we consider this occurs frequently on the most mouldering micaceous precipices, where the giving way of a fragment would toss him some hundred feet on the rocks or into the ocean below, and when he has often a bag of young birds or eggs attached to his body, we may well say, as Shakespeare says of the samphire-gathering on the cliffs of Dover, ' dreadful trade !'

To return to the *erne.* For some years past a very expert and daring fowler, Joseph Matheson by name, had been annually in the habit of robbing the nest of a pair of ernes, which had, from time immemorial, built on a ledge of rock perhaps 400 feet above the level of the sea, on the north-west side af the island of Unst. This year he had as usual ascended the cliff for the same purpose, but finding only two eggs, (the erne always laying *three*, of which one is barren), which he took, he returned after a few days to get the third, supposing it would be then deposited. The eyrie was built on a tolerably broad ledge of rock, and on coming up to the one end of it, the nest itself being concealed from him by a jutting piece of the crag, he was aware that the bird was brooding in it, by seeing its white tail projecting 'beyond the interposing stone. He crept cautiously along the shelf of rock till close to the erne, then suddenly raising himself and throwing his body over the stone, he seized the bird by a wing and leg. The so called king (or in this instance *queen*) of the feathered tribes seemed so completely cowed, that she made no resistance to this rude and unexpected attack, but merely opened her bill, apparently in a furtive attempt to call in the assistance of her lord and master, (who, by the way, was soaring at a safe distance above while the lawless ' spulzie ' was perpetrating), and then resigned herself to her fate. This passiveness of the birdwas the more singular, from her head as well as one of her legs and feet being entirely free, so that the powerful struggle she *could* have made, would either have speedily freed herself, or what is more probable, dragged the spoiler over the precipice. To use the man's own simile, she made 'no more resistance than a hen or a goose would have done in the like circumstances.' He, however, finding her thus passive, leisurely undid his garters, tied up the bill and feet, twisted the wings one round the other, and the vulture eagle lay in her own nest, bound, gagged, and powerless.

The only path by which the man could return was too steep and difficult to allow of his carrying such a heavy bird, and consequently he was obliged to let her fall, so that the unfortunate captive rolled down helpless through the air she had so often cloven with such ease and safety, and met an ignominious death on the rocks below. The successful fowler retraced his steps by another and a safer path, and secured his prize, which, with the egg he obtained at the same time, is now before me, being in possession of my uncle, Thomas Edmondston, Esq. of Buness. The nest was constructed chiefly of heather twigs and the dried stems of *laminaria digitata* uprooted and cast ashore; it was lined with wool, feathers, and 'sinna,' * and contained few of the remains usually found in the nests of birds

---

* This name is applied to the withered herbage of the previous year, and in Norway and Iceland it is given to *carex sylvatica*, which plant, with the *fescue, luzulla maxima*, &c., chiefly compose the grass of the cliffs in Shetland.

of prey, as the young ones had not come out; but a dead guillemot and two kittewakes were found near, which renders it probable that one bird feeds the other while sitting on the eggs. It is also asserted that the male regularly takes his turn at the duty of incubation. The stomach of the bird contained, among some nearly digested fragments, an entire puffin.

" This individual was a very old female in perfect summer plumage, and measured from the point of bill to end of tail 39 inches. The utmost extent of wing, expanded, 93 inches—when closed, 26½ inches."

CHAPTER VIII.

College.

1841–42.

WHEN the winter session of College 1841–42 drew nigh, it was decided, after much anxious deliberation, that both the boys should spend the winter in Edinburgh, residing with their maternal uncle there. Sir William Hooker and other friends, interesting themselves in the great promise and future fame to which the youthful botanist might aspire, strongly recommended that, as a foundation, he should now study for a medical degree. This was also his own great desire. He therefore commenced the prescribed attendance at the various University Classes, and, in every way within reach, increased his botanical knowledge, especially by getting connected with the Edinburgh Botanical Society, of which he became Assistant-Secretary.

The University Session opened on the 1st November

1841, when having matriculated, he attended the Rev. Principal Lee's inaugural address. By a memorandum in his own handwriting, and the Professor's tickets, we find he attended the following classes :—

Senior Latin, . . Professor Pillans.
Chemistry, . . . Dr Hope.
Natural History, . . Professor Jameson.
Private Mathematics, . Mr Pryde.

Private Anatomy, and the New Town Dispensary. He was often, also, at the Royal Infirmary ; always, when permitted, at operations. Of all these lectures, there were notes taken, but such a measure seemed almost needless to impress what he heard on his quick and tenacious memory. Nothing coming before him, however casually, seemed to be overlooked or forgotten. He possessed, as many earnest students do, a great power of abstraction. Completely absorbed in a book or a letter while many voices might be talking around him, he would at a moment turn to some intense, absurd fun, and as quickly again to the most abstruse study. One excellent habit he had, not at all dependent on great natural talent, and, ah ! it would be well if every clever lad would value and acquire it, and that is, never to encroach on the regular hours of rest by sitting up to study. Thomas went to bed early, and generally had eight to ten hours of sound unbroken sleep. For this wholesome habit he was indebted to his education at home, where it was strenuously insisted on, and afterwards became a necessary part of his life, so that, except in a very few short intervals, it was steadily persevered in.

A few extracts from letters will demonstrate the industry with which he prosecuted the various studies to which he applied himself. His uncle of Buness having taken upon himself the necessary expense for the course he was' to pursue, it was to him chiefly that the details of procedure were addressed, although regular and most affectionate letters came to his other relations.

" To the Rev. Charles Clouston,
  " Manse of Sandwick, Orkney.
        " 39 Albany Street, Edinburgh,
          " 22nd November 1841.

" Sir.—I trust you will excuse the liberty I take in addressing you, being personally a stranger to you, but as I have heard much of you as a brother follower of botany, and being next thing to a countryman, (a Shetlander), I hope you will not be offended at my taking the liberty of soliciting information on the following subject. I am just now undertaking the publication of a Flora of Orkney and Shetland, and providing I can get my materials in order, I shall publish it in a month or two. It will be contained in an octavo volume of middle size, and besides short and specific characters and descriptions, will contain *habitats* for the rarer species, and such critical remarks as connect each plant as a native not only of Orkney or Shetland, but also of other parts of Great Britain. The geological and geographical distribution will be particularly attended to.

" Now the subject I would solicit your aid in is the following :—As I have not been nearly so much through Orkney as through my native Shetland, I am much at a loss for *habitats*, &c., to some of the rarer Orcadian plants, and I know no one who is more able than yourself to give me information, and I need not assure you that in that case your communication will be most fully and thankfully acknowledged. There are a few subjects on which I would desire particular information these I shall state in a future letter, if you will favour me with a few lines at your earliest convenience, telling me if you would be disposed to assist me.—And believe me, dear Sir, your most obedient servant,

" Thomas Edmondston, junior."

To the same.

" Edinburgh, 15 December 1841.

" Dear Sir.—I have just received your very kind letter, and have to thank you in the warmest manner for the way you have responded to what I dreaded you might consider intrusion.

" My little book, at least the Shetland part of it, is now in a fair way for completion. The chief subject on which I should be glad to have your assistance is for *habitats* for the rarer Orkney plants ; but I need not say that *any* remarks, critical or otherwise, would be most acceptable. Barry's list cannot be depended on, for many plants he mentions were not natives of Scotland or of Great Britain. He notices *Pisum maritimum* (Lin.) as growing in Orkney. This plant I found three or four years ago in Shetland, and it was the first authenticated instance of its being found in Scotland. What plant could Barry have mistaken for this? It is *Pisum maritimum* of Linnæus, *Lathyrus pisiformis* of Jussieu, and of the three first editions of Hooker's British Flora, and *Lathyrus Maritimus* of the fourth edition of the latter work. I should much like to know if you have ever seen it in Orkney. I have heard that *Ajuga pyramidælis* is found in Orkney, is it so? if it is, what is its station? This is one of our best Alpine plants, and an Orkney specimen would be a great addition to my collection, as I have never seen British specimens in a good state. How many stations have you for the rare and beautiful little *Primula Scotica ?* and is it your opinion that it is permanently distinct as a species from *P. Farinosa ?* This is a point on which botanists are by no means yet agreed, for although very different in habit, yet there does not seem to be permanent specific differences. I can judge but very imperfectly on the subject as my specimens of *P. Scotica* are in a very imperfect state. I should be much gratified by having your opinion on this interesting subject, if you have paid attention to it, and you are doubtless familiar with

P. Scotica in the living state, which is a privilege few botanists enjoy.   I believe *Saxifraga oppositifolia* is found in Hoy.   If you are a collector, and have a spare duplicate of the latter, and also of *Primula Scotica*, I assure you they would be most highly prized by me as valuable additions to my collection, and I should be happy to repay you in kind.   *Sax. oppositifolia* is found but very rarely in Shetland.

"As regards your valuable suggestion concerning the climate, nothing could be more *apropos* in my work. It would be a most valuable addition.   In the register kept by you, have you noticed the temperature by the thermometer regularly? The *monthly mean* temperature would be most interesting.

"I have thrown together the above remarks hastily as they occurred to me ; but I can once more assure you that any observations by you will be most valuable, especially connected with the geological or geographical distribution.   Trusting to have the pleasure of hearing soon again from you, believe me, with best regards,— dear Sir, yours truly,

"Thos. Edmondston, jun."

These were marvellous letters from a lad hardly turned of sixteen.   The very handwriting is bold and original, and evidently dashed off with great rapidity. Mr Clouston lately says of his young and gifted correspondent :—"His very brief and pleasant visit here was for the purpose of collecting materials for his Flora. He wished me to inform him about the botany of Orkney, and I requested that he would come and visit me, and judge for himself, while I should assist him in any way I could. The preface to his Flora and the *Launnaria Cloustoni*, which he did me the honour to name after me, shew that he amply acknowledged any little aid I was able to render him. The two letters above are all that I had from him, except, probably, a note soon after his visit here, (not until August 1844,) when he sent a handsome Shetland scarf to Mrs Clouston ; but though *the scarf has been preserved*, the note has not."

What trifling matters sometimes serve to illustrate the gentle charities that ameliorate society and adorn a generous friendship. A slight article of dress, kept for twenty-one years in memory of an acquaintance of a few days, exhibits as fully the amiability of the living as the attractive qualities of the dead.

                " 22nd October 1841.

" My dear Uncle.—I was very glad to receive your kind note this morning. - - - - I am glad to hear that there are still some seals about Weatherholm. There was a party of *vagabonds* shooting at them when we passed in the packet going to Lerwick. I was out yesterday on a botanising trip as far as Roslin.

" In politics everything is going on swimmingly. The American steam packet has arrived, but has not brought the news of M'Leod's trial. Every body believes that he will be hanged. Our government would seem to be preparing ; for a large squadron was ordered to the Nore some days ago,—it is said to go out to America. I guess they would soon make New York a second edition of St Jean d'Acre. What is most to be feared is the precipitancy of the Canadians, who, it is said, can hardly be restrained from rushing to New York ; and if they do hang M'Leod, the Canadas will rise to a man before fleets and troops can arrive to assist them.

" Every shop window is filled with portraits of ' the Duke of Wellington in the House of Lords,' ' Sir Robert Peel, First Lord of the Treasury,' &c., &c. I have seen a lot of H. B.'s caricatures on the downfall of the Whigs. I shall send you one or two. One represents *the Duke* putting an extinguisher on a candle almost burnt out, called ' Whiggery ' ; its grease, running down the sides of the candlestick, is formed into capital likenesses of Lord Melbourne and Lord J. Russell." - - - -

" Edinburgh, Nov. 1841.

" My dear Uncle.—The heart-rending news * in

---

* The death of a young sister in consequence of a lamentable accident.

papa's letter to me by last post has, I know, plunged you all in as much distress as it has us. But God's will be done. It is not only our duty but our interest to bow to the dispensations of the Most High, and take with meek acquiescence whatever either of good or evil our heavenly Father thinks fit to present us with. - - - - - I am continuing the same round of occupation,—classes during the day, and studying for them at night, occasionally relieved by a little of botany, or 'Blackwood,' or 'Charles O'Malley.' The latter is now finished.

"I have no news to tell you, but what, I am sure, you will be glad to hear,—that the Botanical Society have appointed me assistant-secretary. This mark of distinction you will probably not think much of, as you consider it a sort of 'Pickwick Club' you know. But, I assure you, it will be a considerable feather in my cap. It is attended with no expenses—not much time is expended—will soon be a source of some small emolument—and gives me a 'voice in their counsels.' I am their youngest associate, and yet one of their chief office-bearers. I read a paper on the night of my election on the botany of Shetland, which was well received, so that I could hardly get on sometimes for the cheering. My duties will be, occasionally at the monthly meetings to read the papers of correspondents, and return thanks, in the name of the Society, for donations and communications. - - - -

"There is not a word to tell you about politics. I am perfectly astonished to see every one so marvellously quiet. All seem to have confidence that PEEL will eventually bring forward some great and good measure. The Conservatives think so, because they have every confidence in his matchless ability, and the Whigs, because they think he has committed himself so far in condemning the shuffling policy of the late Ministry.— Remember me most kindly to all."

"22nd December 1841.

- - - - - - - "I am at present thinking of a sort of speculation, which is this. The Botanical Society to print for me a 'Flora of Shetland,' containing a general account of its vegetable productions,—comparing it with other Floras, &c. Two or three botanical journals have strongly recommended me to do it. I am often mentioned in botanical periodicals, and my paper, at last meeting, containing some novel views, was warmly and freely discussed. *Novelty* is the chief thing that can awaken public interest, and from the great attention I have paid to Shetland Botany in various lights and attitudes, I was enabled to give this. Independently of reputation, I expect it may be some little emolument to me; but the chief object I would have in view in coming before the public just now, is to lay something like a foundation on which future efforts may rear a substantial edifice. I am, therefore, writing this Flora; I am bestowing great pains on it, and weighing every thing before committing myself."—T. E.

" 29th December 1841.

" My Dear Uncle.—I have just received your long and kind letter, which I am truly thankful for, and very sensible of your kindness in writing so long a letter. I am always delighted to hear all the little news from Buness, which never fails to awaken remembrances of the many happy hours I have spent there. The society of literary and scientific men, and even all the advantages of Edinburgh, are but poor compensation for the loss of one friend's society, and I never think I was so happy as when seated by your fireside; but that will come again I hope. I have felt all this, particularly at Christmas time. There was none of the roaring fun we were wont to have in Shetland. Biot, Patrick Robertson, and I, spent it quietly together, and remembered our dear absent friends in a glass of ginger beer!

" I am glad you are pleased at the advancement I got in the Botanical Society, as I was sure you would be at anything that did me honour. - - - - - -

" The political world seems quite dull and dead, scarcely even a radical or chartist meeting! Peel seems secure in his own powers, and all seem disposed to be pleased with him, notwithstanding the vituperations of our worthy friends the *Caledonian Mercury* and *Scotsman.* - - - - - - I was at the Theatre Royal last night; the first time in it. It being a holiday, they took half-price for the whole night, and we had some capital comedy and farces. One of Sheridan's fine old comedies was, I thought, excellently performed, but it will be some time before they have the honour of my company again, as I think going to theatres a very useless way of spending time and money. I am working as hard as usual at my classses, and relieve more serious study by my botanical duties at the Society. Dr Balfour has made a most successful *debut* at Glasgow, the scene of his future labours."—T. E.

" 28th January.

" My Dear Uncle.—I wrote you long letters by last mail to Shetland, now three weeks ago; we have never been so long without letters before this winter.* - - - - - - I am busy making the most of my classes. I took the laughing gas yesterday at Dr Hope's (Chemistry), and kicked up a furious row,—fighting like blazes ! - - - - - - I was at Leith yesterday; there is no market for herrings yet, but ling fetches a good average price. - - - - - - - I was at the Infirmary yesterday, seeing a Whalsey man having his leg taken off; he is doing well. - - - - - - There

---

* There was no steam communication then during six months of the year.

is an anti-corn law agitation going on here. Petitions
for signature are at the corner of every street. Another
promising youth and myself have had some amusement
pretending to sign our names to these precious docu-
ments, but, in fact, writing nonsense instead, such as,
' You be blow'd,' ' Corn Law for ever.' ' Down with
agitation.' - - - - - - - -

" 31st January.

" I have this morning your long and very kind
letter of the 12th. I surely need not tell you how
sensible I am of your kindness, and how grateful I feel
for it in writing me so fully, when I know you are often
ill able to transact your more important correspondence.
I was awfully shocked to hear of the calamity that has
again diminished our circle by the death of our good
warm-hearted cousin. I cannot say how much I feel
for you all, especially the poor sisters. I know it must
sink deep into their affectionate hearts. Well I know
I have lost a true and warm-hearted friend. - - -
- - - - - - I am glad you are pleased that I am
going to publish. I was sure you would be, as you
ever are about any thing that does me good. All my
botanical friends here think it will do well, and the
manner you express yourself on the subject will have
the effect of encouraging me on with it. It will not be
large or high priced.

" God bless my dear uncle. Do write when you
can ; your letters always bring back old and cherished

recollections, and are the greatest comfort I look forward to, but I would not be so selfish as to wish it, were you not perfectly able.—Your most affectionate nephew, T. E."

" To Miss Archibald of Broomhill, Shetland.

" Edinburgh, 31st Jan. 1842.

" My very dear Cousin.—This morning's letters brought us the afflictive announcement that my dear cousin Jessie had been taken from us. The ways and workings of the Almighty are inscrutable; but we know this much, that He is merciful as He is just, and that all His dispensations are eventually for the best to His believing people. My own feelings for the loss of one whom I always regarded as an elder sister,—and well I know that no one had a more tender interest in my welfare than she who is now in heaven,—will not allow me to dwell on this afflictive topic, and I trust that you have sought and obtained consolation from the only source.

" I cannot express how much this sudden and second stroke has affected me, ' but whom the Lord loveth he also chasteneth ;' and we all need the rod of correction to subdue our minds, and bring us to acknowledge that we are indeed frail and erring mortals, become liable to sin and death. We must all appear before the dread tribunal one day, and may He in His mercies grant that we may appear there clothed in the righteousness of Him who gave Himself for us. Then, indeed, we shall be happy, while everything here reminds us that this is but a vale of tears and of the shadow of death.

"God bless you, and enable you to bear His pleasure without repining, is the prayer of your affectionate cousin, Thos. Edmondston."

"Edinburgh, 27th Feb. 1842.

"My dear Uncle,—I have little to say in addition to the long letter by last post, and it is now a fortnight since we had letters from the north. It is said there is a Shetland mail in to-day, but I think I should have had letters if the packet had reached Aberdeen. The winter session will be up in six weeks, and I shall not be sorry for a short respite. It has been proposed to me that I should attend Graham (Botany) in summer, so as to make out the year, to count in the medical curriculum. I think there is little doubt he will give me a ticket,—indeed, he as good as offered me one; at all events, strongly recommended my staying and competing for his gold medal, which, he says, 'I should be sure to take.' It is offered as a prize for the best herbarium composed of the plants within a ten miles circuit of Edinburgh. Let me know if you would approve of my remaining and taking out Graham's ticket, or what?

"My Shetland Flora will soon be finished, and I

trust my dear uncle and the rest at home will be sitting in judgment on my ‘maiden effort’; but I shall pray the *Conscripti Patres* to be merciful! I am getting on swimmingly with the Botanical Society.”   -   -   -   -

“ 26th March 1842.

“It is not many days since I last wrote you, but I have a few spare moments just now, and I know you like to hear from me, though I may have little to write about.

“ I am not doing much at present out of the jog-trot business of my classes, and that, too, will soon be up now. I am wearying sometimes oftener to get a few mouthfuls of country air. - - - - I dined at Patrick Robertson’s yesterday. I am often there, and always can be sure of a hearty welcome, and feel myself completely at home. Nothing new in politics since I wrote last. The present ministry are evidently resolved to go on with their plans for the good of the country unwaveringly.”   -   -   -   -

“ 30th March.

“ I had this morning the great pleasure to receive your long and kind letter of the 24th. Only five days from Buness is indeed a *rara avis*, and not, therefore, the less acceptable.   -   -   -   The ‘blawn fish’ was rather soft, as might be expected, when it arrived, but it had the real *gout*, and after it had been hung out a day or two it was delicious. Miss Jameson had not had time to taste her's when I saw her, but I shall soon hear how she liked it. You wish me to give you a screed of politics, but really I don't know where to begin or end. Except a glance at a paper while I am swallowing my breakfast before class time, I am not in the way of hearing political news. The society I chiefly mix in is not at all of a political cast, being for the most part more taken up with the distinctions of plants than the bickerings of politicians. At Patrick Robertson's, where it might be supposed to be discussed, the subject is scarcely mentioned; indeed, it is considered rather a breach of good manners to do so, especially if ladies are present. However, I shall try and gather something or other to tell you in a day or two.

" I spoke to Professor Jameson after lecture to-day, but could not profane his ears in his sanctuary by enquiring about his sister's *blawn fish.* - · - -- Your most affectionate Nephew."

One evening towards the end of April, when the twilight was fast sinking into darkness, the servants at Buness heard some person hail the shore from a small fishing sloop that seemed a stranger. Peter informed his master, who, as any little adventure is rather eagerly welcomed in those parts, wrapped his cloak hastily on, and went to the little quay, desiring his men to return the halloo that was still being repeated at intervals. A loud gruff voice replied, "Its Master Thomas!" and a more youthful one called, "The Marquis—Uncle!" A boat was sent off, and the unexpected guest met his usual hearty welcome. He had longed so for "a taste of the sea," and he wished so earnestly to be allowed to remain during summer for the Botany class and the Professor's prize, that, as this was an extension of the predetermined plan, he justly reasoned arrangements would be more easily carried on after a *viva voce* explanation. He remained about a fortnight, in his usual buoyant spirits, rejoicing in his holiday and his sea voyages, and returned to Edinburgh with the prospect of being home when the summer classes were over in August.

> "Edinburgh, 12th May 1842.
> "My dear Uncle,—I arrived here all safe last night. - - - - - There is to be a sharp competition for the gold medal, and I must commence my labours immediately, for the others (five in all) have the start of me by a fortnight, and with my papers for the Botanical and Wernerian Societies, I shall have my hands full. I shall write by next post, and trust you will excuse this hurried scrawl from your affectionate Nephew."

His uncle having occasion to be a few weeks in Scotland in June, saw him intensely busied in gathering and preparing the plants for the herbarium. When finished it was very complete and handsome. It had beautifully ornamented outside boards—the genera and species scientifically arranged—and the names in illuminated penmanship.

"Edinburgh, 27th July 1842.

"My dearest Mamma,—I am looking forward to letters to-morrow most anxiously. I trust to hear from uncle of his arrival in Lerwick, and that you are better.

"I am particularly engaged just now with the Botanical Society. Babington is here, and working with us at the foreign plants, so we must make the most of our time while such a *shining light* countenances us.

"I am afraid, all things duly considered, that it will be impossible for me to go to Shetland this autumn. I always hoped I might; but finding that the herbarium has occupied so very much time, to the exclusion of almost every thing else this summer, it will take some time to make up my *lee way*, and I promised the Society I would work during the autumn. I told uncle this when he was here, and also that there are one or two publications to be issued before winter, the proceeds of which will, I trust, *do something* for me. This, with private anatomy, which will make the after study more easy, will occupy my time very respectably. *N'est ce pas?*

"I have made some discoveries in the Flora of this

district, which I have written papa about. Biot goes home on Friday. Pat has gone to the Highlands. I have been all day at the Society's rooms. The prizes are to be decided on the 1st. I have no fear of the result.

"Love *ad infinitum.*   Thos. Edmondston, Jun."

But the confident anticipation expressed in the end of the foregoing letter was doomed to disappointment. This circumstance, with its eventualities, was the only *contra temps* that occurred in Thomas Edmondston's short bright career. It involved an act of headlong imprudence, while, at the same time, it displayed much of the acute sensitiveness observable in him from childhood, and a courage and self-reliance we may not altogether condemn. His own statement as to what occurred is as follows:—

"At the beginning of the summer session the Professor of Botany offered two gold medals as prizes to be competed for by the students of his class. The first was offered for the best herbarium collected within ten miles of Edinburgh, between 20th July 1841 and 20th July 1842. The other was for an 'Essay on the Reproductive Functions of Plants.' The conditions were affixed to the door of the class room. I entered into competition for the herbarium prize, fulfilled all the conditions, and sent in my herbarium on the day appointed. It contained between seven and eight hundred species, nearly twenty of which were not formerly noticed in the circuit specified. The 2nd of August being the last of the session, was the day appointed for distributing the prizes to the successful competitors. On the day before (the 1st August), the professor announced to his class that a herbarium (mentioning that having my motto) had been sent to him for competition, which contained some specimens that required *verification* as occurring in the district; at the same time saying, that provided *that* were done it would be entitled to the first prize, being the best he had received."

Young Edmondston happened not to be in the class that day, but as soon as he heard the announcement sought an interview with the professor, which terminated unsatisfactorily, as there was obviously no time left for the pupil to fulfil the new conditions of " verification " by procuring fresh specimens. The prize was adjudged to another on the following day. From a searching inquiry afterwards instituted by Dr Edmondston, who had interviews with the professor and others for the purpose, it seemed clear that, in the first instance, the teacher was indeed startled to find that his (most probably) youngest pupil should have found plants in his own district which he himself had overlooked. And yet in this there was nothing either strange or derogatory to the professor. How many young, ardent, indefatigable students, with physical powers in all their vigour, have made discoveries and observations unattained by far more powerful and accomplished minds, and that merely, or at all events chiefly, by dint of fresher, and, therefore, more acute bodily powers?   But there were other influences also at work to frustrate poor young Edmondston's eager aspirations.   There were, no doubt, secret or only suspected rivals, and mean, jealous fellow-students poisoning the professor's mind against one he had so generously praised and patronised the two preceding years.   This circumstance, also, is one neither rare nor greatly to be blamed, except in so far as it is originated by unworthy passions.   It is most generally compensated by futurity.   So it was in the case before us.   But it first brought about a severe though happily short conflict.

By the first mail to Shetland, after the disappointment about the gold medal, Thomas wrote his friends, smarting sorely under what he believed a cruel wrong. The following is the chief part of one of these letters :

"Edinburgh, 6th August 1842.

"My dear Uncle,—I received your most kind letter this morning. - - - - I have been able to do very little of late. - - - - When full of hope in the morning of life, expecting those who are congenial in pursuits, at least not to retard one, even if they should not help, it *is* vexatious to find hopes disappointed, and petty envy and jealousy occupying the place of the kindly feeling one had anticipated. The temper is (for the time) soured, and a general disgust and morbid misanthropy will creep over one. However, I am learning to bear these things with more Christian resignation, and the lesson will be useful to me in after life. Truly said my great pattern Linnæus—a man, a philosopher, and a Christian,—'When your boat is made of patience and experience, when your rudder is rectitude, and truth your ballast, adverse winds may retard your progress for a time, but you will ultimately regain the haven, not the worse, but greatly the better for your struggle.'

"No man can expect to go through the world without enemies, and the earlier he is trained to bear rubs and misfortunes the better he will be able to combat them afterwards. - - - - The day of awarding the prize came, and a student with not half the number of plants that I had got the prize. - - - - - - - - In my own self-defence I have drawn up a list of the new plants found by me this summer, for the purpose of publishing them in the *Phytologist.*" * - - -

In another letter of the same date we find the indomitable spirit, the beautiful elasticity of temperament asserting itself even while the wound was yet stinging freshly :—

---

* This was done, and the list remained unchallenged, so far as is now remembered.—EDITOR.

"I am working at my Flora. If I can get Balfour or any other professor to patronize it, it will be the making of me. I am also preparing notes on some little understood species,—among them, some of the *Curices.* I have also taken it upon me to take dissecting this autumn. It will save upwards of three guineas in the end, for the ticket is only one guinea *now*, and *subjects* are but half as dear as in the winter session. The class consists of half a dozen studious chaps ; and subjects being good and plentiful, the benefit and the saving will be great. This employs me from 9 to 12. It is at Dr Thomson's rooms.

"With love to every one, believe me, &c.   T. E."

Before the tardy mail could bring him the sympathizing and soothing answers sent from his distant home, the loving circle of friends there were electrified by a short incoherent note, saying he was off to London, where he intended to take any situation he could get, giving no address,—no clue whatever as to his whereabouts or intentions,—although he seemed quite confident he could gain himself a livelihood, and live down the slanders of his enemies. It afterwards appeared he had no intention of misleading or concealing anything from his attached family at home. It was only the perturbed state of his mind that caused the unwitting mystery which chiefly distressed and alarmed them. In fact, notwithstanding the noble efforts he made to

divert his thoughts by turning to *work*, the crushing
of his high hopes, with the accompanying irritating
circumstances, produced such a shock that for many
nights he was wholly deprived of sleep, and all but
brought on a brain fever, so that he threw himself into
the London steamer, scarcely knowing what he did.
After all, perhaps, for his health's sake, it was the best
thing he could have done, although, assuredly, it did
not enter into his calculations that it would be so.
Thus it is, nevertheless, that kind Providence so often
overrules matters, so that from "seeming evil good is
still educed."

Within twelve hours after the receipt of that short
letter, his father was taking a midnight voyage to Lerwick; there reached the mail packet; from Aberdeen
hastened to catch the London train, and surprised his
beloved boy reading in bed before getting up. The son
clung to his father's arms with a burst of loving gratitude. He felt and appreciated the affection that led
him to take such a journey, and poured out confidently
all his vexations and plans. He was in communication
with their friends, and, no doubt, would soon have
found employment, but of course his natural protectors
believed him far too young and inexperienced to be left
drifting on the world. Their greatest dread had been
that he might go abroad. This, however, he had never
supposed would be necessary, and unless it had been so,
he had never contemplated it. With the utmost

docility he obeyed his father's wishes to return home with him at once.

Having reached Edinburgh by train, and awaiting there the sailing of a northward bound vessel, he wrote the following :—

"Edinburgh, 8th October 1842.

"Here, my dearest mamma, after all my misfortunes, I am again, and, I trust, never more to create such distress. I am sure I look back on the last month as a dream, shadowy and fearful. The continued kindness of my dear uncle impresses me with the most heartfelt gratitude, while making me conscious how madly I have acted, and by what interposition of an ever merciful Providence, I was saved from what might have ended in ruin. This has also shewed me how little I can depend on myself, a truly humiliating reflection, when I was endeavouring to persuade myself how little I cared for the injustice and persecution of those I had thought my friends. Were I not convinced that I was not in my right mind after that infernal herbarium business, I should hate myself for ever. Throughout all my life this will be a lesson to me, how, what might at the time have been looked upon as a slight transgression against the laws of strict economy, had nearly ruined me for ever. The herbarium was at the bottom of it all ; in my thoughtless anxiety for putting defeat out of the range of possibility, I was led to the expenditure · of more money than was exactly prudent, or than the thing was worth. Then the shock of the loss of the medal, with its *concomitant circumstances,* so disordered my mind, that I viewed every thing with a diseased imagination, and through a discoloured medium. The tyrannical oppression of my landlady, though I only owed her the rent of two week's lodgings, served to increase my discomfort, but you can see that had I not expended so much on the affair of the medal, I could have discharged my bill weekly as usual. Now, I hope my beloved mamma, *that* matter will still be put right. As to uncle's kindness I can only think,—I cannot speak or write upon the subject.

" Papa is waiting for this letter; and with kindest love to all the dear ones, whom I hope soon to see, I ever am your most devotedly attached son, T. E."

They took the usual sailing packet bound for Lerwick, but the stormy winds of the season attacked them at sea, and, after ten days striving, they were obliged to *return to Leith.* When captain, sailors, and passengers, were during much of the time grievously alarmed at their danger, Thomas alone was completely self possessed and cheerful. As in some previous, and many succeeding occasions of peril, he appeared literally not to have an idea of what physical timidity meant. The isolated solitary circle in Unst suffered dreadful anxiety when no mail, no intelligence reached them. Days drearily grew into weeks of tempest and rain. Before Christmas, however, the travellers safely reached Unst, and thus happily terminated the only act of imprudence on the part of Thomas Edmondston that ever gave a moment's vexation to his relatives. As may be gathered from one of the preceding letters, it was pecuniary embarrassment that finally prompted the rash decision to face the world unaided, and by his own exertions provide for his present wants, and raise himself to the position he never doubted he could and should attain to. He was generous, open-handed to a fault; he knew nothing of the value, or of the care necessary in the spending of money. Had he got the gold medal, in the competition for which he had exceeded his means, he would have thrown himself on his uncle's generosity, and not in vain. But to have lost that for which he had so diligently striven, and to have run himself into debt, (trifling as the amount was), seemed at the time unbearable. Crushed, vexed, and bewildered, he left his clothes with his landlady, and believed that in the world of London he would certainly find a field for the exercise of the acquirements and abilities he felt that he possessed. But he came back to the loving welcome of home, and to the solitude and quiet of Unst, with unabated industry and cheerfulness, settling himself down to his books and letters, his gun and his plants, as if there were no busy enticing world afar, where he might reap greater treasures of knowledge and wisdom than his poor but dear birth place could afford. A happy contented temper is indeed an invaluable blessing to old and young, but in the eager excitable years of early life, is the more rare and enviable.

To Professor Babington.

"Shetland, 23rd January 1843.

"My Dear Sir.—I have at last got the notice of the Cerastium ready, and enclose it for your kind perusal and emendation, along with the drawings. I have been very careful to draw up my description only after comparing a great number of specimens, and ascertaining the constancy of the characters employed. If you will be kind enough to forward it to Newman I will be much obliged; I write him by this post. I am sorry I have not been able to forward the specimens I promised in my last. I have a number of letters to send off to-night, and posts here at the North Pole, are 'like angel visits,' &c. Could you oblige me with a specimen of *Cerastium pedunculatum* to compare with mine. I wish much to have one *from yourself*. What is *C. Pumiluis curtis* of the new list? Hooker gives it as a synonym for *C. Tetrandrum;* a bit of *C. Atrovereus*, or any of the more doubtful *Cerastia* would be very valuable *from you*, and I should be very happy to make any returns in my power.

"Believe me I am always most happy to receive any

criticisms or observations with which you may be pleased to favour me. Do you know any *Algæologist* who would condescend to correspond and exchange specimens with me. I am very hardly situated as regards books and other indispensable facilities for the study of these beauties, and you could not possibly do me a greater favour than to introduce my name to some botanist who has paid attention to these tribes, and who would give me some assistance in them. Do, like a noble botanist, try.

" I wrote you a week or two ago with the *Cerastium latifolium*," &c., &c., " T. E."

In answer to the request contained in the preceding letter, the zealous student was directed to Mrs Griffiths, a well known authority in that department. Most kindly she corresponded with young Edmondston, and he acknowledged Professor Babington's kindness thus :—

" Many thousand thanks for your permission to use your name to Mrs Griffiths. I have written her, and sent her some Shetland *Algæ*.

CHAPTER IX.

Beginning to Teach.

1843-44.

AS the months swiftly rolled on, it was becoming more and more apparent to Thomas and his relations that his love for, and aptitude in acquiring the details of the natural sciences were pointing his way to become an instructor in some of them. The idea of making every one love what was to him so great an enthusiasm, seemed ever present to his mind, so much so, that his attached Unst schoolmaster, the minister, and, indeed, all his friends there, were accustomed to call him " the professor," and address him as such. As the summer of 1843 came brightening on, he proposed to try what he could do in the lecturing way by giving a course in Lerwick on botany.

From the Rev. T. Barclay.*

"Lerwick, 26th June, 1843.

"My dear Sir,—I was favoured with your letter last week, and should have answered it by return of the post had I not thought it best to sound some of your friends and mine on the subject of it before communicating with you.

"Every person to whom I have spoken thinks the subject on which you propose to lecture a very interesting one, and that you are unquestionably qualified to do it ample justice. The only apprehension entertained is people's *want of means* to give you the encouragement you desire, and to procure for themselves the pleasure and the instruction which your lectures and demonstrations would afford. Still, I think it would go hard if you did not muster an attendance sufficient to defray your charges. It would be necessary to make the tickets very low, in order to induce as many as possible to attend; for nothing has a more chilling effect on a lecturer than a scanty audience. I can vouch for that from recent experience, having preached in Tweedie's kirk the first Sunday after the disruption. As you propose to visit Lerwick at all events, I think your best plan would be to give an introductory lecture, to which all that chose to attend should be admitted, and then to propose the formation of a class,

---

* Now Principal of Glasgow University.

intimating terms, &c. I need not add, any influence I may have shall be most cordially exerted to forward your views.—I remain, my dear Sir, yours truly.

"T. Barclay."

"T. Edmondston, Junr., Esq."

It is true that, from its size and small population, there were not resident in the town or its neighbourhood many families of the more highly educated class, but yet, on the whole, we believe few places of its class in Britain could boast a more generally intelligent and appreciating audience. When he had fairly commenced he wrote thus to a friend in England :—

"1st August.

"My lectures are well attended, and some of my pupils are becoming enthusiastic. I have between thirty and forty, which is a good amateur audience for a place like this."

"Lerwick, 6th July 1843.

"My dear Uncle,—I arrived here on Saturday about ten in the forenoon. We got to Rova Head about five, but the wind fell and we cast anchor there till the tide turned, when we got in. Yesterday being Sacrament Sunday, I went to the preaching on Saturday, and in the evening called for Mr Barclay, and staid till pretty late. I have been knocking about all day. I want to

get the Mason Lodge for lecture-room. -   -   -   -   -
I glanced at your newspapers that came by the
steamer." -   -   -   -   -

> "Monday, 13th July.

-   -   -   -   "Well, my first lecture came off with
great *eclat* on Friday.   The room was crammed to its
greatest extent.   We had to send for several more
forms, and a great many had to stand.   They all
seemed pleased, and it is being spoken of, I am told,
with high praise.   I was slightly nervous for the first
two or three sentences, but very soon was as cool as if
none but you and Peter were present.   They all seemed
particularly pleased with the demonstrations, and altogether I have reason to be satisfied with my success.
A great deal of time is taken up in gathering plants for
exhibition." -   -   -   -

> "Thursday night.

"I am just come from lecture.   Got on famously,
and am glad to see the interest displayed in what they
are pleased to term my 'lucid explanations.'   It was
all extempore, except a page of notes.   More tickets
have been sold.   I believe I shall have abundance of
profit to clear all expenses.

"260 whales have been killed at Ura Firth.   Large
shoals of them have been seen on the west side.   I
wish some would come your way.   A Greenland brig

has arrived with 4100 seals. They have a live one on board, and I went to see it. It is different from any I have ever seen or heard of. It has a long snout, very thick round the shoulders (although lean), and small below."

" 16th July.

- - - - "I am very glad of this lecturing business to get me into the habit of *regular* systematic working, as it has been rather desultory of late; but I must work now, and pretty hard too. There are endless things to be done. The very endeavour to dress up a science in a style sufficiently popular for my audience, is more difficult than it would be to acquire a new one. Botany is quite the rage at present, and I am sending for a supply of books by the steamer. I have eight or ten pupils with me when I go to gather plants, which is rather a nuisance, for I cannot walk so fast as if I were alone, nor can ladies leap dykes and wade into bogs, or do many other things appertaining to practical botany. - - - - - -

- - - - - "There was a dancing school ball on Friday night. All the *dons* were there, but *beaux* were very scarce, and accordingly were held in high repute. I sat still for the first three dances, studying the figures, and then danced quadrilles and country dances the whole evening. There is nothing in this world like a little *brass*. By its means I passed for an excellent dancer, and in fact, was declared the chief beau of the party! This is what may be termed 'coming out' in a new character; but variety is a grand thing, and blarney passes current in most situations. We had an agreeable evening, however, and Charlie Duncan, Charlie Barclay, and myself kicked up a considerable row. Since new characters are *all the go*, I think I shall come out as musician next.

"I have had a peep at the *Scotsman* just arrived. *They* say there will be a split in the Cabinet, and that Lord Aberdeen will positively resign; but its no believing what *they* say—the scoundrels! Spain also seems in a sweet mess. There will be certainly another civil war in that peaceable, orderly, well-disposed country! Walker says O'Connell was advised to come to Edinburgh to hold a repeal meeting, but he said he would be 'noosed' in the castle if he left Ireland. This looks as if he were afraid, and I trust they'll muzzle him yet."

"22nd July, Saturday morning.

- - - - - "I have an excursion to-day. I am looking forward to letters from home in the afternoon. I dined at Sound yesterday; am to dine with the Sheriff to-day. - - - - - Every one continues kind and attentive and *respectful*, as in duty bound, to their *venerable and venerated professor*. I am inclined to laugh sometimes at my rather novel position, but am getting a little accustomed to it, and endeavour to be-seem myself with all becoming gravity. Archie Greig and some others are turning somewhat *uproarious* with cheering in the class room, so I shall have to take old Hope's plan, and threaten ' to expel those gentle-men from the room ?'"

" Monday.

" The excursion on Saturday came off very well. I explained all the plants we met with, and shewed them the quickest and easiest method of finding out the names by the book. The lecture in the evening went off as usual. I am just now on the history and pro-perties of the better known and more extensively useful plants in the arts, medicine, &c., such as corn, cotton, dyeing plants, &c.

" This has been my first idle day since I came, as my next lecture will be all demonstration, so, as I was wearying for a *shot*, borrowed a gun, and went to Bressay. I shot seven plovers and four pigeons, besides some kittiwakes and willcocks. The pigeons, three of the plovers, and all the gulls, were killed on wing. I am sure you will be glad to hear that I have found three specimens again of the *Cynosurus echinatus* near the old place in Bressay. I have sent one of them and a note for the *Phytologist.* T. E."

While thus in the full enjoyment of popularity and

of the work he loved best, the youthful lecturer was laid on a sickbed by measles. Let himself describe his progress.

> " Lerwick, 10th August 1843.

" My Dear Uncle.—In my last I was scarcely able to scratch two or three lines to tell you I was seized with measles. To-day is my first down-stairs. Though feeling excessively weak and giddy, I think I am equal to the task of jotting down the progress of my ' case.' - - - - - - It has given me great pleasure in the course of my short illness, to see the desire among my friends to show me every possible kindness and attention. Not one of them but has called several times, and often sent twice a day to enquire for me. To-day I have from Gardie House got a very kind note, and a pot of honey and some preserves. Altogether, I am beginning to think there are worse berths in the world than a ' popular lecturer.'

" The doctor says I shall likely go out to-morrow, and that I may lecture on Tuesday. I trust, dear uncle, that you have not been anxious about me. I am afraid mamma will have been so, but I hope papa and you, knowing the *non-dangerous* nature of the disease, will not have been alarmed. For my own part, had it not occurred at such a vexatious time, I should have been glad to have *got them over.* T. E."

" 14th August.

" Since writing you on Thursday I have been gradually improving. I am now quite strong, but, of course, not sufficiently so to take any liberties with myself. I know well the disastrous consequences of cold after measles, and I have been careful to guard against it. The worst effect they seem to have had is on my eyes. The acute pain in them, at the moment I am writing, is tormenting. After reading or writing a quarter of an hour, I am obliged to intermit for an hour before I can resume. I trust this will improve, or it will be a bad business for me. But Dr Cowie, and his brother, have advised me to wear coloured glass preserves.

" Oh ! the poor ' Boys' o' Deal.' What a melancholy, unfortunate accident !* It is the will of Providence, and our duty is to bear it with patience, but truly a more destitute set of families than are thus left, could not be found in Shetland.

" Above thirty passengers have come by the steamer, the largest number, I believe, since she began. Mr Barclay returned. The church here was declared vacant yesterday by Mr Hamilton. Mr Barclay preached a most excellent sermon in the afternoon. I think he *beats* Mr Robertson of Ellon, and all the others I have ever heard, *all to sticks.* - - - - I have no more to tell you of any interest. My eyes are hinting pretty strongly

---

* **Loss of one of the ling fishing bouts.**

to me to leave off. I hope to resume my lectures on Tuesday, but if my eyes are no better I shall have to curtail them. I had one ready when I was taken ill, and by little and little I have managed to get up another, so that for some days I shall have little to write."

"Monday, August.

"You would be surprised at not hearing from me by Thursday's post. This is how it happened. I had been in Bressay gathering plants for the evening lecture. The room was rather dark, and the strain on my eyes, with the previous fatigue, made me quite useless with headache and sore eyes. When I got home, I threw myself on the sofa to get a rest and fell asleep, not waking till past eleven,—of course too late for the north post. I am now quite well and strong as ever. I took leave on Saturday, after having had a very full attendance at the excursion that day. I was cheered of course prodigiously. The lecture was principally on the growing of trees in Shetland, and all expressed themselves highly pleased. I am very glad that they are over; and, I do assure you, I am very happy I commenced them.

"I am afraid I will not get home to-morrow as I expected. I have not, since I recovered, been able to make the calls I ought to make, considering the great kindness I have experienced. Mr Playfair has invited a party to meet me, and as I have been in a ' public capacity,' I may have to get up a speech ! Then the washerwoman has got all my clothes to be *fumigated* before I go home, so I shall remain another week. - - - - I heard one of the finest possible sermons from Mr Barclay yesterday. He preaches his farewell next Sunday ; he merely mentioned the fact of leaving, and there were one hundred pocket handkerchiefs up. Every one regrets his going, and thinks Lerwick will never get such another. - - - - Kindest love to all.—From your most affectionate nephew, T. E."

The ensuing winter, 1843–4, was again passed in Buness ; in the first instance invigorating his health, which had suffered considerably after measles, by the exercise in boats, and walking out with his collecting box, or his gun, to which he had been so early accustomed, and to which a residence in towns was so opposed, that he ever fancied himself as in a prison, when compelled to be located in such parts. But the long evenings and many wet stormy days of " Shetland weather" were occupied in preparing the " Flora " for the press, writing papers for periodicals, and carrying on his voluminous correspondence. He was asked by his aunt one day, how he managed to pay for all the letters he sent ?—it was then the early days of penny postage. " Oh !" he replied in his own merry way, " the jolliest easy thing in the world ; just write "paid" on them, and they go free in uncle's bag." When weather permitted he dredged on the coast for Edward Forbes, with whom he regulary corresponded. There remain, also, rough notes of at least two intended small works,—the one, " A particular account of the birds found in Shetland," and the other entitled " Conversations on Botany," evidently intended as an elementary book for the young. He was also much engaged with a work on a new system of classification of plants, allusions to which are made in some subsequent letters, but what became of this voluminous manuscript has never been discovered. He read a good deal of French this winter. He also began Spanish, with no other book than an old Bible in that language that happened to be in his father's library, little thinking under what circumstances the slight familiarity with the language, thus acquired, would afterwards prove so serviceable.

From the *Phytologist.* Vol. I., p. 772.

" It will perhaps interest the readers of the *Phytologist* to know that I have this year again found *Cynosurus echinatus* in Bressay, Shetland, about one hundred yards from where I found it in 1840. I obtained only three rather small specimens, but this fact proves the perseverance of the plant in the locality, and shews the propriety of reckoning it in the Scottish Flora. If such a request be not considered presumptuous, might I mention, through the medium of your pages, that if any of your correspondents could furnish me with even the *loan* of a south of England specimen of *C. echinatus* it would be conferring a great obligation on me. The Shetland specimens, both those collected at first and also now, differ much from my foreign specimens; the latter are admirably and characteristically figured in Parnell's beautiful 'Grasses of Scotland.' They differ from the Shetland form in having a much more *dense, roundish* spike, which is covered with a somewhat heavy pubescence totally absent from the Shetland specimens. I should much like to see an English specimen of this interesting grass, to ascertain which form my plant agrees with."*

This is all we have heard of the *Cynosurus echinatus* in Bressay. Sir W. Hooker's opinion has been therefore proved correct, as was to be anticipated, and the plant was only a visitant of a year or two. Without doubt some seed had got imported, no one knows how, and the uncongenial climate allowed it but short existence.

" *Note by the Editor of the* ' Phytologist.'—Among the plants mentioned in the following communication by Mr Gibson, as having been collected by himself in the vale of Calder, is *Cynosurus echinatus.* We have no doubt Mr Gibson will feel pleasure in complying with Mr Edmondston's request. We also should be much gratified by receipt of a specimen from each of the localities discovered by these gentlemen."

Perhaps the following may contain some hints not unacceptable to young students of the beautiful and attractive science of Botany :—

From the *Phytologist.*

" I observe your correspondent's enquiry regarding the formation of a herbarium, &c. The plan which I have adopted in arranging a rather extensive collection is the following :—

" In all the best herbaria the specimens are *glued* to the paper ; that this is far preferable to securing them by slips or thread, as practised by some, does not, I think, admit of a doubt. Besides making the specimens more easy of reference, it is more expeditously accomplished, and the constant breaking up of the slips is obviated ; besides, there are many plants which cannot well be attached by that means, such as the leaves of *Atropa Belladonna*, the very compound ones of many *Umbellifera*, &c., where if slips are applied in sufficient number to fasten the specimen fairly to the paper, both the beauty and character of it are greatly diminished ; then again the fruit of grasses, carices, compositæ, the petals of roses, and other species bearing fugacious flowers, are almost sure to be eventually lost. Under all these circumstances, I think it will be evident that fastening them in this manner is preferable to the other method by slips of paper. Thin glue should always be used, never gum or paste, as these are apt to turn mouldy, and, also, after a time to give way. It should be carefully applied with a pretty large and soft brush, and immediately committed to the press and paper used for drying plants, to remain there till thoroughly dry. The paper I use is large printing paper, thick and strong, about 17 by $9\frac{1}{2}$ inches. I have some of half sheets cut in two, and others in four, the folio size being intended for such plants as the *Rumices*, most ferns, grasses, *Carices*, &c. ; the quarto for those of the size of *Sedum*, *Telephium*, *Geraniums*, &c., and the octavo for all such small species as the *Arenarias*, *Saxifragas*, &c. In this way only one specimen is put on each piece of paper. I have then a sheet of coarse stiff cartridge paper for each *species*, about a fourth of an inch larger every way than the other sheets ; within this is laid the specimen or specimens glued to the other paper, with the station, date, or any other particulars written on the latter ; then on the lower left hand corner of the large sheet, I write the name of the species, and I include all belonging to the same genus in another rather larger sheet, on which are written the name of the genus, class, order, &c. The genera may be arranged according to the system adopted by the collector, and made up in tolerably small bundles, not *bound* at the back, but secured instead by strings, or straps and buckles, at each side. This mode of arranging a herbarium I find to be the most convenient for reference and enlargement, as well as the most economical, and the collection admits of being laid much smoother and flatter than if the leaves of paper were all of one size.

"It is desirable sometimes to have specimens *loose* for examination; indeed, this is almost the only recommendation in favour of having them only partially fastened to the paper. In all *doubtful* or interesting plants it is very necessary to have at least the most essential parts loose; and a piece of paper, folded somewhat like a letter envelope, and fastened by a wafer or a little gum to any part of the inside of the *species sheet*, should always contain the flowers and fruit of the *Umbelliferæ, Carices, Cruciferæ*, &c.

"As I am on the subject of *herbaria*, allow me a few words on the *drying* of plants. However simple the operation, it is one by no means well understood. I shall mention the way which, in my hands, seems to take up least time and trouble, and to dry plants more perfectly than any other I have made trial of. It appears to me, that one cause of our seeing so many imperfectly and clumsily dried specimens is from botanists not using enough paper between the layers of specimens, and from not applying sufficient pressure *at first*. I never employ less than twelve sheets of thick absorbent paper for any plants, twenty-four for strong or succulent species, and a board between every layer or two of specimens. The weight at first ought generally to be not less than two cwt. This amount of pressure very speedily expels the moisture from the plant, without giving it time to shrivel up or change colour. The specimens lie in this way one, or perhaps two days, and are then taken out and all the paper changed, and half the weight or less applied for two or three days. No more changing is necessary, and in a week at most, from the time of gathering, the plants will be found to be perfectly dry. If any one would import the thick coarse paper used by German botanists for drying plants, and which we here never see unless coming with plants from that country, it would be conferring a great boon on British botanists; for the great superiority of the German specimens is evidently in a great measure owing to the superior paper for drying they possess. I made trial of this paper among some experiments instituted on the drying of plants last summer, and I found they dried in half the time required for those preserved with the common kind of paper. In conclusion, I would beg to caution inexperienced botanists against using hot water in the preparation of *sedums, agraphis*, and other succulent plants, or, indeed, for any specimens whatever; for however well they may look, they are entirely useless as *specimens*, for the hot water utterly spoils the character of the plant, it being impossible to dissect and analyse them, and unless pasting plants on the walls of rooms comes into fashion, I am quite at a loss to conceive the use of it. By proper care and attention to having the plants *quite dry* before committing them to press, specimens may be preserved fully as beautifully, and infinitely more usefully, than by the *hot water cure.*   T. E."

"Baltasound, Shetland,
"15th June 1843."

To Professor Babington.

"Buness, Shetland,
"20th Feb. 1844.

"My dear Sir,—I yesterday received · yours of 29th January.   I wrote you a few days ago, enclosing a specimen of *Bromus velutinus.*

"As to my Shetland Flora, I never thought that local floras, as a general rule, should be more than a list of names with *habitats.*   My object in appending characters will only be to endeavour to put a key to the vegetable productions of their country in the hands of my fellow Shetlanders, and for this reason, also, I proposed arranging it according to the Linnæan system. I intend to add a list according to the natural system. These arrangements have not, however, been completed, and, although the book is nearly written, after circumstances may call me to alter my plan in accordance with your views.   Much will doubtless depend on these universal *tyrants,* the booksellers, for I shall not publish a work of the kind at my own expense. - - - T. E."

To Mrs Griffiths, Torquay.

" Baltasound, 19th March, 1844.

" Dear Madam.—Your kind letter reached me a few days ago. I am greatly obliged for the information contained in it, as also for the interesting specimens. I am especially obliged for the *Asperœaccus.* Your opinion is of course final as regards the genus of the plant. I have broken my microscope, and being so far distant from any place where the damage can be repaired, I am just now at a stand still in Cryptogamic Botany. I enclose a specimen of *Craccium rubrum,* which, so far as I recollect, was gathered at the same time and place as the specimen on which you have detected *Isthmia obliguata;* the plant is so very minute that I am uncertain, on an examination only with the lens, whether the parasite is present or not.*

" I confess that the more I study the marine *Algœ,* the more I am puzzled with the various forms which the same species assume. All acquatic plants, I think, are subject to the same, whether phœnogamic or cryptogamic, and I can easily see that great experience is often necessary to decide to what species some anomalous forms belong. *Laurencia primitifida, Dumoulia filiformis,* and *Rhodomenia palmata,* are every day confusing me by the strange inconstant forms they assume, and this not always occasioned by

---

* Mrs Griffiths decided in the affirmative on this point.

difference of situation, for some of the most opposite forms occur side by side. I am at present like yourself much occupied, as I am to leave Shetland in a week or two. If you write again, however, before hearing from me, address here as usual, and it will follow me. I shall be happy to do my best for Miss Griffiths' collection of mosses. When convenient let me have her list of wants. Please present to her my best thanks for the interesting *Borrera*. I should be delighted to receive the other cryptogamia you mention, as well as any *Algæ* when quite convenient, and believe me, very respectfully yours," T. E.

In April 1844, strengthened and ready for another campaign, Thomas accompanied his uncle as far as Aberdeen, with the intention of devoting the fine season to botanizing in the Highlands of Scotland, and, if opportunity offered, giving lectures in some one or other of the country towns. The opportunity did occur, and after making arrangements with his bookseller for putting the at last completed Flora of Shetland to press, he set out for Elgin.

To Professor Balfour, Glasgow.

"Aberdeen, 1st May 1844.

"My dear Sir,—I am about to publish a Flora of Shetland (of which I enclose a prospectus) by subscription. It will be a small affair, and as such I have to ask your permission for the liberty of dedicating it to you, as my *first* botanical friend, and for whom I, in common with all who know you, entertain an equal respect and esteem. The bookseller here who takes charge of it, will go on with the publishing, provided a certain number of subscribers previously come forward, and he will trust to chance for the remainder. This number I trust I will obtain among my botanical friends. Considering the interest attached to the flora of a remote district like Shetland, and the increasing sense of the importance of local floras, I have been induced to adopt this mode of publication at the recomendation of Dr George Johnston; it is somewhat troublesome, but I must put up with that. Hoping to hear from you as soon as convenient.

" I have written along with copies of my prospectus to most of my botanical friends and correspondents, and have sent by post copies to about eighty botanists with whom I am not acquainted. I have, also, requested Johnston to notice it in the *Annals*, and Luxford in the *Phytologist*, and I think the intention ought to be pretty well known. - - - - - Believe me, my dear Sir, very faithfully yours, T. E."

From Dr Balfour to Thomas Edmondston, Jr.

" Glasgow, 3rd May 1844.

" My dear Sir.—I am glad to hear that you purpose publishing a Flora of Shetland. I feel much flattered by your kindness in wishing to dedicate it to me; I am the more proud of the honour as coming from one of my early pupils. I shall have pleasure in inserting my name among the subscribers, and I shall do what I can to get subscriptions, &c. I shall lay the prospectus before the members of the Botanical Society here. You should send prospectus to Gourlie, Adamson, and Lyon. Wishing all success, I am yours sincerely,

"J. H. B."

To Dr Edmondston.

"Elgin, 24th May 1844.

"My dearest Papa.—I arrived here last night safe and sound on the outside of the coach,—left Aberdeen at seven A.M., arrived here about three P.M. I got my letters at the Post-office before I started; your's and Biot's were most acceptable. There were a number of others from botanists ordering the 'Flora' We shall get on very well I doubt not. I have letters to several literati and influential men here from my ever kind friend Macgillivray. I must get my advertisement ready for the newspaper, which is published to-morrow. I think the lectures will begin early next week. I will need to wait a little to let the good folks of this highly aristocratic town ascertain what a luminary has arrived from the 'far north' to enlighten them. I have as yet seen little of the place, but it seems a most lovely town, and the old cathedral magnificent. The situation and country around it is really beautiful. I had no idea that Morayshire was so pretty.

- - - - - - " I have some idea of improving the 'artificial system' by engrafting on that of Linnæus the *artificial* not the *natural* system of Jussieu, which would form subdivisions to the Linnæan classes, the unwieldy bulk of which is their practical difficulty.

" I will write particulars of my adventures here as soon in the next week as possible, and give you an account of all my proceedings.—With kindest love to all, your most affectionate son,   T. E."

As soon as the necessary arrangements could be completed, the lectures on botany commenced at Elgin, and also a course at Forres. Between these places the young lecturer had to travel on the intermediate days by stage coach, and it is a proof of his versatility and readiness, that although the subject was the same, the treatment and illustrations were different at the two places.* The introductory and valedictory lectures only were committed to writing. Before leaving Elgin he offered to give a lecture on the more extensive subject of zoology for the benefit of the interesting museum there. A few notices from the newspapers of the day will conclude this slight account of his visit to Elgin.

---

* Each also quite different from those delivered at Lerwick the preceding summer.

Extract from the *Elgin Courant.*

" Mr Edmondston delivered his introductory lecture on botany in the museum here to a highly select audience.

" Mr E. explained in a clear and perspicuous manner, with much ease and energy of delivery, and also great eloquence of language, 1*st*, The direct utility of a scientific knowledge of plants as conducive to the welfare of man, and 2*dly*, Recomended its prosecution as an agreeable and elegant pursuit.

" The lecture throughout was most interesting and instructive, and listened to with great attention. We would again impress upon the citizens of Elgin, not to let slip the opportunity of acquiring at these lectures, the knowledge which Mr Edmondston is so well qualified to impart.

From the *Elgin Courant.*

" Mr Edmondston's lecture on zoology for the benefit of the funds of the museum was delivered yesterday.

" The attendance we are happy to say was very large, thus showing not only the interest taken in the museum, but also the deservedly high estimation in which the lecturer is held, who, although yet a very young man, has by a course of persevering and laborious study, attained a position in science probably never occupied by one so early in life, and who has been delighting our citizens by pouring forth the stores of his own rich mind.

" We are sorry we cannot afford space to give an abstract of Mr Edmondston's lecture from the multiplicity of subjects he touched on ; but on all he seemed equally at home, and probably there has rarely been so large an amount of information delivered in the space of two hours."

From the *Forres Gazette* of Friday, 5th July 1844.

" Lectures on Botany.—Mr Edmondston, a talented young gentleman from the North, has been enlightening the lieges here upon this delightful science during last month. His abilities as a lecturer are of a very superior order. He appears to have the most perfect acquaintance with his subjects, and he communicates his knowledge in the most plain, pointed, and practical manner possible, and chiefly extempore. We were much gratified to observe that a goodly number of the ladies had availed themselves of the benefit of these prelections."

From the *Forres Gazette* of Saturday, 3rd Augt. 1844.

" Botanical Lectures.—Mr Edmondston concluded his course of lectures on botany on the 8th ult. by a comprehensive and appropriate lecture on the kindred subjects of zoology, physical geography, and medicine, and after complimenting the ladies and gentlemen of

Forres for the patronage he had received, and returning thanks for the personal kindness he had experienced among them, intimated that next season he would again have the pleasure of addressing them on this delightful study. During his stay here Mr E. made several excursions, accompanied by his practical class, and we are happy to say they succeeded in descrying several plants which were hitherto undiscovered by the botanists of Morayshire."

To Professor Babington.

"Elgin, 7th June 1844.

"My dear Sir,—Your long and kind letter has just reached me. Allow me to thank you most sincerely for the friendly hints it contains, which I shall not fail to profit by. Now, first, as to my papers in the 'Phytologist' on classification, I wish to impress on the minds of botanists the necessity of considering the mind of a beginner as a *tabula rasa*, and to do with him as Linnæus did with the science generally. Commence with a simple index, or what you please to term it. Call the Linnæan the initiatory, and the Natural the advanced system, and keep both in their proper places. This is the amount of my argument, and I never dreamt of censuring as useless or absurd a system which the *illuminati* of the science are agreed on ought to be received. The natural is just in its proper place as regards R. Brown; the artificial as regards one of my students here ; and even in teaching a short popular class, I am far from losing sight of the utility of the natural system. My strictures on that scheme are, I conceive, applicable to it in this view, but would be fallacious in the other ; for a line of reasoning may be legitimate against the *abuse* of a thing which is not so against the *use* of the same.

"With regard to nomenclature, I think the primary principle ought to be,—retain or re-instate the *oldest* name, and never mind whether another has been generally received or not. Great care and persevering consultation of books is requisite in doing this. Again : a name which is the same in zoology and in botany, as *Ammophila* and *Liparis*, ought certainly not to be retained.

"As to the distinctive characters, of course you have a perfect right to your opinion, and there is every likelihood of your being right and I wrong, seeing you have so much more experience and such superior facilities in consulting authors. Consequently, I should have every disposition, when we differed on the relative value of a character, to bend my opinion to yours. - - - - - - I shall study the *Ranunculi* this season, and shall be happy to change my opinion and adopt yours if possible.

"I shall trouble you with some *Hieracia* presently, one of which, if it puzzles you as effectually as it has done me, will not be easily despatched. I have gathered many excellent plants here.

- - - - "I am very busy. I have two classes here,—a forenoon one for ladies and gentlemen, and an evening one for gardeners, &c., on three days of the week ; and on two days another class at Forres, twelve miles distant. I have also to give a lecture on zoology next week. - - —Most faithfully yours, T. E."

"Elgin, 20th June 1844.

"My dear Brother,—As I have not written you for some time, I shall address this letter to you, and it must just do for all, for I am in a most awful hurry. I have got your letter, and also one from mamma, of both of which I was very glad.

"I have just now (half-past twelve noon) returned from an excursion to Fochabers (nine miles distant) with Mr Stobbs of Nairn, Mr Gordon of Birnie, and Mr Brander of Duffin. We drove out in a barouche of the former gentleman's. Left this at half-past five, botanized and returned ; and as I have to lecture at Forres to-night, I must be off there in a few minutes.

"My zoological lecture for the benefit of the museum came off yesterday with great *eclat*. The house crammed—neither sitting or standing room—all the fashionable lords, baronets, &c.—and all seemed well pleased. I have a good class at Forres (from twenty to thirty), but not so many here, but my gardeners in the evenings make up.

"Next week will finish me in Elgin. I have to be a week longer at Forres, and then start for Aberdeen, off to the Highlands, and then down to Shetland in the beginning of August. I will need some rest then, for I am working hard here.

"Take the measure of the muzzle of my double-barrel accurately with a piece of wood, and then cut a piece of paper to the size, so that I may know the bore for some cartridges, and send it to me in your first letter. Be sure and dry plenty of the plants. Every one is most kind to me here. I only regret that I have no time to accept all the invitations I get. The lairds and country gentlemen are for my opinions regarding their gardens, and not a plantation of trees has been cut down that I have not been asked to come and tell the age of the trees, &c., so I am quite a 'professor,' and 'up in the world.'

"Poor Barclay's funeral was yesterday, but I could not go, as it was at my lecture hour.

"Kindest love to all the bairns, papa, mamma, and aunt Mary. Remember me kindly to the minister, Peter and all enquirers.—Your most affectionate brother, T. E."

CHAPTER X.

Progress and Professorship.

1844–45.

URING young Edmondston's stay in Moray-
shire, although he was there partly as a
teacher of his favourite science, he learnt
much more than he taught. Especially
in the difficult department of the Cryptogamic plants
he gained great experience, and made several discoveries. No pains, no fatigue, no researches were spared,
that he might perfect himself in this extensive and
minute branch of botanical science. He availed himself of the assistance of Mrs Griffiths of Torquay, and
her accomplished daughter, after introducing himself as
their correspondent. They never met in this world,
but he often mentioned their kindness to him with
pride and pleasure.

Untiring enthusiasm seems to have been the hand-
maid that led our stripling naturalist into all the bye-

ways, as well as highways, of every sort of learning which his age and opportunities permitted him to attend to. And what, we would ask, avails the finest intellect and the most exalted talent without zeal and industry? One of his Morayshire kind friends writes lately how well he remembered accompanying Mr Edmondston a distance of many miles "just that he might see the night-flowering *cereas*, and his extacies on the occasion."

On leaving Morayshire, our young botanist set out upon what was a most eagerly desired excursion to the mountains of Aberdeenshire,—in fact, his dream for years past.

The note-book carried with him on the excursion to Glen Callater, &c., contains lists of the plants he gathered, descriptions and drawings in pen and ink of any that were new or remarkable, and on the board at the beginning is this inscription,—"Oh Dei Sapientia in Rebus Naturalibus!" and in Greek, beneath his name on the fly-leaf, is something equivalent to "Plants are my passion."

He drew up a full account of the ramble, but it is too long for insertion here. A shorter, but very interesting description of one day's adventures we shall give from the pen of his congenial companion and afterwards constant correspondent, Mr Hewitt Watson, mentioned in the letter that immediately follows.

" Castleton, Braemar, 24th July 1844.

" My dear Uncle,—I am just starting for Clova, and have but little time for writing, but I must drop a line to tell you how I got on. I wrote last from Banchory. I reached Kincardine O'Neil that night, walked to Aboyne next morning to breakfast, and reached Castleton (34 miles) by half-past four P.M. I have never been off my feet since. Glen Castleton, Ben Avon, Ben-na-Buich, Ben Mac Dhui, and Loch-na-Garr have all been visited. I was at Camlachie yesterday, which is a part of Clova.

" As to discoveries they have been very numerous, especially mosses and lichens. Of the latter I have found an entirely new *genus*, a most singular plant. I got the two rarest British plants in Camlachie—*Gentiana nivalis* and *Soachur alpinus*, in a new station.

" Who did I find here but Mr Hewitt Watson, ' mine ancient enemy' ! He has been out with me at several of the places. He is a most delightful, frank, gentlemanly man, and most kind, even respectful, to the ' marquis professor.' - - - - - ."

Mr H. Watson writes in February 1866,—" I well recollect our first meeting. I was staying at the inn at Castleton, in Braemar, for the purpose of measuring the altitudes at which the various wild plants ceased to grow on the mountains around. He came into the room as a new arrival, and caught sight of one of the japanned collecting boxes peculiar to botanists. Looking at the box, then at me, the only person in the room, then again at the box, he said in a joyful and jocose tone, ' I think I have met with one of my own craft.' He was not slow in letting me know his own name, and when told that it was already familiar to me, his curiosity was aroused to draw out mine. He did not succeed in this attempt, however, until some short time after, when we were joined by Mr Gardiner, (Dundee), who was also staying at Castleton. On Mr Gardiner addressing me by name, Mr Edmondston of course found that he had indeed met with ' one of his own craft,' and a correspondent besides ; for this was several months after the date of his first letter to me. We had several rambles over the Braemar mountains, in quest of botanical rarities. One of these journeys was across the intervening ridge of the Grampians, from Castleton to Clova in Forfarshire. We started in good time in the morning, and expected to reach Kirkton Inn in Glen Clova by early afternoon.

" But the plants of the Aberdeenshire rocks proved so attractive to Mr Edmondston, that no prophecy of a coming fog could frighten him forward in sufficient time to get across the high table land before we became enveloped in dense fog and driving rain. We tried long to find a safe descent down the rocks of Glen Dole, the head of Glen Clova, so as to reach the stream which would have been our guide to the inn some miles below, but were always foiled by the steepness of the crags and the denseness of the fog. At length when nine o'clock came, it was too evident that we must choose between remaining on the mountain top all night, wet, weary, and famished, or striking down *any* declivity, in order to reach the low country. We followed a stream downwards, and shortly before midnight got inside a shepherd's hut. Our kindly host rose from his bed, made a fire, warmed some water, and mixed oatmeal in it, thus giving us the most welcome meal perhaps that I ever tasted. Next morning he guided us over the hill (from Glen Prosen, if I rightly remember the name of his glen) into Glen Phee, a short lateral Glen at the head of Glen Clova. We then saw that much of our time the preceding day must have been wasted in endeavouring to find a track down the precipituous rocks of Glen Phee, mistaken for those of Glen Dole, this latter being the more direct continuation of Glen Clova, and much easier to descend into from the moory summits above. Shortly after our arrival at Clova another young traveller came in, who had been out on the hills through the night along with a shepherd guide. They had missed their way, and had not gained the welcome shelter of a summer hut or shieling. Thus, bad as our plight had appeared, there were two others in a worse condition not far from us on the same fog covered hills."

The above narrative is identical in substance (though much shorter) with that by Edmondston himself very soon after the event. The youthful tourist adds the following characteristic sentences :—

" Such was one of our botanical excursions.

" The pursuit of science is not without enlivening and agreeable excitement. Natural science, especially, cannot be successfully cultivated by sitting in your arm-chair in your snug library. Indeed no. You must roam over hills, wade through marshes, climb rocks, explore deserts, scour sea shore—yea, even examine sea depths. All these accomplished,—and assisted by good health, a sound conscience, and plenty of enthusiasm, —I hesitate not to say, the pursuit of the divine goddess *knowledge* takes a high stand among earthly pleasures. Such, at all events, is our idea. If you are a botanist you will appreciate it ; if you are not, why you ought to be—that's all !"

T. Edmondston, Esq. of Buness.

" Lerwick, 12th Aug. 1844.

" My dear Uncle,—Here I am, safe and sound at last. I arrived by the steamer yesterday morning at six, after a very pleasant passage from Kirkwall. I spent a remarkably agreeable week in Orkney. Visited Mr Clousten, and was at Mr Watts of Skaill, &c., &c. I found fifteen plants not hitherto known in

Orkney, though none of them are either new or very rare. Of all my adventures more when we meet, which, I trust, will be to-morrow evening ; though I write this in case of accidents. I shall ship per ' Rattlesnake.' I wish I were home to-day, instead of loitering here. I dined at the Sheriff's yesterday along with a Belgian officer."

To H. C. Watson, Esq.

> " Baltasound, Shetland.
>
> " 21st August 1844.

" My dear Sir.—I reached home about ten days ago, after spending a week in Orkney on my way. I did not find anything of great interest there, although I added several species to its Flora. I visited several of the stations for *Primula Scotica*, and found abundance of the plant, but nearly all past. I have to-day gathered great plenty of our *Cerastium*, and shall send you and Mr Dennis specimens as soon as they are sufficiently dry, and also duplicates for the Society's distribution.

" I suppose long before this you will be domiciled in Surrey, and quite recovered from your *pull* round Glen Shee, and subsequent comfortable nap in the shieling of Glen Prosen, not to speak of the *peeling* at the fire, and the oatmeal brose. The lamentable figure we cut on that eventful night never recurs to my imagination without provoking the exercise of my risible muscles. I encountered old Reid at Ballater on my way to Aberdeen, and returned him the stick I so cooly borrowed."

The two following short letters will prove how little relating to his favourite study ever escaped the vigilant observation of Thomas Edmondston.

To Sir William Hooker.

" Baltasound, Shetland.
" 23rd August 1844.

" My dear Sir.—My principal object in dropping you these few lines is, to acquaint you with a rather interesting fact regarding that much disputed plant *Rubus articus.* While in Morayshire lately, I observed it cultivated in the garden of a nurseryman at Forres, and he assured me that the original plant from which his stock had been reared was brought from Cairngorm by a lady who has now unfortunately left the country, but who was well acquainted with botany, and gave the plant to Mr Grigor under its proper name, and as one of the rarest British plants. Perhaps this fact tending to establish this most interesting little plant as a denizen of Britain, might be worthy of being recorded, in order to put botanists who may be visiting that district on the look-out for it.

" I have made several rather interesting discoveries this season. Among them a *Thiracium*, a rose, and a *Trifolium*, all apparently new. I mean, however, to investigate them more thoroughly before venturing to add other species to these already over burdened genera. My father and uncle desire their kind remembrances. - - - - - - Most respectfully yours, T. E."

To Sir William Hooker.

" Baltasound, Shetland,

" 1st October 1844.

" My dear Sir.—Your kind note, for which many thanks, reached me by last post. You may be sure if the reputed discoverer of *Rubus articus* on Cairngorm had been accessible, I would have endeavoured to ascertain more regarding the plant. The lady was a Miss Robertson, sister to a Mr Robertson, who formerly was master of an academy near Forres. Both left the country some years ago, and no one knows where they now are, but it is supposed at the Cape of Good Hope. If I can make out her address I will write, notwithstanding the distance. I believe the lady knew botany well, and she gave the plant as a *great prize* to Mr Grigor under its true name. - - - - - With much respect, my dear Sir, most truly yours, T. E."

When personally in communication with Mr H. C. Watson, it appears he had requested that gentleman's influence to obtain for him a Curatorship of the London Botanical Society, with which Mr Watson as an amateur had some connection, and there was some succeeding correspondence on that matter. Thomas Edmondston was now so entirely imbued with the ambition to become an eminent naturalist, and so confident that therein lay his great strength, that he and his friends soon came to the conclusion it would be desirable he should devote himself in the meantime to his beloved botany, with the view of prosecuting it as a profession. Mr Watson in the most friendly manner gave him suggestions thus :—

" You in conjunction with your natural guardians are the proper parties to determine whether it be prudent and advisable to give up the medical for the botanical profession. The former is doubtless much overstocked, but there will always be room for practitioners who unite competent knowledge of their art with personal conduct calculated to please and gain respect. In botany there is no such certainty. On the contrary, average botanists are out of pocket by the pursuit, so many following it for the direct intellectual gratification (mingled with some variety) independently of any expectation of profit. University Chairs and some other offices are open to competition; but where the offices are few, and candidates many, there can be little certainty for one individual. My own impression of yourself is, that you can, and probably will acquire so good a kowledge of botany as to give you a very good chance among candidates for such offices." - - - -

It turned out so that Thomas did not obtain the desired appointment. He went over to Shetland for a couple of months. It was there arranged that he should spend the winter in Aberdeen. Whence, on his return, he wrote thus to Mr Watson :—

To Mr Watson.

       " Aberdeen, 27th October 1844.

- - - - - - " I have, with the consent of my friends, abandoned the medical profession for that of Natural History. How it may turn out, God knows, but the pursuit of natural science has now become a *second* life to me, and as essential to me as my *first*.

" I am going to remain here during the winter for the purpose of attending Macgillivray's lectures, having the benefit of his fine museum of Natural History, and perfecting myself in some elementary knowledge in different branches of the science. I hope that if you hear of any situation becoming vacant, of which you think I might have a chance, you will let me know. I should be most happy always to have the benefit of your advice, which your great experience in such matters so well qualifies you to give.

" I have been working away in Shetland, dredging principally, and have added many *Algæ* to my former list. I am superintending the printing of my little ' Flora.' As soon as I get it off my hands, I intend publishing some account of my Morayshire novelties.

" I am exceedingly anxious to get into correspondence with some foreign Cryptogamist. I correspond with almost all the eminent British cultivators of that department, and would consequently be able to give British species for foreign *desiderata*. I would prefer a German or a Swiss Correspondent, principally for mosses and lichens, but also should be very glad if you know any sea-coast botanist who studies *Algæ*. I should be happy to give British Phanogamæ for foreign Cryptogamia. If you could manage this for me I should be eternally obliged. If the gentleman could not write English, he might write in French or Latin, (not German of which I know nothing.")

Whether it were for the better or not, so far as the young aspirant was concerned, that he did not obtain the situation in London, who shall say? Doubtless the disappointment was intended for good by the All-wise Disposer of our lot. Indeed, in as far as we may judge, there is little doubt that his winter's study in Aberdeen, under the excellent Macgillivray's able teaching, and almost paternal surveillance, promoted young Edmondston's improvement in all branches of natural science, as well as botany. The appointment in London would, in all probability, have made him an accomplished botanist; Macgillivray made him a naturalist. On the study of shells and insects he entered with his usual zeal,—his previous knowledge in these departments being only slight and preliminary. The following account of a supposed new shell was laid by Macgillivray before his class, and this is the label by which the Professor distinguished it in his collection :—

" *Pecten Macgillivraii.*

Length,	- - - -	1 10
Height,	- - - -	1 9½
Breadth,	- - - -	6

" First found by Professor Edmondston, and presented by him to Dr Macgillivray, Professor Natural History Marischal College, Aberdeen."

An eminent conchologist of the present day, however, gives it as his opinion that the so called *Pecten Macgillivraii* is only a very beautiful variety of another species,* and so far as is known to the present writer, only that one specimen was ever obtained.

" Aberdeen, 10th Nov. 1844.

" My dear brother.—I have barely time to drop a few lines, which I would have done before, but have been much occupied, and had a good deal to write. I have now fairly settled, and am very comfortable. I am only attending two college classes, Natural Philosophy, and Natural History, and I practise draw-

---

* P. Oporcularia.

ing in the evening. Macgillivray has, however, two hours daily, viz., from nine to ten generally, taken up with examinations, and eleven to twelve the regular lecture. He has about forty-five students, but they are regularly stupid, as well as stupid looking, in their exquisitely ragged red gowns. They have been all examined, but hitherto he has not had me up at all.

" We have had awful weather. The mail packet (from Shetland) has lain here a week, and could not get over the bar, and some of the steamers much longer. A Dutchman, laden with bones, was smashed to pieces on the pier a few days ago. All the men were saved, principally through the bravery of an Aberdeen pilot, who jumped into the water and gained the wreck with a rope, by which the crew got safe ashore.

" The ' Magnus Troil ' is to call here on her way from Leith to take in some wood. I shall send you a little powder and shot by her. I hope you have got me some birds ; I am very anxious to have the wild fowl eggs, as the gentleman is in a hurry for them. - - - - My dear Biot, your most affectionate brother, T. E."

" Aberdeen, 10th Nov. 1844.

" My dear Uncle.— - - - - - I am just *vegetating* away very agreeably ; no weather for rambles, so my migrations are confined to the college, where I work several urs (besides the hours of lectures) in Macgillivray's museum ; he is most kind to me. I am also most comfortable as to lodgings. I am reading on entomology, and working at drawing in the evenings. - - - - I have made two or three short walks into the country, but have found nothing novel as yet. Clarke is sanguine as to the success of the book. Amen, so let it be! I was a good deal amused at a caricature of 'the Duke' the other day. It represented him as an old lady, and the Queen and Louis Phillipe as two children, brother and sister, who had been on the eve of quarrelling. The old lady was saying, 'There, be good children ;—go and kiss your little sister, and don't talk of fighting any more.'

" I have not seen a paper since I came here, and know nothing of things political. There has been a terrible succession of south-east gales. Terrible as I have seen the sea in Shetland, I never saw anything so magnificent as on this coast for the last week. For about eighteen miles there is a flat sandy beach, and the water extremely shallow for two or three miles out, consequently the waves were breaking upon the ground more than a mile out. It was truly the most magnificent sight I ever saw. Macgillivray's lectures will be most instructive and entertaining. He has about fifty pupils.

" You will see that I can have little to tell you new regarding my different undertakings. I am noting down ideas relative to the 'classification' matter. I think that the best and most authoritative form of publishing a full explanation of my views, together with a history of previous and contemporaneous systems, and the exposition of the metaphysical principles on which I conceive the arrangements of natural objects may and ought to be conducted, will be, as 'Philosophy of Botany' reducing, not only the mere classification, but also, the structural and physiological principles on which that should be founded, to order and system. This plan would bring out many views, daily and nightly dawning on me, sometimes faintly and inexpressively, and sometimes in full force. I believe that all the works of God are perfect, and it would be contrary to all analogy, drawn from the consideration of physical laws and phenomena, to conceive that animal and vegetable structure, fitted for certain functions, is not also subject to certain immutable laws.—With kind love to all, ever your most affectionate nephew."

" 22nd November 1844.

" My dear Uncle.—After sending off my last letter, your kind and more welcome letter of the 4th came in. What had delayed it that it did not come with the others, I do not know. I certainly think a post very dull when I do not see your well known hand, it looks *hame like*, and its kindness always cheers me on. You say you miss me, indeed I may with interest reciprocate the sentiment, for I many a time wish myself at Buness, were it but for a moment, and often imagine to myself what you are employed about; especially in the twilight, I often shut my eyes and see all familiar faces as vividly as if they were before me. I feel very dull sometimes, but must just *go ahead*, as the Yankees say. I quite agree with Papa and you now, that I am better here than in London this winter. I will get a prodigious addition to my knowledge in many ways.

" Many, many thousand thanks for your kind and liberal offer regarding my publication ' On the New System.' I spoke to Clarke about it, and he is perfectly ready to print any thing on those terms. As soon as the Flora is out, I shall set about it, first trying some Londoner who works in that way, if he will not take and print it *sans condition*. I would entitle it, ' The Philosophy of Botany,' and sketch and criticize all the systems that have been propounded. I think it could be made a capital thing."

To H. C. Watson, Esq.

" Aberdeen, 24th Nov. 1844.

" My dear Sir.—Your note has just come in. As you are still of the same opinion relative to my *Cerastium*, I shall cancel my former name and remarks, and publish it as a variety, as you have the advantage of being able to compare it with a much larger suite of specimens than I have access to.

" I quite agree with you as to modern *splittomania*. British naturalists seem engaged at present in every department of the science in a race with foreigners after novelty. The absurdities daily promulgated in Botany (especially Cryptogamia and Zoology) are enough to make one laugh. Every dreamy vision that floats before the optics of some German transcendentalist must be ten times more mystified by the importers of these precious 'novelties,' and the *ignus fatui* which dance through the brains of the French will be received without a question of their palpable absurdities *out-Heroded.* Where this folly is to stop, and when natural history is to become a science of pure reason and of common sense, heaven only knows? *Query* :—Could not your phrenologists endeavour to repress the redundancy of ' ideality ' so plentifully manifested of late by ' young natural history.'—Ever, my dear Sir, most faithfully yours, T. E."

The Andersonian University of Glasgow was founded by Mr John Anderson, son of the Reverend James Anderson, minister of Roseneath, in Dumbartonshire, who was born there in 1726. He was educated partly in Stirling, and afterwards in Glasgow. In the latter city he became Professor of Oriental Literature to the University in the thirtieth year of his age, and, in 1760, he was appointed to the Chair of Moral Philosophy, which he filled with much zeal and success during the rest of his life.

To his customary course of lectures, Professor Anderson added one of a more popular kind twice a week, illustrated by experiments. He called it his *Anti-toga* class, in contra-distinction to the regular academical one,—students in the latter being obliged to wear red gowns. For the use of this class he began to collect specimens of the different objects in Natural History, which he increased to a large collection, and it became the nucleus of the excellent museum now belonging to the institution.

On the death of Professor Anderson in 1796, he left the whole of his property towards founding the college that bears his name. It was undoubtedly the first that afforded to all classes of the community the means of studying various branches of literature and science without restrictions of any sort, and at such pecuniary rates as brought the instruction within the reach of the tradesman or artizan. This project was ably and energetically carried out by Professor Anderson's trus tees and executors. The same year he died, the first lecturer on Natural Philosophy (Dr Garnett) had a large class of ladies and gentlemen, in a room hired for the purpose. In due time and by the help of other liberal philanthrophists, the ardent wishes of the founder were fulfilled, by increasing the number of professorships, obtaining suitable buildings, and extending gratis in- struction to the artificers of Glasgow on the principles and powers of mechanics.

At the present time (1868) the Andersonian Institution

has a complete staff of able professors on all the subjects actually taught in the universities. It is a competent school of medicine, and, besides the regular and duly recognised classes in literature, science, and philosophy, has courses of weekly evening lectures and classes, for the nominal fee of half-a-crown, on mechanics, chemistry, physiology, botany, and music,—thus completely realising the desires of Professor Anderson as to " a college for the people."

           " Aberdeen, 17th December 1844.

" My dearest Uncle.—A long and most dreary time has passed since I heard from you,—nearly a month having elapsed since the packet left this, and she only reached it again yesterday. She brought me your letters of 21st and 28th November, as well as three from papa, and one from mamma.

" The first thing of importance I have to tell you, is about a speculation I have embarked in, with a good deal of hesitation, as it was impossible to get advice from you or papa in time ; it is this.—The professorship of Botany in the Andersonian University of Glasgow is vacant, and two or three days ago a friend brought me a paper containing an advertisement for testimonials of candidates to be lodged. I immediately wrote to Dr Balfour to know about it ; he promptly replied. It appears there is no salary attached, but the fees must constitute the professor's income ; but he said, 'an active energetic person like you, would make something good out of it.' I consulted with Macgillivray, and told him how I was situated, that I could not get advice from home in time. He strongly advised me to become a candidate, and offered testimonials, and all assistance in his power. He said, it would be, could I get it, an excellent *step*, and then, as there is no one but the very aged professor to lecture on Natural History in Glasgow, and an admirable museum in Anderson's College, I might get a good Natural History class in winter. Moreover, the college is a regularly chartered and very respectable medical school. Its teachers have the name and *status* of professors, and very eminent botanists have filled that chair. All these and various other reasons, determined me to become a candidate, and I have accordingly written to all my influential friends for testimonials, and shall apply for it in due form. The election takes place on the 15th January, so you will see that no time was to be lost. If I am fortunate enough to succeed, (though I shall not be disappointed if I do not). I think I might as well be a professor in Glasgow as doing anything, and if it does not pay, why it can soon be given up; it is but a three months course at all events, and should the worst come to the worst, and there be no chance of a winter class, I could remain in Shetland during that season, and resume my duties or resign them in spring.

" These are my ideas in trying this *dodge*. If I get it, and am lucky, I might make a living tolerably well, and far more respectably than as a curator. My name and writings would acquire great additional weight, and, altogether, I might soon be a 'great little man.' I dare say my next (if the packet is as long away this time) may give an idea of how the election would go. Let me hear all your opinions on this head. Macgillivray continues singularly kind and confidential to me." - - - - - -

" 18th December.

" I wrote you yesterday, but as the packet cannot sail till to-morrow, I send a few lines additional.

- - - - - " I have got an excellent testimonial from my kind friend Dr Balfour. I met one of my Forres pupils to-day, just come off the coach. He says he signed a testimonial there in my favour last night. So my friends are not letting grass grow under their feet. Who knows but I may wear a gown soon. ' Nothing venture, nothing win.'

" Kind love to every one. I don't know if you will get this before ' Yule day.' I will have no Christmas this year. There are only two holidays (Christmas and New year's day) at this confounded college, and no Saturdays to ourselves. Remember me in the Whip-coll toast. But I need not tell you; I well know I am never forgotten. I get dull and dreary sometimes, but work the harder to forget it." T. E.

"16th January 1845.

" About the professorship. This state of suspense is tantalizing. By the advice of my friends here, I set off for Glasgow a fortnight ago; got to Edinburgh that evening, and went to Glasgow same night. I called on all the Directors, leaving copies of my testimonials with them. Uncle D. happened to be in Glasgow, and staid a day, going among all his friends who had any influence in the matter. I returned to Edinburgh on Friday at midnight; staid with uncle D. Next day went to Currie to see the Barclays, and next morning at five started for Aberdeen, which I reached at six P.M., most unenviably knocked up. I had great ado and expense seeing the Directors as it was New-year week, and all were out of town. From what I saw and heard I feel sure the *spec.* would be a good one for me. Some of the professors have splendid classes, and even should the botany not prove very lucrative, which I do not expect, as Balfour is there, a Natural History class, assisted by the splendid museum they have, could not fail to do something. Dr Couper, the professsor of Natural History in the college, is old, and my plan would be to open with Botanical and Natural History classes every day for the regular students, and popular

Botanical lectures three times a week, and it will be bad indeed if I do not make something decent.

" I am sorry to see by your last letter that you are not very sanguine about the matter. I am not surprised at it, as my former lecturing speculations were not the most profitable in the world. ' We must, however, walk before we can run,' and it is scarcely to be expected that at ' my age ' I am all at once to fall into a fine situation in a profession where they are so few and far between, and so many candidates. If I do get this I have made a firm resolve, that I will live within what I can earn myself, and I have perfect confidence that you will, in that event, and on that understanding, set me a-going decently. Such a situation would give me *status* and authority in the science, and enable me with far superior effect to illustrate my name, and come forward with a good chance of success for the first thing that might offer in any branch of Natural History. All my friends and correspondents, better judges than myself, agree in these views. Enough of this, my next will announce whether I am a professor or in *statu quo.*

" The Flora is in the binder's hands still. I fully expected to have had a copy to send you by this mail. Macgillivray and I are as *croose* as ever. We have a long walk together every day, and dispute about systems and classification, birds, shells, and minerals, as fraternally as possible. He is lecturing on insects just now, and I am very busy endeavouring to acquire a competent knowledge of this branch, of which I have been hitherto very ignorant.

" I have little else to tell you about. I see literally nobody ; never see a paper, and am as ignorant of what is going on in the world as if I were in Kamschatka. I cannot find time for these things. If at the end of this session I become a teacher, I cannot expect to have much time to myself as a student, so that the present opportunity is precious, being probably the last I can afford under such favourable circumstances for acquiring knowledge." - - . - - -

To Professor Babington.

" Aberdeen, January 1845.

" My dear Sir.—Yours has just reached me ; many thanks for the testimonial. I am happy to say that I have obtained certificates of my qualifications from some of our first naturalists. I as yet know nothing about how the election may run, or if any other candidate is likely to come forward. It matters little as to the name of the college,—whether ' University ' or ' Institution.' The days have happily gone by when mere *names* carried undue weight, and it is now, I think, the *men* more than the titles that are looked to. Yet, if I am correctly informed, the ' Andersonian College' has a title to be so called, seeing that it is a medical school, and its tickets qualify for the different boards of examination. I have been so busy for these few days, that I have not yet found time to send the *Hieracium* to J. Ball. We shall see what he says about it.

" As to my remaining here to study medicine, I may remark, that I have *for the present* at least abandoned that profession. Whether I may resume it, should I obtain the lectureship or otherwise, will be a matter for consideration. I came here this winter for the purpose of studying Natural History, under, as I consider him the first Naturalist in Europe, Dr Macgillivray, and otherwise of perfecting myself in some branches in which I was deficient. My after plans will have to be duly weighed.

" I have done nothing of course in Phœnogamic Botany ; I have however found some interesting Cryptogamiœ.

" Wishing you a happy New year.—Believe me faithfully yours. T. E."

" Aberdeen, 25th January 1845.

" My dearest Mamma.—Your three letters of the 6th, 9th, and 16th inst. arrived this morning. Macgillivray also showed me a laconic epistle from papa, as to whether I was alive or dead. You will before now have learnt that my absence at Glasgow occasioned your not hearing. You are a wrong prophet for once, for hear, and tremble ! I am a *bona fide* professional individual, and have received official intimation of my induction into the delectable situation of Professor of

Botanical Science in the Andersonian Metropolis of western Scotland.

" There's a Johnsonian paragraph !

" I will have to go there as soon as the lectures here are done in the beginning of March.   There would still be a fortnight of this session remaining then, but it is taken up with examinations for admittance into the more advanced classes next session.

" I am very sorry you have been so unwell.   All the children will have grown ' out of kenning' before I can see them again.   I am thinking great long to be home again, and am rather *shaky* at the work to be gone through, but,—

> ' Forward, onward, foot and horsemen !
> To the charge, oh, gallant horsemen !'

 - - - - - " I sent the little book to Biot, as a present for his trouble about the eggs.   Kindest love to all.   Tell Baby, for her peculiar satisfaction, she has the distinguished honour of being sister to a learned professor.   God bless you all.   T. E."

" Aberdeen, 25th January 1845.

" My dear Uncle.—To-day the packet has brought three notes from mamma, the latest the 16th.

" I am happy to tell you that on Thursday evening I received official intimation of my election as Professor of Botany to the Andersonian University.

" The Secretary wished to know when I would be ready to commence, and I told him that I intended opening the campaign with Botanical and Natural History Lectures in April. I am also Professor of Natural History, and *ex officio* Conservator of the Museum. Macgillivray has taken a most prodigious interest in the business. No mortal here knew I was trying, but every one got hold of it yesterday morning, and I am nothing but 'Professor' in the class like fun. Mac. is proud of this elevation of his pupil. I must now to business, and write my lectures; of course the work will be hard, but eight hours writing a day will, I calculate, nearly suffice for the more difficult parts, and the rest I must trust to writing day by day. It is highly necessary to have a good course the first year; the great thing is a beginning. It cannot be that conducting two classes in a town like Glasgow, I will not make a living, and during the recesses I would likely get engagements to lecture in 'Mechanics Institutes,' and stuff of that sort, in the neighbouring towns. I have no fear of getting on tolerably in time, if God spare me life and health. I will not shrink from any labour in order to form for myself a reputation which will command me the first good opening which presents itself.

" I must leave for Glasgow by the beginning of March. There is nothing done in the college here after that time but examinations, and I must be on the spot for two reasons; the first, because I can't write the great part of my lectures without knowing the specimens in the museum; and the second, to form acquaintances among the people connected with the college, and endeavour to get up classes. I also wish to try and publish a 'Text Book.' Of course I will not be able to go to Shetland till August, when, God willing, we shall meet again. Perhaps though you will be coming southwards in spring again, which I do hope you shall, and I hope you will see me lecturing to large classes. This Andersonian College is much better for getting up classes than almost any other, especially for subjects which non-professional people attend to, as there is so large a number of trustees (eighty-one), and these have so much influence amongst a large body of the community, and send their friends and acquaintances; consequently the classes of chemistry, and some others, are extremely large.

" I fully expected to have sent a copy of my book by this mail but they have been keeping it back in order to see if ' Professor ' could not be put on the title page.

" My life drags on in its usual monotonous course. How I have envied you the *Yule* at Buness. I have been picturing all the *tableau* of the Christmas ceremonies. The fearful trial of the drinking healths in the dining-room by the lassies in the morning, and Freddy's jogging head and elbows in ' Lucky can ye link ony,' in the evening. I got into a brown study in the class on ' Auld Yule Day,' and did not hear Mac. till he had three times called me up to be examined. Kind love to all hands. Tell the minister how prophetic his constant ' professoring ' of me has turned out, and that I will hold him a conjuror henceforth. Kind remembrances to P., S., C., and all old cronies.—Your most affectionate nephew,   T. E."

" I intend getting an L.L.D. very soon ; I can manage it easily."

From Professor Macgillivray to Dr Edmondston.
                " Aberdeen, 26th January 1845.

" My dear Sir.—Your son will no doubt have written. The reason of his having missed one of the packets was, I believe, his having been absent a few days on occasion of his applying for the Andersonian Professorship of Botany, which he has obtained. His conduct has all along been most exemplary, and he has gone fairly to work as a student, regularly keeping up with the business of the class, and although infinitely superior to the rest, submitting like them to examination. I often walk with him to the shore, and fishing station, for mollusca, zoophytes, and the like. He is now about as fond of zoology as of botany, and is also anxious to have a general knowledge of geology, on which subject we enter in a few days."

To H. C. Watson, Esq.

"Aberdeen, 2nd February 1845.

"My dear Sir.—Yours of the 30th has just reached me. Many thanks for your kind wishes. I am looking more to Natural History Lectures than to the Botany as a means of procuring the *needful.* That subject is almost new to Glasgow, and aided by the excellent museum they have in the Andersonian, I think I might draw an audience.

"I do not expect many botanical pupils, as Balfour is very popular. Thanks for the hint regarding diagrams, it shall be taken advantage of, as making a large number of coloured drawings takes up a great deal of time, and I have had work enough to prepare for two classes. I am just now writing lectures on Animal Physiology."

- - - - - - - -

"Aberdeen, 8th March 1845.

"My dear Uncle.—I was beginning to weary much to hear from you when your kind and welcome letter came in this morning. I expected to have been away before now, but I wished the session to be fairly through, so that I lost nothing by having my classes. The botheration of properly stowing away my various collections, &c., has been very great. I was to have left, however, on Tuesday last, but a party of friends insisted on giving me a supper, which accordingly came off on Wednesday last in Machardy's hotel here. About thirty sat down to supper, but many more came in afterwards. Mr Speed, an advocate, was in the chair. We had a magnificent supper, and a most respectable company,—two of the King's College medical lecturers, two or three M.D.'s, and several advocates and solicitors. The chairman made a splendid speech in proposing my health, and I did my best in returning thanks. You see I am coming out rather. I believe I am very popular here, and, I trust, by a due attention to honourable and gentlemanly conduct to acquire the same where I am going. I have had very hard work of late; you may believe that writing and composing from four till twelve or later, with scarcely any intermission, is no joke. I have stood it well however, and, thank heaven, my eyes have held out better than I anticipated, although now they are beginning to trouble me, but I will be able to give them a little rest.

" Well ! my book is published at last. A copy goes by this post."

Not having access to any other reviews of the " Shetland Flora," except the following, from the pen of Hewitt C. Watson, Esquire, it is extracted from the *Phytologist,* (vol. ii., p. 438), abridged.

" Circumstances unimportant to the reader of the *Phytologist* interfered with an earlier notice of the ' Flora of Shetland,' published by Mr Edmondston, when about to quit the shores of Britain on an important botanical expedition, which is likely to occupy him for several years,—(*Phyt.*, ii. 185.) It seems that Mr Edmondston is a Shetland *rara avis* in his botanical acquirements, since we are told in the introduction to his volume, that he has never heard of any native that had studied the science saving himself. The ground was new and all his own; but novelty has its disadvantages along with its pleasures. The botanist who writes a flora of a cluster of islets, whereon dwelleth no second votary of the floral goddess, is likely to find few purchasers, and still fewer readers of his book. He must look for the latter at least, among those who occupy themselves with the geographical relations of plants. And indeed from the position of the Shetland Isles, like a conecting step between Great Britain and the more arctic islands subject to the crown of Denmark, a list of their plants will possess more geographical interest than usually attaches to a local flora for a very limited track. Until their floral productions were investigated by Mr Edmondston, these 'hundred isles' remained almost a *terra incognito* in a botanical view; and hence, however small its usefulness to the non-botanical islanders, the 'Flora of Shetland' is, nevertheless, a publication of some importance in the literature of botany.

" The volume includes a list of all the species *(fungi excepted)* which have been detected in the isles by the zealous author of the work. The phanerogamic portion of the list comprises about three hundred and thirty species; adding thirteen *Filices*, four species of *Equisetum*, and three of *Lycopodium*, we have an islet flora of three hundred and fifty species, exclusive of the strictly cellular plants. Although the author intimates that the group of isles has not been fully examined, we believe this numerical result may be accepted as a probable approximation to their true floral census, which is not likely to exceed four hundred species, even should it hereafter be raised to that number. The *data* afforded by the neighbouring islands, both southward and northward of Shetland, appear to justify this supposition. Messrs Babington and Balfour detected three hundred and thirty-eight species in the outer Hebrides, during a short tour in those more southerly isles, at the most favourable season of the year for ascertaining their plants. The number reported for the Orkney isles indeed exceeds four hundred, but the list is brought under that number by deducting many species which have been reported on authority botanically insufficient, and which are very unlikely to be found so far north. The flora of the Faroe isles, as reported by Mr Trevelyan, includes only two hundred and eighty species, while that of Iceland embraces three hundred and seventy species. Thus there seems fair reason to believe that Mr Edmondston's industry and research have supplied us with a creditably copious and pretty complete list of Shetland plants, although some few of the species may have been left out, but, doubtless, a goodly number of those enumerated in his volume, more especially the agricultural weeds, owe their existence in Shetland to the operations and importations of farmers or others.

" The geographical notices introductory to the list of plants, and remarks scattered through the list itself, are deserving of attention. And on the whole, though not free from some of the defects of haste and youthful inexperience, the ' Flora of Shetland ' is a creditable evidence to the author's ability and industry of research."

" Glasgow, 3rd April.

" My dear Uncle.—I wrote you from Edinburgh about ten days ago. - - - - - On coming here, I of course called on the Secretary, and was by him introduced to my future colleagues. They all received me most cordially, and I took my seat as a Member of the Medical Faculty on Saturday. The Directors seem in every way disposed to befriend me. They wished me to take an inventory of the museum, which I have been busy doing, and have laid a long report before them, containing several plans for the improvement of the collection. I have also seen most of my friends here. I intend giving popular lectures on mineralogy and geology twice a week, £1, 1s. a ticket. I have been paying great attention to the subject, and being just *off the irons*, think I shall get on. It is the most *taking* department of the science. Our summer lectures commence on the 6th May. My hour is eleven forenoon, and the geological hour likely three P.M. The museum is a most admirable one. I have directions to draw up a full catalogue, which is to be printed as soon as ready. I was at a meeting of the Philosophical Society, where Balfour read a paper the other night. I spoke for nearly half-an-hour on a theoretical point, and was much applauded. The 25th August is the day appointed for distributing the prizes and examining the medical students. It is unlike the Edinburgh system, quite a public affair. I am made examinator on physiology, and also one of the judges of a surgical prize essay, whereat I am *funking* a little ; but I hope a grave countenance and a white neckcloth may carry me through, though, alas ! my medical lore is now but very rusty.

" I am thinking great long for Shetland now, and dreaming about it and you all every night. I was shooting rabbits with Biot, Peter, and Charley all last night. However, I will enjoy it all the more when I do come, which will be in August, please God. I was never so long absent from home on a stretch yet, and, I trust, wont be again. I am hoping to hear from you on Wednesday next by the steamer.—With kindest love to all, ever believe me, my dearest Uncle, most affectionately yours,   T. E."

It may not be amiss to give here a copy of the

printed notice circulated in Glasgow at this time, corroborating what has already been more than once mentioned,—the indomitable energy with which Thomas Edmondston set about any task, however herculean. It will be remembered that he was only in the middle of his twentieth year, and yet confidently undertaking several courses of lectures in the most populous and important city of Scotland,—the third, if not the second, in the British Isles.

" He was slightly but symetrically formed, his height scarcely attaining to middle size. Yet the shapely head, with its close dark curls and full whiskers, the high intellectual brow, and the quick beaming eye, added to the lines which severe study had imprinted on his noble countenance, gave him the look of being a year or two older than he was. His carriage and manners were refined and gentlemanly, but although he always dressed well and in good taste, the sombre colours, loose fit, and somewhat careless adjustment of his clothes, announced the student rather than the young man of society and of the world.

"POPULAR
"LECTURES ON GEOLOGY.

——

"MR THOMAS EDMONDSTON,
" F.B.S.E. & L., &c., &c.

" *Professor of Botany in the Andersonian University.*

" Begs to announce that he intends forming a Class

for GEOLOGY and MINERALOGY, with the application of these subjects to Mining, Agriculture, the Arts, &c., in the Hall of the *Andersonian University.*

" *The Lectures to commence on Monday 12th May,*

" At 8 o'Clock P.M.,

" And to continue on Mondays and Thursdays throughout the Summer Session. They will be Illustrated by Drawings and Diagrams, and by the extensive collection of Minerals and Fossils (amounting to upwards of 3000 Specimens) in the Museum of the University.

" FEE, for the Course, £1, 1s.

" MR EDMONDSTON'S LECTURES and DEMONSTRATIONS on BOTANY will commence on TUESDAY the 6th MAY, at Eleven o'Clock, A.M.

" Excursions on the Saturdays.

" FEE, for the Course, £1, 11s. 6d.

" Certificates of attendance on these Lectures qualify for Examination before the Universities of Oxford, Cambridge, London, Aberdeen, and St Andrews; all the Royal Colleges of Surgeons in Great Britain and Ireland; the faculty of Physicians and Surgeons in Glasgow; and the Army, Navy, and East India Boards.

" *N.B.* This being Mr E.'s First Course, Tickets taken now will be perpetual.

" PRINTED IN THE GLASGOW HERALD OFFICE."

The following letter gives us a passing glimpse of one of these self-taught aspiring geniuses who occasionally start up among the peasantry, especially of Scotland. One would like to know the after career of this "journeyman bootmaker" who writes such a correct and in its way remarkable epistle ; but we can only gather from Professor Balfour's letter a week later, that Mr Edmondston had mentioned the circumstance, but that he had "forgotten to give the address," which, however, Moore had not stated particularly. We may feel assured that either of these young professors would give every encouragement to the aspirations after knowledge of the intelligent tradesman.

From John Moore, Shoemaker.

> " Tradeston, Glasgow,
> " 3rd May 1845.

" Sir.—I wish to enter your classes on botany, mineralogy, and geology, but as I am only a journeyman bootmaker, if you would take work from me instead of money I could give you material and workmanship not inferior to what you would get in the best shops of the city, and at a cheaper rate.

" If you be so kind as agree to the above proposal, you will much oblige, Sir, yours respectfully.

> " John Moore "

" *P.S.* Please have an answer and I shall call on Monday.

" Thomas Edmondston, Esq."

CHAPTER XI.

𝕱ar 𝕮ountries.

1845.

" MAN proposes, God disposes." After all the eager desires and strenuous efforts to attain a situation where he might become independent of other resources than his own, after he had happily attained it, and had addressed himself so energetically to its duties,—duties which very few youths of his age would have attempted, —an aspect wholly unexpected was given to his future prospects by the following letter from Professor Edward Forbes.

" 6, Craig's Court, Charing Cross, London,
" 29th April 1845.

" Dear Edmondston.—Before stating what I write about, I must request an *immediate* answer by return of post to this.

" An expedition is going out to the Pacific and California. It *sails in a fortnight.* This morning I have been sent for to the admiralty to say whether I could recommend a naturalist at a moment's notice, as Prince Albert had desired that a naturalist should be appointed to accompany the expedition. The salary will be between £250 and £300 a year, finding mess out of it. This I consider good pay. Now it seems to me that this would be an admirable opportunity for you, both to pursue your scientific aims, and to lay the basis of a distinguished reputation. It is very short notice, but I went to the Oregon on a shorter, having got all ready in a week. It may lead to much better things than your Andersonian appointment could possibly do.

" Now, if you write at once, saying that you would like to go (there is no time to consult friends at a distance), I will do everything in my power to get you appointed, and can almost promise you the appointment. Should it be so, you will have to come to London at once to prepare.

" There will be no time to get any replies to any letter of yours to Shetland, but I feel sure both your father and uncle could desire no better prospect for you.

" Write at once, as everything depends upon promptitude. In haste.—Ever yours, Signed, Ed. Forbes."

" Glasgow, 2nd May 1845.

" My dear Uncle.—Your letter reached me to-day. Before saying anything more, let me advise you of a serious step. This morning brought me the enclosed letter from Edward Forbes, wishing me to go out on the South Pacific Expedition as naturalist, on a salary of £250 to £300 *per annum.* You will see, as he says, that no time is allowed for receiving advices from home. As the expedition sails in a fortnight, I can conceive but one way, and uncle D., (who is here to-day), and my other friends cordially concur, and that is to accept the appointment. Forbes says he can as good as promise it, and, I doubt not, early next week I will receive orders to join my ship. I am writing Forbes, therefore, accepting his kind offer.

" This appointment is of all others the most desirable I can conceive. Going out in a man-of-war, under the auspices of government, and even directly under those of the Prince ; a very handsome salary of which I cannot spend more than £60 per annum ; a country to be explored new to science ; a fine climate ; everything combines to render it the most eligible thing that could happen. I would be certain of a good appointment when I came home again, if God spares me. One thing clouds the prospect. You may easily guess how distressed I will be to leave the country without seeing you all. I do not know how long the expedition may remain out ; this I will hear from Forbes, and let you know. It will likely be for a year or two, or possibly more. Yet, if I do go, I trust in the mercy of God we may yet meet.

" I know from your long and well tried affection for me, that you will feel much distressed at my sudden departure in so sudden a manner, yet, I also know, you have my good so much at heart, that were you here you would at once consent. I fear much that this news will, for the first at least, distress mamma in her present weak state, therefore I do not write her. You will also tell papa, and consult together on the subject. Although I write to *accept*, there would likely be time for a letter to reach me in London, and if you wish to *veto* the proceedings, (which, however, I cannot contemplate), there will be time. I can say but little about any thing but this new affair, and will be somewhat on the *tenter hooks* till I hear from Forbes. From the terms in which he writes, however, I feel quite sure of the appointment, but of course I will not throw up the professorship till I hear from him.

" As regards money matters I hope, if I go, I will get some advanced from the Admiralty for *outfit*. I am much hurried. I will write fully next week, when my fate will be decided.—Ever your most affectionate nephew, T. E."

" Write under cover to Professor Edward Forbes."

To Professor Macgillivray, Aberdeen.

" Glasgow, 2nd May 1845.

" My dear Sir.—Your letter reached me in due course;

many thanks for it. I think it likely that I will not deliver even my introductory lecture, and that the 'professorship' will be demitted almost as soon as acquired. Yesterday morning I received a letter from Edward Forbes, stating that a government expedition was to sail to the Pacific and California in a fortnight; that, at the eleventh hour, Prince Albert had requested that a naturalist be appointed, and the Admiralty had sent for him (Forbes) to recommend one on a moment's notice. He writes me in consequence, strongly recommending me to go, and saying, if I chose, he could as good as promise me the appointment. I, accordingly, immediately wrote, joyfully accepting, and expect to hear again on Monday, when, if the answer is favourable, I will start on Tuesday morning for London. This is hurried work, and no time to consult my friends at home; but it will, I believe, be an admirable thing for me. The salary is £300 per annum; how long they may remain out I do not know. It is a fine field for scientific research; an excellent climate; a very handsome remuneration, and the prospect of getting something good on my return.

" I was intending during the summer to lecture on botany twice a week at Greenock, in addition to my advertised lectures here. I trust, however, next week to leave the Clyde far behind me. Hurrah! for Natural History! Who says it is a bad profession!

" Many a time I thank my stars I attended your

lectures last winter, as the knowledge then acquired, is now of the most vital use to me.

" I trust on my return (D.V.) to see you well again. Believe me, my dear sir, I shall ever entertain the most lively sense of your kindness to me. I may never be able, even very trivially to return it, but the feelings of gratitude, respect, and friendship, will never be obliterated.

" I should like much to hear from you before I go, and if I do start I will write you from London. A letter would reach me here if you wrote *immediately* on receipt of this, so pray do, and tell me if I can do any thing for you in London. I hope to bring you home a large stock of birds, shells, &c., and trust that we may have a long talk over my adventures, if I am spared to return. My kind regards to Mrs Macgillivray and your family, and ever believe me, my dear Sir, most faithfully yours, T. E."

From Dr Edmondston.

" Baltasound, 8th May 1845.

" My dearest Thomas.—Your letter to your uncle of the 1st inst. has agitated me a good deal from the idea of your being so far from us ; and partly a surprise, though for long I suspected a similar pursuit awaited you. I hope our letters to-day will reach you. One point in your letter I fervently thank God as a good omen. It breathes affectionate confidence and docility. It is, when you still leave the *veto* with us who have your honour and interest so deeply at heart. We do not, however, balk your laudable zeal and enterprise. The salary is good. It is under the wing of government. It will, or ought to, give you repose and leisure for thought, reflection, ay ! even health ; for your mind, body, and spirits, have been for months too much agitated for your strength and age, and it will, if God spares you, give you at once an unassailable name and *status*, to which the Andersonian point was a good step and title. Above all, it will compel your too fervid intellect and brain to necessary repose, and tend to mature and consolidate your constitution, and remove you from the petty and distressing annoyances of pecuniary difficulty. So far so well. On the other side, much will depend on the nature of the expedition, the vessel, and those who have charge of it, for comfort, facility, and safety.

" Of course you will leave us ample information how to communicate with you in your ' devious wanderings.' Your mother viewing your present prospects as, humanly speaking, prosperous, bears up well under the idea of long separation. I hope you can find no difficulty in getting sufficient advance for necessary outfit,—plenty of warm clothing, books, and implements.

" Now you will find the good of Macgillivray's course, mapping out to you the boundaries and localities of Natural History. Your previous studies in Natural

Philosophy, Medicine, and Anatomy will also tell, and your education in Shetland, itself a kind of *barbarous* colony, all whets and matures your own powers of observation. - - - - - You will become what I so early *vaticinated*, 'Lin. the Little,' if God spare you, and you act according to the rules of prudence and religion. I fear the climate of the warm parts of the Pacific, especially in surveying lagoons and inlets. May God preserve you,—use the means of safety, leave the result to His providence.

" My dearest son, in one sense this is a joyous epoch for you, in another it is solemn. The scene is untried, and you can hardly expect that all those whose hearts beat now so warm and so true to you, will be alive to welcome your return ; but God will be ever with you, to protect and console you, if you seek Him as He has directed you. This is the grand thing. Even to the natural eye the moral nature (that is the will and the motives) is superior to the intellect, which is only one of its servants. Revealed religion, also, never fails to recognize the *heart*, not the *head*, as the man.

" If you should never again hear from your father, take this as his last earnest counsel, to view as the substantial paramount business of your life, to prepare for a glorious future in the world to come. Again, my dearest Thomas, farewell.—Your ever tenderly affectionate father. L. E."

From his Mother.

"Baltasound, 8th May 1845.

"My dearest Tom.—The short notice, and surprise of your letter, almost takes from me the ability to say a word to you, but yet I must say, that my *reason* tells me the appointment is what we ought to have wished for you, and yet the distance and the uncertainty makes me only alive to the *feeling* that you are to be so far from us; however, we all think you did right in accepting it, and may God, of His mercy, turn it out for your good. With His blessing all will go well with you, and, oh! I pray you, seek *it* fervently and constantly, and be sure of your mother's prayers many times when you are sleeping. The bairns are all well, I will not let them cease to speak of you. - - - - May heaven's blessings be ever with you my dearest boy.

From Mr Biot Edmondston.

"Baltasound, 8th May 1845.

"My dearest Brother.—How can I express our astonishment yesterday when your letters reached us regarding the intended *expedition*, of which you are to be naturalist. Both papa and uncle seem to think it is the best thing that could be, but they are both writing you fully. - - - - This is only, my dear Tom, to bid you good bye, and praying that God may preserve your life from the many dangers you, in all probability, must incur, and hoping you will not run any needless hazards, for the sake of those who are so much interested in your welfare, and who love you so much. Again farewell, and may God bless you, my dear Tom, will be my constant prayer till spared to meet again.— Believe me to be ever your most affectionate brother.

" B. E."

To Dr Edmondston.

" London, 14th May 1845.

" My dearest Papa.—I would have written you before regarding the eventful step I have taken, had I not been aware that you would consider the letters I have written to uncle the same as if they had been to yourself, and really writing twice over the same thing is an irksome task, without any good resulting from it. In a letter I am to-day writing uncle, I have given a journal of my various adventures since leaving Glasgow, to that I must refer as containing the mere narrative of my proceedings.

" I have been here a week to-day, and certainly never was more knocked about in all my life. There is such an immensity of apparatus for the collection and preservation of quadrupeds, birds, reptiles, fishes, insects, plants, shells, rocks, and fossils required, that I have done nothing but run from Regent Street to Bishopsgate ever since I came. And then there are dinners and soirees, and parties and breakfasts, and society meetings, where I must go to see this naturalist and that, to get directions, and hints and advices; I am indeed almost sick of preparing for a Natural History Expedition,—such comes of hurried departures. However, I hope that we may get things at least tolerably to rights. The Admiralty supply me with certain things, such as, paper for drying plants, alcohol and glass bottles for spirituous preparations, and a few things of that sort, but I must be at a great out-lay myself, especially as, in case of accidents, a duplicate assortment of nearly every thing is required. Books also are an important item; clothes also, and shoes sufficient for three or four years tear and wear, together with bedding, my share of the mess furniture, table cloths, towels, candles, even down to soap, all have to be bought and mess paid out of my advanced quarter's salary. So I have enough to scheme and think about to make ends meet, I can tell you.

" Our expedition consists of a fine twenty-eight gun frigate, the ' Herald,' Captain Kellet. She carries her full complement of officers, men, and marines, I suppose in case of a brush with *Jonathan*. We are accompanied by the ' Pandora,' a brigantine, as tender. We call at the Canaries and Rio as we go out, and at Valparaiso, &c., on 'tother side Cape Horn. Our immediate object, however, is to survey the coast of the Californian Gulf and New Albion (the Oregon territory). The ' Erebus' and 'Terror,' commanded by Franklin and Crozier, are expected, about the same time that we have finished this, to have made the North-west passage, but if they do not then come to us, we are, I believe, to go as far north as Behring's Straits. Wyld, the Queen's geographer, however, not only does not think they will make the passage, but does not believe they will ever be seen again. They themselves are much more sanguine, and the officers are taking out *dancing shoes* for a grand ball we are all to have at Valparaiso when we meet. God knows how many of these expectations are to be realised.

" All the naturalists here are on ' tip top expectation ' regarding the good things I am to bring home. The British Museum folks are half-mad about it, as scarcely any thing is known from the west coasts. There will certainly be a splended coast to be examined, if God grant me life and health for that purpose.

Of course I was for the first a good deal embarrassed what to do, there not being time to hear from you at home ; but the advantages are so palpable, that my mind is quite at rest regarding your approbation. I fear mamma will be much distressed at the idea of my going away for so long a time ; indeed, I have scarcely courage to write to her, yet I trust all will be for the best, and I will come home well and hearty to find you all the same, and get a snug professorship, or some other berth, which will enable me to spend with you the remainder of our lives. There will be some stories of 'Hawkeyes,' and Sioux and grisly bears to tell too. I am getting a good armament of guns, pistols, rifles, &c., for the expedition.

" I was at the Geological Society, Somerset House, last night. Buckland, Sir Henry de la Beche, Phillips, Sedgewick, Mansell, Lyell, and last though not least, old Von Buch—he is here just now, looking as green and fresh as a daisy. I got introduced to all these, and besides to the Marquis of Northampton, the Bishop of Norwich, &c., &c.

" I will be a *great* little man on my return, let some folks laugh and sneer as they please. I cannot sufficiently thank Providence, and your advice, that I went to Aberdeen last winter. Had I not done so, I feel certain none of this good fortune would have attended me; and even if 'it had, I could not have been one quarter so competent as I now feel myself to be, to do justice to the opportunity. I go to a meeting of the Entomological Club to-night. I hope to hear from home to-morrow. I will write of course before I leave, either from London or Portsmouth. Meantime, farewell, may God bless you all.—Your ever affectionate son.   T. E."

" London, 17th May 1845.

" My dearest Mamma.—Well, the die is cast! and here I am, Her Majesty's officer, and to join my ship in the early part of the week. I am writing long letters to papa and uncle, containing every sort of news I can think of. I don't believe the ' Herald' will sail for some time, at least from Plymouth.

" I daresay you feel much distressed at the thought of my going so far away, yet I feel equally sure that your strong reason will tell you, that it is the best thing for me, and I also hope, that though I am barely arrived at the age when most people quit their mother's apron strings, I have had some little, alas ! some dearly bought experience in the world. Still, I know you will feel, and so do I ; although constant occupation drives away many rising thoughts that will doubtless occur to you. But courage, dearest mother ! my fate will be a higher one than to be extinguished now. My star is in the ascendant, and I will yet return, brown and weather beaten, but having laid a strong foundation for future fame and fortune. Something has always whispered ' futurity' into my ear, and I see the dream of my boyish ambition will be realised. I was promising myself much delight in seeing you all in August, but it must now be postponed. Perhaps we may not be away so long as we think. I fear I will have got out of the dear bairns' minds ; don't let them forget me. I am going to-day to get a daguerotype taken for you, and shall send it by post, so that you may see me sometimes exactly as I now am.

" I will write again before I leave. My heart is very full, and I can say but little, but God ever bless you, dearest mamma, think of, and pray for, your devotedly affectionate son, T. E."

The following narrative is evidently the commencement of his journal, extended from short-hand notes, but its continuation, in a cypher of his own invention it is understood, has unfortunately been lost.

" *June* 1845.—It was with no small degree of pleasure that I exchanged the prospect of the hard summer work that was staring me in the face, with much to do, and, in all probability, little to get, for the roving life of a naturalist at large, and, consigning my intending pupils to any one who might choose to occupy my vacated place, with joyous alacrity made my preparations for starting from Glasgow. Tuesday, the 6th May, was appointed for my opening lecture. When I came to the college at the time appointed, the President, Secretary, and others of the Directors, were waiting me. But, instead of delivering my ' Introductory,' I briefly vacated my seat, and informed the worthy Andersonians that their eminent Botanical Professor was now about to depart, seeking elsewhere the fame and fortune not likely to be acquired in Glasgow. After taking leave of the worthy Mr and Mrs Balfour, with whom I had been staying, and one or two other friends, on the following day I started for Greenock by rail. At the latter place I picked up the Liverpool boat, and at nine next morning we arrived at the great maritime metropolis of Britain. I rested till four at Liverpool; called on R. R. Henderson, and Mr Coventry. At four I left by the swift train for London, and truly it may be called ' swift,' for at ten we were at Euston Square, London, having stopped half-an-hour at Birmingham, besides numerous other short stoppages. I took a cab to Evan's hotel, Covent Garden, where I thought I was in some sort near home, seeing that my dear uncle always put up there. Next morning I went to my kind friend Forbes, who introduced me to Captain Beaufort at the Admiralty. A day or two afterwards, I obtained my Admiralty letter of appointment and advance of salary. On the 19th I went down to Sheerness, but returned the same day, and finally joined my home for so long on Wednesday the 21st.

" My time in London was very agreeably spent. I was introduced by Forbes to most of the London naturalists. My first essay was at a soiree given by the Reverend T. V. Hope, President of the Entomological Society. I there met Yarrell, Grant, Waterhouse, Doubleday, Newport, Heppert, and others. Mr Yarrell is a most excellent, kind, warm hearted, and hospitable old bachelor. He invited me to breakfast with him next morning, and shewed me all the attention in his power. It is impossible to know him and not to like him. I went another evening with him to the Zoological Society of which he is President. Like other societies it is, I think, a kind of *humbug*. Grant was very affable to me; he recollected my father well. He is a man of the regular old Wernerian stamp, and looks like a rugged Scotch birch transplanted among exotics. He has not, I think, realized the promise he gave before he left Scotland, of being an industrous comparative anatomist and minute naturalist. I was frequently at the British Museum, and went one night to a meeting of the Entomological Club in Doubleday's house; spent an evening with Hooker at Kew; dined with Mr Cumming, a jovial, worthy old blade, who has the finest collection of shells in the world. I dined one day along with Forbes and Van Voorst on board the hulk at Woolwich, with the officers of the 'Erebus' and 'Terror.' Harry Goodsir goes as assistant surgeon and naturalist.

"Sheerness is an infamous hole! Nobody lives in it but dockyard 'mates.' I was two or three times on shore with our officers, and two or three times in London. At last, after being heartily sick of the locality, we weighed, and went out to the little Nore. After a rather tedious passage we arrived at Plymouth, and finally set sail for the southern hemisphere on the 26th June."

We trust that besides details having merely personal reference to the bright and loveable subject of these memorials, there may be found scattered here and there points of general interest and information. It will probably be inferred that the profession of a naturalist is no easy one, either in respect to the pains necessary for acquiring a competent understanding of it, or the attention continually demanded in keeping up with its ever unfolding stores and new discoveries. The realms of nature are so grand, so diversified, and require an intellect of such powers and versatility, it seems marvellous that one mind could attain the amount of information young Edmondston had gathered, since his first rambles on the Shetland fields until his appointment in the honourable and responsible post where we now find him. When presented to some of the first men of science, he modestly met their investigation, and was hailed by them as a brother assistant.   From Forbes and Hooker and Darwin he received letters or verbal instructions as to his work,—work that one would think a lad yet under twenty years of age must have shrunk from.   Sir William Hooker directs him to the highest mountains ; to Cryptogamia and sea weeds ; wishes for seeds and live plants in hermetically sealed glass, and refers him to the most erudite foreign books as his study.   Edward Forbes wants every thing from the sea depths.   Another begs for bats ; another for butterflies ; a third for fossils, and a fourth for beetles.   Darwin advises him to take a good stock of small steel rat-traps, with which to catch *rodents ;* he begs also, that all facts may be noted relating to the elevation of the land, especially where it is so grandly displayed as in South America, and on the

Californian coast to ascertain in what latitude great angular esoteric boulders have been transported by floating ice, over plains and across wide valleys; and finally, a complete geology of the Mauritius! What must have been the appreciation entertained by these eminent men of their young friend!

HE, to whom we are indebted for all our powers, and who, in His wise providence, appoints our place, alone knows whether a tithe of the expectations formed of the young naturalist would have been realized had his life been prolonged. At all events, we can tell what he intended, and what he aspired after, and it is ever our highest wisdom to leave to the unfolding of *hereafter*, the reasons or dispensations which now appear inscrutably dark.

> " H. M. S. Herald,
> " Nore, 28th May 1845.

" My dear Uncle.—Here I am now fairly on my way into the great world. I joined the ship at Sheerness on Wednesday. We have come out here this morning, and are now at anchor, waiting for final sailing orders from the Port Admiral. We expect to leave for Plymouth to-morrow or next day.

" I was so excessively busy in London that I had really little or no time for any thing, but just buying the necessary articles for so long a cruise. - - - I like what I have seen of shipboard very well indeed, and my messmates are very pleasant fellows. The Captain is first rate, and a perfect gentleman, and shews me the greatest kindness and consideration. The arrangements of the mess are, every member pays £30 entry money, and £2 monthly. It is a very expensive mess, but we cannot help it, as so much has to be provided before we leave England. I have also furnished my cabin with a chest of drawers, wash-stand, sheets, blankets, towels, &c., and the mess share of table-cloths, plate, &c., so I have had enough to do. Our vessel is a beauty, twenty-six guns, three hundred and fifty men, besides marines; twelve mids., some of them the smallest you ever saw; some of them, poor fellows, will get a browning before they see old England again. I can tell you little more of our route than I did in my last. We do not yet know how we shall come home, but most likely round by the Cape and Australia, so we shall make a circumnavigatory cruise of it. We shall be at Teneriffe, and Madeira, Rio, the Falklands, Valparaiso, Guyaquill, Lima, Gallipagos, Cocos, Panama, and, in short, north of the places you can trace on the map from the Rio Plata to 60° north latitude, which, I believe will be the north limit of our cruise. How little did I think a month ago, when preparing for a hard summer's work, lecturing, and mounting the white *choker* and grave *phiz* of a 'professor,' that I should so soon be walking the deck of a frigate, in blue and anchor buttons, preparing to circumnavigate the globe.

" Now that I have noted down these memoranda, I have to acknowledge receipt of your letter of the 8th. It, together with those from papa and mamma, gave me great pleasure from the circumstance of your agreeing with me on the advisability of the step I had taken. At the same time the familiar handwritings, carrying a thousand associations, brought the idea of my separation still more forcibly to my mind. Isolated as I must be for long from those bound by the ties of love and relationship, and thrown among strangers, who of course can feel no interest in me beyond what my own conduct can call up, I will yet live in the good hope that we may in this life be permitted to re-unite, and that in old Buness our united thanks may be given to God for another happy meeting. This is my constant prayer. Often will old familiar faces, scenes, and events rise before me. My ever dear uncle ! I knew not till now how dear ! in fancy how often I will yet be present, though in the body so far away. And well I know I will not be forgotten, but when on the stormy ocean, or in the sultry forests of South America, I will, I know, be thought and spoken of as much as if I were only in Balta. I know not what I would not give just to spend one day among you, but I daresay it is better as it is. I hope to hear again from you before we leave, and I will of course write from Plymouth. I wish we were fairly on our journey, for this lingering here is idle work.

" I believe I have little more to say of any interest.
Our life is monotonous enough ; breakfast at eight ;
lunch at one ; dinner at six, and to bed between ten
and twelve. The intervals I fill up with reading and
writing, laying down plans of action, and noting, as they
occur to me, things to be particularly attended to.   I
have got a good library of books, and we have a large
chart room under the poop, where I have shelves and
a table for my study, which is very convenient, as of
course neither in the gun room, nor in my little crib of
a cabin, can study be carried on to advantage. I am
trusting to hear from you when we arrive at Plymouth.
We may dawdle a month there for ought I know ; that
port being a sort of sailor's heaven, which they are always unwilling to quit. Kind love to U. S. - - -
And ever believe me, my dear Uncle, your most attached
and grateful Nephew,   T. E."

> " H. M. S. Herald.
> " The Nore, 30th May 1845.

" My dearest Mamma.—I have scarcely had courage
to write you, considering the long time it will likely be
before I can see you again.   Yet after all it is the best .
thing that could, according to all human appearance,
have happened to me, and I am sure you will consider
it as such, and, consequently, be reconciled to the separation. Still I was promising myself so much pleasure

in seeing you all in August, that I do feel, notwithstanding the bright prospect before me, very keenly.

"I have been on board now more than a week, and no word of our sailing yet. We shall be a few days at Plymouth, and then, hey, for Madeira and South America! We shall be a month at the Falkland Islands. The way you will have to write to me is 'H. M. S. Herald, Panama, South America, *via* West Indies. You will require to pay 8d. or 1s., or something of that sort, at Lerwick, to ensure the safe transit, It will this way be November or December before I can hear again, but there is no other sure way of catching us. You will hear very frequently from me as there will be always opportunities of sending home.

"I am, of course, doing little here, except making such little preparations for sea as are possible. I do not expect we shall be more than three years absent if we come home again by Cape Horn, perhaps less, but, of course, longer if we go round the world.

"I have got a daguerotype of my handsome visage for you, so that you will be able to know what effect a circumnavigatory cruise will have had on me when I get back again.

"I like my messmates very much, they are very pleasant fellows, and the captain is an exceedingly agreeable man. They have got distinct orders to give me every facility for investigation and collecting at the express desire of the Prince (consort), and orders have been sent out to the Governers of the Falklands, and the various British Consuls, to assist in every way.

" I hope to find another letter from home awaiting me at Plymouth.   I will write from thence ; meantime farewell.—Your ever affectionate son,   T. E."

" *P. S.* I send the portrait to-day by post, separately.

' H. M. S. Herald.

'· The Nore, 30th May 1845.

" My dearest Papa.—Your letter last week was a great comfort to me, both from its containing so much good counsel, and also shewing me that you did not disapprove of the step, which, one way or the other, I was obliged to take independent of your advice.   If I am spared, I cannot but think it will be greatly for my advantage, and having youth and all I have learned only fermenting in my head, I will be in a situation to make the most of my opportunities.   My being so long away from you all must be a heavy balance on the other side, and I am well prepared many a time to wish myself at home again ; however, we must just ' wander in the wilds' for a time first.

" I will endeavour, to the best of my ability, to fulfil your wishes.   Never fear for my being too fool-hardy ; I have too bright a prospect before me to allow of my throwing away my life needlesly, though I have sufficient confidence in myself to think, that if I am compelled into danger, I will face it like a man.

" I like what little I have seen of my messmates very much. The surgeon is a most intelligent man ; has been in almost every quarter of the world ; speaks half-a-dozen languages, and has a *penchant* for natural history, so he is for me a very agreeable companion. The other officers are also very pleasant fellows. I have mentioned all little particulars in my letter to uncle, and that you will of course see. - - - - - -

" Now for a little bit of business while I recollect. As you know I will be rather more exposed to dangers now than at home, and it is well to be prepared for the worst, I have judged it right to *leave a will* in case of anything happening to me. It is in the hands of my agents, Messrs ——————, who hold my power of attorney, and to whom my quarterly bills will be re-mitted as they become due. I am also going to insure my life at Plymouth for £300 ; Messrs ——— have sent the papers. You, jointly with them, are my executors.

" I don't intend, notwithstanding these precautions, to get *blüved* however, but we all know that accidents do sometimes happen, even in the best regulated families. I shall write again from Plymouth.—Your ever affectionate Son,   T. E."

" H. M. S. Herald,
" Devonport, 17th June 1845.

" My dear Brother.—I would have written you before now, but I have had so much to do, and so many things to attend to, that time has often been very scant. You would, however, always know my motions from my letters to papa or uncle. It is about a week since we came here; we are only in to provision the ship, and a few days now will see us at sea. It will be a long time ere I see you again, and if God spare us to meet, you will be a full grown man, and I a weather beaten traveller. You will doubtless soon be going into the great world to buffet your way, I trust, to fame and fortune. Ever, my dear Biot, next to your duty to God, and to your fellow men, keep a laudable ambition uppermost; aim high, and if you should fail in attaining the elevation to which you aspire, you will, at least, rise above mediocrity. Try to gain what has been called 'a niche in the temple of fame,' and you will have the proud consciousness that men will speak of you with respect and admiration when you are sleeping in the grave. All men are not placed in position to acquire eminence in arms, literature, or science, but every man can render himself more or less famous, and at least send down his name to his successors as an honest man, and such, has well been said, to be 'the noblest work of God.'

" I am about to leave Britain, and will be absent four or five years. When I return, I trust to find you occupying a respectable position in society. I suspect I am booked for a vagabond life. Naturalists are a wandering race, and I am of a rather restless turn;

though I may get some berth on my return, which will enable me to cultivate my own 'vine and fig tree' (metaphorically at least) at home. I will write before I leave finally, meantime, farewell, and may God bless you.—Ever your most affectionate Brother,   T. E."

" H. M. S. Herald.
" Devonport, 17th June 1845.

" My dearest Uncle.—I have little to tell you, but of course you will expect to hear. We left Sheerness on the 6th at noon, and were five days coming down Channel,—no very auspicious augury of quick passages. We were two days becalmed off the Isle of Wight. I have been busy getting sundry fittings for my cabin. If I can manage it, I have some idea of taking a start to Torquay to see Mrs Griffiths, but I have still many things to get here. The weather is very hot, and we are wearing duck jackets and trousers. They say it is warmer than it usually is at Madeira, but I can do with the heat very well through the day, only at night it is most disagreeable.

" I have been practising with my rifle, and *bulls-eyed* the mark twice out of five shots at 50 yards, without a rest. It is now nearly two months since I was summoned in such a thundering hurry. Had we known, I could easily have gone down to Shetland to see you all before starting on my long long voyage. God's will be done. The rest from hard study has done me a great deal of

R

good. I am delighted to find I shall be able to write frequently, as, while we are surveying the coast, the ' Pandora' will be sent from time to time to Panama, with and for dispatches, &c." - - - - -

" Plymouth, 25th June 1845.

" My dearest Mamma.—I am just on the eve of leaving England now, after so long a delay. The only word I can say is, farewell. Although you are all so many miles away, and although my pen cannot indite what I feel, you can easily conceive, that the old rocks of Shetland, and the beloved household faces, rise pre-eminent among the objects left behind. God ever bless you all. My eyes swim, and I am, I know not why, almost unable to write. Should I never see you again, dearest mamma, my last breath will be for your happiness. God bless you ! God bless you ! And He will ! Kiss the dear bairns for their brother Tom ; he will be long away, and he will be much altered ere they meet again, but they may be sure that many a time, perhaps in the midst of danger and death, his thoughts will wander to where they are. Adieu ! adieu ! We shall meet again !   T. E."

" Plymouth, 25th June 1845.

" My dear Uncle.—I have been, I confess, much disappointed in not getting a letter from you before I started. Now, however, we are indeed setting off, to bid a long, perhaps to many of us, in all likelihood to some, a last adieu to old England, and many a coast of salt water, and ray of a hot sun must beat on us, before we can again see the white cliffs of the Channel. I have passed some very pleasant days here with the Rev. Mr Hore, who is a very nice fellow ; and with an exceedingly pleasant family. The captain has just come on board ; and there's the pipe !—' All hands, make sail !' Signal ditto to the ' Pandora' ! ' Hoist away main royals !' Adieu ! adieu ! Farewell ! God bless you !" T. E.

" *P. S.* Write regularly to Panama."

"H. M. S. Herald,
"At Sea, 12th July 1845.

" My dear Uncle.—As I trust about this time to-morrow we shall be at anchor in Santa Cruz, Teneriffe, from whence we shall be able to send letters home, I commence this, and shall finish it after we arrive. We left Plymouth on the 25th ultimo. I wrote you a hurried note while they were making sail, and sent it ashore in the bum boat. After leaving old England we had two or three days of moderate weather, though the wind was contrary, but from the Chops of the Channel, and right across the Bay of Biscay, we had a succession of S. E. gales, and a terrible sea running. Our consort, the ' Pandora,' lost one of her quarter boats and stove the other, while we slightly sprung our foremast, which, however, was splendidly 'fished,' and made all right. After we made Cape Finisterre, ten days after our departure from Plymouth, and got clear of the confounded Bay of Biscay, the most delightful weather set in, occasional calms, but the wind quite fair, when there was any, and extremely warm, almost too much so. We passed Porte Santo and Madeira yesterday, and expect to see the Peak of Teneriffe to-night, as the breeze has freshened to-day and is quite fair.

" I shall not be sorry to have a day or two on shore, as we are seventeen days at sea, an unusually tedious passage. I have got quite accustomed to the ship now, and feel almost as much at home as if I were ashore. One mercy is, I have had only about two hours of sea sickness, and eat like a shark. The greatest inconvenience I feel is the intolerable heat at night, our gun room and cabins being two decks down (on the lower deck), so that there is scarcely a possibility of sleeping. I generally walk the deck during the first, and part of the middle watches, and then turn in on the top of the clothes. The nights are certainly most lovely,—a cloudless sky, and cool sea breeze, without any of the frosty, or rheumatism laden feeling of a British night. Once I get a little accustomed to the heat, I shall feel very comfortable. With respect to the captain and my messmates, I am most comfortable I dined in the captain's cabin yesterday. A more agreeable, genial character I never met. In the evening all hands were piped to sky-larking ; the men were singing and dancing on the main deck, and discipline for the time suspended. The *mids.* were set to boxing, single stick, &c., and what reminded me vividly of the kitchen of Buness on *Yule* night, 'a game-cock play, the captain backing one against the first *Luff.*, and playing *bottle holder* to admiration. I thought of Peter tripping up Biot and myself a couple of years ago, and how little I then thought I should be witnessing the same pastime on the deck of a frigate in this latitude. One thing more important is, that the captain has appointed the senior midshipman as my assistant, to be solely under my orders ; so he now ranks ' naturalist's assistant,' and is a very intelligent young man. It will enable me to get through twice the work I otherwise could do, as he will speedily learn to skin birds, dry plants, and otherwise take a great deal off my hands, so as to enable me to pay much more attention to the more scientific part of my duties."

" 13th Santa Cruz, Teneriffe.

" We have just *come to*, off this lovely little town. Giant mountains, and above all, the far famed Peak, are looming above us. Date palms are waving in the land breeze, an azure sky, masses of volcanic lava, scoriæ, and ashes, all form a scene new, as delightful to me. Added to this, a quarantine boat is alongside, containing six olive coloured vagabond looking Spaniards, like villanously dirty Irishmen, but ten times uglier ! I hope to get ashore in a short time. The appearance of the gentlemen alongside is, however, so highly unprepossessing, that I shall take care to carry a couple of British bull dogs (alias pistols) in my pocket, which, indeed, is a necessary precaution here." T. E.

" H. M. S. Herald,

" Santa Cruz, Teneriffe, 13th July 1845.

" My dearest Mamma.—Here I am at last in a foreign port. We dropped anchor here an hour ago, and I am waiting for the captain's coming on board from the consul, to go on shore for my first ramble on foreign ground.

" Every thing around us bears an aspect as different from what I have hitherto been accustomed to as can well be. The island is a most singular looking one, wholly of volcanic origin. It is, as it were, a mass of rugged and fantastically shaped peaks, piled one on top of the other, with deep and rugged ravines running down to the sea edge, their sides covered with volcanic ashes and cinders. The town is a gaudy looking little place, with party-coloured houses and neat looking gardens, but, except a date palm here and there, there is little wood to be seen. The snow-capped Peak, looking delightfully cool in the burning weather, is the chief feature in the landscape. How shall I describe the prepossesing looking natives? such a ragged, dirty, ruffian looking set ! The ship is surrounded by boats with fruit, eggs, onions, bread, &c. ; our fellows are jumping into the boats, pitching the unfortunate owners overboard, where, not being burdened with clothes, they are swimming about like olive coloured seals, swearing and shouting all the Spanish and Portuguese oaths, and calling for vengeance on *los Inglese* in the name of all the saints in the Calendar. ' Jack ' is laughing, and devouring their bananas, grapes, apricots, and other good things *sans* remorse, and, perhaps, *sans* payment. So much for *los Espanos ;* these are certainly very far from being a noble looking people.

" I have been studying Spanish during the passage, and what with that and my own beloved science, having a good library in its various departments, the time passes well enough. I have not even been sea sick. Kindest love to all the dear bairns, also Biot, who cannot now be termed a ' bairn,' else the naturalist to the Californian Expedition would have to consider himself prematurely promoted. The same to aunty Mary. My best blessings be ever with you all.—Your most affectionate son, T. E."

" H. M. S. Herald,

" Off Cape St Roque, Brazil, 9th Aug. 1845.

" My dear Biot.—I know you will like to hear from me, and as I shall have so much to write, besides my duty to attend to at Rio, I intend now to spend a leisure hour in scribbling a few lines. I hope you would all receive the letters safely I forwarded from Teneriffe; they were sent by a Danish schooner, which was to land the mail bag somewhere in the Channel. After we left Teneriffe we got a steady north-west wind (trade wind), which carried us delightfully along until within five or six degrees of the equator. There unsteady winds, calms, and terrible rains annoyed us not a little, added to which, the heat was most intense. We were rather lucky in getting rid of these 'variables' as they are called, and about a degree and a-half on the north side of the equator, we got a steady south-east trade wind, under which the 'Herald' is now walking away towards Rio. The day before yesterday we passed close to the island of Fernando de Noronca, which you will see, by reference to the map, lies off Cape St Roque, the eastern extremity of South America. To-day the land about Pernambuco was discernible from the mast head, and as we are now running along the land as fast as this old dull-sailing jackass of a frigate can be expected to do, I suppose ten days or a fortnight will see us at Rio, the capital of Brazil.

" Nothing of course can be expected to occur on board a vessel of a character likely to amuse or interest those at a distance. I have long ago worn off the strangeness of living on board; in fact, I should be rather astonished to waken in the morning and find myself in a steady four post bedstead on shore; not that I prefer the sea, or should not like to stretch my legs on land, but that I have got so far accustomed, that for a little it would be the shore that would feel strange now. The only incident worth mentioning was the shaving match, in commemoration of our crossing the equator. This most disagreeable ceremony was duly performed on all hands who had not before crossed the line. It has been so often described that it is familiar to every one ; yet a short narration may amuse you. In the first place, all those to be shaved are ordered below, and sentries placed at the hatchways. I was second on the list, and on my name being called by Neptune's secretary, two ' constables' bandaged my eyes, and led me on deck. As soon as I got on the quarterdeck, I was half smothered with buckets of salt water poured over me, and the engine playing right into my face. I was then seated on a plank placed over the main hatchway, and under which, on the main-deck, was a large sail filled with water, with two or three sailors swimming about in it. Neptune, (repre-sented by an old captain of the foretop), with his wife and child, was seated on a gun carriage. A number of questions were asked me, to which I answered nothing, keeping my mouth firmly shut. My face was then lathered with a villanous composition of tar and grease thickened with oatmeal, and Neptune's private physi-cian, opining that I must be faint, thrust up my nose a cork, with half-a-dozen needles stuck in it, by way of scent bottle, thereupon the plank was withdrawn from beneath me, and I tnmbled headlong into the sail full of water below ; the sailors who were in it seized me as soon as I fell, ducking me under water ; at last, half drowned, I managed to scramble out, and doubling up a *middy,* who was preparing a bucket of water for me as I emerged, I gained the quarterdeck, and was soon assisting in serving the others the same way.   The ship was a queer spectacle during the whole affray ; discipline was for the time suspended, and the captain and officers were enjoying the fun, and got as well soused as any. We were all dressed in duck trousers and shirts only, consequently the wetting did not much hurt us.   Some of our *neophytes* got very roughly handled ; indeed, I wonder some were not drowned, they were so pertinaciously kept under water by the ' bears ' or fellows in the sail." - - - - - T. E.

" H. M. S. Herald,

" Rio-de-Janeiro, 22nd Aug. 1845.

" My dearest Papa.—Here I am in a regular terrestrial paradise.   We arrived here three days ago, and shall remain two more.   We had a tedious but not otherwise disagreeable passage from Teneriffe.   We called at no place, and only saw land once, viz., the island of Fernando de Noronca, off Cape St Roque, the first land we made.   No language can describe, no pencil depict, the faintest shadow of this magnificent bay, universally acknowledged to be the finest in the world.   It is eight or ten leagues long; everywhere studded with lovely islands, and singularly shaped mountains down to the sea-shore, covered with palms, casuarinas, cotton trees, aloes, and agathotes; beautiful sandy beaches. The two fine and most picturesque looking cities of Rio-de-Janeiro and Praia Grande, (the latter on the opposite side of the bay), and an immense background of stupendous mountains, form a *coup d' œil* that cannot be imagined, but must be seen. This is the commencement of spring or end of winter, and the mornings and evenings are delicious, although the middle of the day is most oppressive.

" How shall I describe my feelings on my first ' wandering in the wilds' of a Brazilian forest. The first thing that strikes a British botanist is, that all the plants are ligneous,—scarcely a single herbacious species. It would be different later in the season, when the singular parasitic *orchidæ*, would make their appearance. Cotton trees of various species are very common; coffee, and indigo, weeds, *Nicotiana tabacum*, arborescent, and also every where *Casuarinas, Eriodendrons, Musus*, arborescent, beautiful flowered *Solanaeæ* and *Compositæ*, magnificent shrubby *Passifloras, Petunias, Convolvoli, Bignonias, Cassias; Jasminum, Oxalis*, and a host of others. I have been of course laden every day, and have procured several apparently new species. Some of the *Fuci* are identical with south of England species. The profusion, size, and beauty of the insects is also astonishing. You cannot lift a leaf without seeing silver and gold coloured beetles and locusts, of the most brilliant metallic lustre, and singular forms, two or three inches long; while butterflies, six or eight inches across the wings, float languidly in the hot air. The only drawback is the enormous and lavish profusion, so that one scarcely knows which to take. I have been very fortunate in finding a good Saxon botanist here, Dr Lippold. We have made several excursions together. I have not neglected seeing as much of the town and people as I could. Nine-tenths of the population are negro slaves; beauties, and no mistake! The town of Rio is a very large one, streets narrow, but otherwise good, very fine shops, and every thing can be got here as well as in London, though three times the price. Most of the natives can speak French. Some of the hotels and churches are very fine buildings. This is not a good season for fruit; oranges, bananas, and pine apples, are the principal. A dozen of the first, each as large as a child's head, and the finest in the world, can be bought for a 'dump,' (a little less than our penny), pine apples a shilling each, and not nearly so good as the English! You may be sure, after living so long on salt junk and biscuit, I enjoy the land fare.

"I have to detail the zoology of my stay here to Forbes, and botany to Hooker; so what with all this, my diary, preservation of specimens, and describing species, every moment I can spare from collecting is intensely occupied.

" There are several British brigs of war here, mostly occupied in the prevention of the slave trade ; also Yankee and Brazilian ships of war. I dined on board the ' Pandora,' along with three of the American officers. One of them especially, a ' Vermonter,' amused us all ' a few.' Addressing me, he remarked, that, ' a down-east cat fish crawler would beat H. M. S. Herald in a race,' and offered to bet his ' head against a brass farthing, that she never had sailed seven knots.' I told him, his ' head was of little or no use to me, while even a brass farthing was, but I would bet a dollar, and refer to the log;' on which, ' Yankee doodle' hauled off, refused to bet, and got laughed at.

" I am, thank heaven, well ; health and energy as good as ever I had. I think the warm climate will agree better with me than I supposed." - - - -

" Rio-de-Janeiro, 22nd Aug. 1845.

" My dear Uncle.— - - - - This bay is universally accounted the finest in the world, and I certainly think it deserves all its reputation. It is quite impossible to magnify its varied beauties, in fact, description fails us altogether ; nothing can give an adequate idea of such a most lovely place. To me it is a perfect paradise. Plants, shells, and insects are so numerous, so new and beautiful, that I am almost bewildered at the lavish profusion of the glorious works of God. No country in the world is to be compared to Brazil in the variety of its natural productions, consequently, there is no place which is so properly the elysium of the naturalist. As this city is the capital of the empire, its neighbourhood has been well explored; yet I feel assured that I have found several undescribed species. The reason is obvious. Every month, nay, almost every week, brings with it a new series of plants, and if you go to identically the same spot a fortnight after you had visited it, you will find an entirely different vegetation, so exhaustless seem the stores of nature. Just now is the end of winter here, yet the woods are full of the most beautiful flowers. The evenings and mornings are very pleasant, that is to say, not much warmer than the south of England in summer; but the middle of the day, from ten till three, is oppressively hot. I have been out every day, and spend great part of the night in putting by my plants. This is a healthy place, especially at this season, none of the villanous fevers that are common in Mexico and the Spanish Main. In a fortnight after leaving this we shall get into a climate colder than Shetland. Hurricanes of snow and hail blow off the mouth of the Rio-de-la-Plata, and in the Falkland Islands, which will be our next resting place, and the climate is very inhospitable. Old Cape Horn will then have to be passed; then into the hot latitudes of Chili and Peru. Many a time have I wished, when the stifling hot breeze has been blowing into my cabin, that I could, even for a moment, feel the cool blast blowing up *the Voe.* I dare say, by the time this reaches you, you will be getting cold enough weather, but almost any degree of cold, I think, is better than extreme heat. Artificial heat you may create, cold you cannot; you must suffer on, and puff and blow, sometimes during the live-long night, in a heat almost sufficient to roast a beef steak. Once we pass San Blas or Monterey, on the lower Californian coast, it will not be so hot, and we will go far enough north to freeze our noses off.

" I have shot nothing but a few humming birds here. In fact, one can scarcely carry a gun and botanize at the same time here. The *Baagies** and *Kittiwakes* are common even here, and associated with the Frigate bird, &c., of the tropics. They sit on the water, and, pursuing the flying fish, behave exactly as they do after the herring in Shetland. - - - - - Of the Brazilians the less one knows the better, I believe. Assassinations are every day occurrences; and if a man is accused in the public prints of murdering another, he merely defends himself by letter, the law (?) never troubling itself about them. Thus, for example, the following is the title of a letter in the *Journal de Commercio,* (translated) :—' The answer of Ovidio de Carvallis e Silva, ex-

---

* Great black backed gull.

municipal judge of Pinchery, to the false, malicious, and unfounded accusation, regarding his connection with the murderers of Raimondo do Sousa Brevas.' The said Raimondo was found in the street with seven knives sticking in his back, and his head so battered with bludgeons, that, except for his clothes, he could not have been recognised. What sort of a country is it where such things are common occurrences !

" The principal distinguishing feature of the town, is the immense number of slaves. Nineteen-twentieths of the people you see in the streets are negroes, half naked, ugly wretches they are. Fat monks, with black cassocks and shovel hats, and a cord round their waists, swarm in all directions, while the city is full of churches, convents, and monasteries. ' The nearer the church, the farther from grace.' The native ladies are never seen in the street, but by going to the public places, the museum, or opera, plenty of pretty faces show that the Brazilians yield to no nation in that respect. One curious fact amused me much. Whenever one of the men goes from home, even for a day or two, he sends his wife to a large convent kept for the purpose, named, *Il convent dos maritos*, where she is kept securely locked up till his return," T. E.

" H. M. S. Herald, 7th Sept. 1845.

" Off Monte-Video, Rio-de-la-Plata.

" My dearest Mamma.—We are just now becalmed

a little to the southward of the Rio-de-la-Plata, and as there is a great probability we shall be able to send letters home by Rio from the Falklands, by a Riote schooner we expect to find there, I commence this letter, though, in good sooth, materials to write about are somewhat scanty. I wrote papa, uncle, Biot, and aunty, fully from Rio-de-Janeiro. We left that loveliest spot of earth on the 28th, and are consequently about twelve days at sea. We expect to gain the Falklands in eight or ten days more, but are just now tantalized with calms, fog, and rain. The weather is very cold; pea-jackets, blue trousers, and blankets, are now in requisition. In fact, the change had commenced before we left Rio, where the one day I was broiling, in white trousers and jacket, no vest, and straw hat, and the next, after a heavy fall of rain, with thunder and lightening, shivering in Flushing togs, and a sou'-wester. This change gave me an attack of fever and dysentery, which, however, speedily yielded to the usual remedies, and now, in a climate much like Shetland, or rather the highlands, while all around are shivering in cold and rheumatism, I feel all alive, and enjoy amazingly the contrast between the sickening heat we have had and the present more congenial temperature. In fact, much as all seaman fear and hate Cape Horn, I shall almost regret when that dreaded boundary is passed, and we lose the cold of the antartic regions for the heat of Chili and Mexico. However, we shall be there in the cold season. Since leaving Rio, we have been lucky in having fair winds, and tolerably moderate weather. Only once we were obliged to strip all sail, and scud under bare poles for a part of the night. We got storm-sails bent, and all preparations were made to encounter the 'pamperos,' or hurricanes so frequent off la-Plata, especially at this season, but we have been agreeably disappointed, and we now congratulate ourselves on being nearly out of their latitude.

" 15th September.—Something interrupted my writing at the above point, and since, it has been almost impossible to take pen in hand. My self congratulations at getting out of the latitude of storms were rather premature, and somewhat prophetic, for on the night of the 7th a very heavy gale came on, which has continued with little intermission until now; the wind, besides being contrary, and the sea so rough, that we durst not lay to. In consequence we have had a very unpleasant week, and the most disagreeable of it was, sometimes the momentary expectation of seeing our poor little consort the 'Pandora' get some terrible damage. She has stood it out with nothing more serious than losing a couple of boats, some bulwarks, and other deck work. We have suffered no damage, thank God, at least nothing to speak of. The wind is still contrary, but more moderate, and as we are now not more than four hundred miles from the Falklands, I trust another week will see us there. Still the cry is, ' I

wish we were round Cape Horn !' The temperature is
several degrees below the freezing point, and, as our arrangements are mostly made for warm weather, we are
ill prepared for such cold. Thus, we have no fire in any
part of the ship except the galley, and consequently
the temperature of the gun-room is rather *cool.* All
these little discomforts, however, must just be cheer-
fully submitted to, and I should say, a voyage of this
sort was a very good school to teach a man the necessity
of dispensing with some of the home luxuries of life."

" Falkland Islands, 28th Sept.

" We arrived here safely on the 19th. As I am
writing my adventures here to papa, and uncle, I need
not repeat them, as of course you will see those letters.
As I am exceedingly busy you will, I know, excuse a
longer letter. I could linger over my pen for hours,
and fancy myself at home, but with the prospect of
being called when the boats leave the ship at five in
the morning, one must get to bed before twelve, and it
is fast approaching that hour. Our time is about three
hours astern of English time, consequently you are all
now asleep, as I will be very shortly. I often, often think
of the dear bairns ; they will be much changed, and I
almost an old man when I return,—you know I am past
twenty now ! I trust you are not keeping Biot much
longer at home. Depend on it, a boy or man cannot
learn soon enough to trust to some extent to himself ;

and though, for the first, his experience may be dearly bought, it will be the more valuable, and the better remembered. Mary will be quite a woman too. I shall take her away to keep a little box I intend to have somewhere in the suburbs of London when I return, and get a berth of £200 or £300 a-year. I am as yet wavering between Kensington and the Hampstead Road; so please have her duly educated, with a view to purveying good shrimps and muffins. Well! one must dream now and then; and who knows? My air-built castles have been hitherto more than realised. Adieu! and God ever bless you all, is the constant prayer of, my beloved mother, your devoted son, T. E."

"Falkland Islands, 23rd Sept.

"Dearest Father.— - - - - This dreary archipelago,—the head quarters of storms, wild geese, and penguins,—certainly much resembles Shetland, though less picturesque and diversified. The few miserable huts here which they dignify by the name of a settlement, serves rather to augment than to relieve the desolate aspect, so striking by contrast with lovely Brazil. The population of the settlement is about one hundred and fifty men, women, and children. They are composed partly of a small party of engineers, (Lieutenant Moody, of that corps, is governor), partly of English settlers, and partly of Gauchos, from the Buenos Ayrean Pampas. These last are the most singular ; they are generally half-breeds between Spaniards and South American Indians, dark, desperate looking fellows ; can nail a man's ear to his own door with a knife, twenty yards off; the finest horsemen in the world ; think nothing of seizing a furious wild bull by the horns with the *lazo*, and as little of sticking a man as a pig. They much require the red coats to keep them in order. They are kept here for the purpose of catching wild cattle, on which the subsistence of the people depends. Wild as this place is, I have enjoyed my rambles much. I have not yet been able to go into the interior, but hope to do so, and get a shot at a wild bull. I have waited here in order to procure live plants of the *Tussac* for Kew ; this I accomplished yesterday. I went with a boat to the chief place where it grows in huge clumps, in a soil half sand, half peat. You may judge my delight at seeing this singular and most interesting grass in its native wilds. Little did we think, not very long ago, when chatting about it in the parlour ' up the way,' how soon I should be wandering among it. I was happily able to procure a number of young live plants for Sir William Hooker, and plenty of specimens in fine flower. Unfortunately it is much too early for seed, else I would send you some in this letter. The plants will be sent home in a closed glass case, *via* Rio, and I shall tell Sir William, to endeavour to send you some plants, if they reach England alive. It is a noble grass, and how I should like to see some fine tufts of it in your garden, if God spares me to return.   Such a place for shooting as this is! The *furor sportsman meusis* frequently overcomes the *botanicus*, and in going out, I am sometimes obliged to leave my gun on board, else the plants brought home would be few.   Four species of magnificent geese actually swarm, one of them cannot fly (*Anser brochyptera*), and all are so tame that a gun is almost superfluous.   Two vultures, and a large hawk (*Polyborus*), are common, three or four ducks, two or three gulls, one a new species, and a most lovely bird. Snipes swarm, and a white bellied shag in myriads ; penguins of course, dotterel, and lots of small birds.   The great black backed gull here, as at Rio, is quite at home.   It is the only wild and wary bird, and, although mixed with such incongrous associates, it speaks to me of the ' Hammers,' the ' Skerry o' da Soond,' the ' Gyo,' and the ' Muckle Head.' *   Rabbits are numerous in some places, and other game too multifarious for detail. The breeding season is just commencing, this month answering to our March. The plants, therefore, are chiefly out of flower.   The formation hereabouts is quartz and gneiss, and is covered with peat.   A species of *myrtus*, a *Gaultheria*, and a small compound flowered shrub, supply the places of heath and blacberry. The hills are low, and the land is every where intersected with

---

* Vernacular names of Unst localities.

long *voes*, quite like our own. I have no idea how long we shall be here, likely not many days, so I must make the best use of my time, and consequently work from morning till night. It is very different preparing numerous specimens in different branches of Natural History on board a man-of-war and on shore. Cramped for want of room, and twenty unavoidable obstacles are in one's way here. Still I must persevere ; fame and fortune are, I trust, before me, to the extent at least I have ever wished, viz., a competency, and a name as a naturalist ; and, if God spare me, they will speak of me when I am crumbling away.

" I dined, along with the captain, at the governor's ; he is a very gentlemanly, well-informed man, has a very comfortable house, and fine library. I am afraid you will scarcely be able to read this disconnected epistle, but I am writing after a hard day spent in skinning birds in the cold, and my fingers are stiff enough. I am writing mamma, and uncle, and perhaps this rigmarole, bad as it is, may amuse you a little. I must be concluding now, for I have to be off at six to-morrow morning to dredge, and must now turn in to my narrow crib for some sleep. God bless you all.—My dearest friend, good night."

" Falkland Islands, 28th Sept.

" My dear Uncle.— - - - - - We have been very unfortunate in the weather ; not a single decent day since we arrived. Gales so furious that even in this harbour (the finest and most sheltered I ever saw) we cannot get ashore without our eight oared cutter; and then the furious squalls of snow and sleet render botanizing a most uncomfortable pursuit. Notwithstanding these drawbacks, I have been working from morning till night. My berth is really no sinecure while we are in port, though at sea I should sometimes like a little more to do. I think this place would be a very agreeable one for a time, were the equinoctial gales, which are in force just now, over, and the spring a little more advanced. I am told they have very fine weather in summer. Perhaps my liking to it arises from its resemblance to the poor old islands so many thousand miles away. I am continually finding a ' Basta voe,' or a ' Durie voe,' among the retired inlets, and was much delighted the other day at finding a very perfect little ' Hoonie.' Every now and then, however, a flock of penguins, a huge albatross, or an ugly vulture, hovering over my head, destroys the illusion, and I am forced to awaken from my dream of home, with a sigh, to confess that I am nearly at its antipodes. I often wish for Charlie here; something better than ' scarfs ' and ' scories ' are to be picked up. Every creek and hole swarms with wild geese, and ducks, so tame that I have pulled into the midst of a flock, and the men knocked them down with their oars. I killed twenty brace in about three hours; the ship is hung round with them; snipe are also plentiful. All the birds are tame, even hawks.

" There is a large hawk, or rather small eagle, which is so impudent and intrusive, that you cannot lay down your game-bag for an instant, but one of them is sure to pounce on it; several of them have got shattered bodies for their impertinence. An immense vulture is also sometimes seen, but rarely. I lay down on the ground yesterday, and, being considerably fatigued, fell fast asleep. When I awoke, two of these vultures were sitting about forty yards off, looking at me with a most evil eye, as if speculating on the probability of my being in a fit state to afford them a banquet. I speedily let them know that I was alive and kicking, for I 'up stick' and, before they could get out of my range, *doused* one. He measures thirteen feet between the wings. There are lots of seals, but only in . the outer islets, and I have only seen one or two swimming about. Weather has prevented me from making a two or three days excursion I was meditating into the interior. As there are no houses, one must sleep in the open air, and that is not comfortable in a gale of wind and snow, with thermometer three or four degrees below the freezing point. I have, in consequence, missed shooting one of the wild bulls which are to be found here. Both these and wild horses are common about twenty miles from the settlement. The Gauchos go out once a week, and having caught the animals with the *lazo*, bring to the settlement as much beef as will last a week. They live almost entirely on beef, as there is no corn or other vegetables grown on the island as yet. The place is under martial law, and rations are served out to all the men once a week, amply sufficient to serve a man, his wife, and child. They consist of fresh beef, pork, peas, biscuit, rum, flour, suet, raisins, salt, pepper, mustard, and vinegar. Each man gets ten pounds of beef, and his other rations are nearly twice what is allowed in the navy. In addition to these rations, each man in the government pay gets 3s. 6d. a day, and those working for private individuals, or any kind of artificers, can easily earn 6s. or 8s. a day. In consequence of this, a working man doing nothing but cutting up the peat to admit of laying down roads, or building rough quays, or such like work, can lay by £40 or £50 for his summer's earnings, and much more by piece work in winter. The government could employ several hundred more hands at the same rate. I am quite astonished that more attention is not paid to this place in the way of emigration. Though the climate is rigorous during winter, there is little snow, and the summer is very fine, and it is perhaps the most healthy place in the world. I wish that a few of your non-paying tenants were shipped out here. I have to make a report to the Colonial Government at home, regarding the natural production, and facilities for emigration possessed by this place, and, I doubt not, it will speedily become a flourishing colony.

" I have now scribbled a good deal, and time presses. I am writing papa and mamma, and as of course you will see those letters, what is omitted in the one, will perhaps be found in the other. I expect this will reach you sometime about Christmas. My *Yule* will be spent, please God, in one of the hottest districts of the world, somewhere on the coast of Peru. You wont forget the absent 'Gooshman' on that festive morning. He will be a sunburnt, weather-beaten character when he returns. Even in the short months I have been away, you would scarcely know me were I to pop in upon you. I am burnt nearly black by the sun of Brazil, and my face being covered by a Russian like beard, I dare say I am very unlike what I was."

" Off Cape Horn, 11th Oct.

" I wrote three or four letters at the Falklands, which were left with the Governor, to be forwarded to Rio by the first opportunity. - - - -

" We were all mighty glad to get away, though it was 'out of the frying pan into the fire,' with a vengeance. We had about a day of fair wind, but since that, oh, such weather! gale succeeding gale, and always in our teeth, driving the poor old ship to the southward and eastward. We parted company with the 'Pandora' in a snow storm, shortly after leaving the Falklands, and she being a much better sailer than we are, I suppose she will get round long before us ; yet the weather has been so bad, we can't help being anxious for her. Of a truth, this same Cape Horn amply deserves the not very amiable character it has received ; last night, however, it out-did itself, and blew not a storm, but a regular hurricane. We could shew no sail but a main trysail, and mizen staysail, and she was making six knots of leeway. The captain, first lieutenant, and master, were on deck all night, and many a time none on board thought the vessel would get off her beam ends again. Luckily we had a good moon, and by its light the scene was most awful and sublime. We carried away gangway boards, and other light affairs, but the old ship stood it bravely on the whole, and, thank God, we found ourselves still above water in the morning. Nothwithstanding that the hatches were battened down we shipped two seas, which smashed the sashes of the gun-room windows, and quite flooded us below. The weather is intensely cold, and the appearance of enormous icebergs vividly explains that we are in an inhospitable region of the earth, or rather *sea*, besides contributing to make us nervous regarding our safety, seeing that they are no small items in the dangers of a voyage round ' the Horn.' "

" 12th November.

" We have at length surmounted the pains and

perils attendant on a passage round the stormy cape. On the 8th we sighted land, being the Cordillera of the Andes above the island of Chiloe. For a few days previously we had had fine weather, though not very warm, and we had good reason to call this splendid ocean 'the Pacific.' Almost immediately after we had made sufficient westing and borne up, the boisterous sea seemed to become smooth as by a miracle, and we glided easily and happily on. On the 9th we looked into the entrance of the bay of Valdivia, merely to see if the Admiral on the station was there. Finding he was not, we stood out again, and yesterday ran into Talcahuano bay, or la Concepcion, as it is generally called, from the town of that name about eight miles inland. Our chief object in going in here was to land me, for I had requested, if possible, to be landed here, and left to find my way on to Valparaiso to rejoin the ship,—my intention being to skirt the great chain of the Andes which bounds Chili. I would thus not only have seen a country little explored by naturalists, but would have passed through a tract of land abounding in gold, silver, and copper, the examination of which is inculcated in my instructions. But, alas ! 'the best laid schemes of mice and men gang aft ajee.' On consulting the residents, it was found that the necessary horses to perform so long and arduous a journey, and a guide, could not be procured in less than three or four days, and the distance to Valparaiso being three hundred miles or more, and the captain not being able to allow me more than a fortnight's leave of absence, I was most reluctlantly compelled to give up the idea. I had gone on shore all prepared with tent, baggage, &c., but had to return on board 'with my thumb in my cheek.'

" Talcahuano is a small seaport, which ten years ago was altogether destroyed by an earthquake. Earthquakes here defy the industry of man, and paralyze all exertion ; for who will invest capital for the improvement of a country every moment liable to be swallowed up ! We were here much gratified by ascertaining the safety of the Pandora. She is a fortnight a-head of us, having touched that time ago at Talcahuana for fuel. We ascertained also that the admiral is supposed to be at the Sandwich Islands or Tahiti, and not expected on the South American coast for six weeks at least. I trust this may have the effect of delaying us at Valparaiso, or Callao, when my long cherished project of exploring the mighty Andes may yet be gratified.

" We expect to reach Valparaiso to-morrow or next day, when I shall immediately start with as long a leave as I can obtain, and lead an independent shore life as much as possible, although I am now sufficiently accustomed to our life on board ship to bear it without any great inconvenience. It is true, it is not a life capable of much enjoyment, and the rather dull routine and wearisome etiquette of a man-of-war suits little the roving spirit of a naturalist. But notwithstanding all our petty annoyances from bad weather, wet, and poor living, I enjoy (thanks be to God for all his undeserved mercies) the best of health, and only wait the opportunity to work again ' like a Trojan.' The glimpse I had during the few hours we staid at Talcahuano impresses me strongly in favour of Chili. The climate is delicious, and the immense profusion of beautiful flowers (for it is here just the end of spring) tantalized me terribly, and added to the regret I felt at being compelled to forego my expedition. I am determined, however, to get to the Andes, if within the limits of possibility, for few or no botanists have been in central Chili for many years, and if I were only lucky enough to do any thing in the *mine discovery* line, it would be a grand thing for me ! I am wearying sadly for letters from home, and hope that we shall do no surveying this year south of Panama, else it will be long before I can expect to see the letters which will of course be waiting there. You will never imagine, in its full extent, how anxiously I look forward to receiving them. On board ship there is little to distract the attention, and the very dissimilarity of every thing one sees, by the force of comparison the more draws one's thoughts towards home, and the beloved friends there. Night and day I pray to God to grant that we may meet again ; and I cannot imagine on earth greater happiness, than if I could for one short day be wafted to your fireside again. The minutest particular is stereotyped in my mind, and no distance of time or space can dim or eradicate it. Often, when perhaps you little think, my thoughts are so roving, I pace the deck, picturing to myself what you may be doing or saying, and fancying that perhaps you may even just then be saying, 'I wonder what the poor Gooshman is about,' and I fancy to myself whether if I suddenly dropped in now,—come up by the packet for example, and Peter, and Charlie were to come on board, whether they would know me, with my sunburnt face, and a beard like a Russian. I think *you* would still *twig* me, if I were to walk in upon you. It may seem needless to ponder these things, but really the happiest times from home are spent in anticipating our return, and *he* has a poor share of manly feeling who is ashamed to own, that thus he often thinks of his home, and his dear friends there."

To the Rev. Mr H.

     " On the Voyage to Valparaiso.

- - - - " After encountering the usual allowance of ' pamperos ' off the Rio-de-la-Plata, on the 19th September we reached the Falkland Islands, where we staid till the 30th. Alas! alas! what a miserable change from the palm and acacia groves of Brazil! - - - . - There are also wild horses, one of which I shot in one of my rambles, and dined off him in the following manner :—A large round mass of flesh, the skin adhering, is cut off and roasted on the fire, hide downwards ; this is termed, ‘ carné con cuero,’ or ‘ flesh with the skin,’ and to a ravenously hungry naturalist, a piece of colt's flesh treated in this manner, albeit roasted five minutes after the animal was galloping over the hills, and eaten without bread or salt, is no contemptible grub. You may laugh at my Tartar banquet, but had I not come across the unfortunate *cheval* which furnished our meal, I had serious thoughts of supping on a turkey buzzard, which might have been rather tough, and somewhat carrion tasted.

" As it was the end of winter, scarcely a single plant was in flower, and the heath was covered with tufts of withered grasses, and *Cyperaceæ.* I got some very good Cryptogamia, especially lichens, five *Stictae* and *Usneæ*, a good many *Algæ*, one species, a large *Iridea*, scarcely differs from *I. edulis*, unless in size, it is sometimes four or five feet long. The shore is everywhere belted by an enormous growth of *Macrocystis pyrifera*, which extends to the depth of eight or ten fathoms, and renders landing in a boat frequently very difficult, or almost impossible. It grows in an immense matted mass, the stems being very slender, and each lanceolate, toothed leaf, having at the base a large oblong vesicle. From its excessively branched and entangled growth, it is almost impossible to ascertain the length of any one plant, but I have unravelled thirty-three feet without any appearance of end, and, I doubt not, it attains one hundred feet, or even much more. Another giant Alga is also abundant, the *Lessonia fuscescens,* before whose dimensions our *Laminaria bulbosa* and *digitata* sink into insignificance ; the enormous stems seem more like the trunks of trees as they lie on the sea-beach than any thing else. The upper part of the stem is divided into an immense number of dichotomous branches, each of which is terminated by a lanceolate frond. Oh ! this charming Cape Horn ! it amply deserves its character ; gale after gale, storm after storm, hurricane after hurricane. I wish you could have seen three gales we have had, when we were scudding under bare poles. I never saw any thing so magnificent ; but that ill makes up for other discomforts. The wind is always dead against, and we are half thinking that we must be distantly related to the ' Flying Dutchman.' We leak like a spout besides, and I have six inches water in my cabin every morning. It is doubtless very pleasant, in awaking during the night, to be lulled to sleep again by the gentle music of running water in your bed-chamber; but I am so unromantic as to prefer the contrary. However, one must put up with these small discomforts at sea ; and in a week or two, the trade winds and blue sky of the Pacific will, we trust, welcome us, and waft us moderately to Valparaiso."

" H. M. S. Herald, Nov. 1845.

" One day's sail from Valparaiso.

" My dearest Father.—I have not a great deal to talk about just now, seeing that I have at intervals during our voyage, been noting down anything that I thought might be interesting in letters to mamma and uncle, and as of course letters to any one of you are equally addressed to all, I need not recapitulate, but leave the one letter to fill up the deficiencies of the others. It is, consequently, unnecessary to tell you of all the gales and discomfort we have endured during our forty-five days passage from the Falklands. Of course storms were to be expected, but though most of our officers are old voyagers in these latitudes, they had none of them before seen such bad weather. It was just about the time of the South Vernal Equinox, and blew incessantly. Contrary winds drove us almost as far south as the ' New Shetlands,' and we suffered severely from cold. Firing was very short, and if we had not had plenty of warm clothing, we should have been badly off. The ship is not fitted up for a cold climate ; she has no stoves any where below, and the arrangements for ventilation, however comfortable in warm weather, &c., do not do when the temperature sinks five or six degrees below the freezing point. We saw a very large iceberg in 59° S. Lat."

" Valparaiso, 26th November.

" On the 16th we arrived here, after a nice passage from Talcahuano. The following day I hired three horses and a guide, and started inland. I rode forty-five miles that day to the village of Quillota, a most lovely place, situated in a valley surrounded by the mountains of the Sierra Campana, and about fifty miles from the Cordillera. I enjoyed the ride amazingly, and was speedily laden with the most beautiful plants. I never saw of course so splendid a *Flora;* that of Brazil is more curious and imposing certainly, but I prefer the Chilian. The characteristic genera are, *Calceolaria, Fuschia, Gentiana, Amarythis, Spelobuna, Canothu, Hesperis, Dracæna,* and beautiful shrubby *Labratæ* and *Compositæ.* The scenery along the road is magnificent. All Chili is hilly, and the glimpses we got of the snow-capped Andes on the one hand, and the Pacific on the other, were beautiful in the extreme. Quillota is a large valley, watered by the Con-con river, which descends from the Cordillera. With the Andes in view you may be sure I did not sleep long next morning, but started at daybreak, and that night slept alongside of a patch of perpetual snow. Our bivouac was very cold. We slept on the sheepskins which form the Chilian saddle. A poncho, or Chilian cloak, and a great-coat, were my only coverings, but we lighted a good fire, cooked two pigeons I had shot, with some rice, drank our ' mate' (Paraguay tea), smoked a cigar to keep off the mosquitos, and slept like tops. We rambled and rode about the ridges and valleys of the Cordillera for the three following days. The plants are very few, but those I got, pretty and interesting. No animals almost ascend so high, except the condor, many of which we saw. The last day I was there, while we were descending a steep pass, I came upon seven sitting on a peak about forty yards distant. I sent a rifle ball through the neck of a splendid fellow. He measured 8 feet, 4 inches across the wings, and a bird so massively built I never saw. A puma had been committing great ravages among the cattle at the foot of the Cordillera, and I was just calculating whether I could spare a day to go and find him, when we overtook four men, one of whom carried *El leon*, as they call him, dead of course, across his saddle. They had killed him that morning, having hunted him with dogs into a tree, lasso'd, and dispatched him with their knives. The puma measured 6 feet, 9 inches. The four fellows bivouacked with us that night, to my considerable uneasiness, and the exquisite terror of my guide, for these mountaineers are more than half banditti, call themselves, *guardos del camino* (guards of the road), and levy black mail, if not with the courage, at least with the perseverance of Rob Roy. They talked big at first, but my double-barrelled gun and rifle, and the *accidental* removal of my poncho shewing a brace of pistols at my belt, and treating their hints for money with quiet nonchalance, speedily silenced these fellows, for they are at least as great cowards as bullies. The guide and I judged it right, however, to watch turn about during the night, and I was very glad when we started at daybreak for Quillota. I had only a week's leave, and the three following days were spent botanizing the Sierra Campana. These hills are higher than the Grampians, but are nothing compared to the Cordillera. I got a great variety of plants, many of them new ones, and the day before yesterday returned to Valparaiso thoroughly laden.

" I know not when we sail; likely not for ten days at least. I have seen little of Valparaiso. The town is very picturesquely situated on a steep hill. It is large and thriving, and there are many English residents. I intend to deliver one or two letters of introduction to-day, and take a day or two's rest, for I have been hard worked. Thank God, I am in the best of health and spirits. The climate agrees well with me, and is not very hot; that is to say, the thermometer is seldom above eighty degrees.

" *30th November.*—I believe we sail the day after to-morrow, and the mail is being made up, so I must be concluding this epistle. I have been busy collecting shells and dredging here, and have made an excellent collection of these, as well as of plants." · - · -

" Valparaiso, 30th November.

" My dearest Mother.— - - - - - - Since I returned from my excursion, I have been working at the natural history around the city, chiefly marine zoology, and have obtained many interesting results, especially bearing on the new theories of the Zoust distribution of animal life, and its bearings on geology ; a subject which Edward Forbes very successfully commenced in the eastern Mediterranean, and which I am carrying out as far as I can. We are to sail in a day or two. We shall reach Callao, the seaport of Lima. I suppose in a fortnight. I shall like much to see Lima, ' the city of palaces,' as the South Americans call it ; it is said to be a most splendid old Spanish town. After that we go to the Gallipagos, an uninhabited volcanic archipelago, perhaps the most singular and anomalous group of islands in the world. Every plant and animal in them is peculiar, and found no where else, while it seems the last spot on earth where certain creatures yet linger, now only found fossil elsewhere. Such are huge herbivorous and marine lizards, like the *Plesiosaurus* of geologists, enormous land tortoises, &c. I anticipate much pleasure in spending a few days there. After that our destination is unknown, except to the captain, and he tells no one.

" Every day we get more anxious to reach Panama to hear from home. You will before this time have got my letters from Rio, and will likely soon be receiving those I left at the Falklands. I cannot expect you will get this in less than three months or one hundred days. You must not get anxious when some time elapses between the arrivals of my letters ; for of course there is a great deal of uncertainty in the posts, and sometimes we may even be many months without an opportunity to England. Never, dearest mamma, omit writing me once every two months, or oftener. You cannot form an idea what a comfort it will be to me, far from home, among strangers, none of whom of course have congenial feelings with myself, to receive letters which will make me fancy myself again with you, and which tell me of *home*, that little talismanic word that transports the mind of the wayworn wanderer so far away, to the scene of his happy childhood. I feel most at sea the want of some one of congenial tastes and habits. Were it not that I have my beloved natural history,— my true and early mistress, who has soothed many an uneasy hour, and to whom in any vexation I can fly, with the assurance of finding speedy comfort,—I would sometimes find myself very *ennuyée*. I have tried to inoculate several of my messmates. The purser is a man of great and versatile talents, and I do not despair of making a geologist of him. The wide range, and the sublime speculations of that noble science, naturally captivate a man of expanded mind ; but the difficulty is to make the necessity of *detail* apparent and palatable ; for many a man flies into the region of speculation without having plumed his wing with *facts*, and then blames the science instead of his own rashness, when he tumbles to the ground. There's a metaphor for you! Amn't I becoming a philosopher!

" I am spinning out a letter about nothing, but, to tell the truth, I feel loth to lay down my pen when once I have taken it up ; it is our only method of communication, and I cling to it. I have written both papa and uncle long letters; and outlines of my motions and adventures are there detailed. Many a queer adventure do I have too ! in fact my life on shore is a succession of them of one sort or another,—small and great, grave and gay. I keep a minute diary, and it will give you some amusement some time or other.

" My bivouacs in the Cordillera were Salvator Rosa-ish enough. Here is a sketch ;—Time, sunset ; place, by the side of a rill, running from a patch of eternal snow on the Sierra de San Carlos. Above me lowered the gigantic Andes, some of them just putting on a night-cap of fog. Below, the broad valley of Quillota, its green vineyards, and waving orchards, and the Con-Con river winding like a silver thread through it, while far away the glassy Pacific stretched its broad and placid water. Over all, the deep blue sky, contrasted beautifully with the pale rose-coloured clouds which always accompany a Chilian sunset. All is still as death where we are. My guide is habitually taciturn, besides which he speaks no English; my Spanish is yet imperfect for continuous conversation, and, above all, he is engaged in the agreeable office of cooking a dish of *casauela* (or a fowl stewed with rice and other vegetables), which is sending forth a steam very acceptable to hungry men. On the grass is stretched a handsome young man, dressed in a *poncho* (or square parti-coloured cloak, with a hole in the middle for the head, and thence falling over the shoulders). Enormous boots of untanned leather cover the lower man, and a broad-brimmed *sombrero* shades his expressive features, albeit the sun has peeled of a few feet of skin. This good-looking youth is Me! your worship! The *casauela* is cooked; *mate*, or Paraguay tea, is made in two small pumpkin shells, and sucked into the mouth through a reed. The plants are put in paper; the horses' fore feet tied together; the sheepskins which form the Chilian saddle spread near the fire; the latter is replenished; the caps of rifle and pistols renewed, and somewhere placed handy, for there are pumas and robbers plenty on the skirts of the Andes, and a prayer is breathed to that God who watches over His people, whether in desert or city, and the weary travellers sink to sleep as if their beds were of down, to dream of home, and be awakened next morning, by a South American sun beating on their faces.

" I need hardly add my kindest, warmest, love to you all. May God ever shield and watch over you, is the fervent prayer of, my dearest Mamma, your devotedly attached son,   T. E."

     " H. M. S. Herald,

      " Callao Road, 23rd December 1845.

" My dearest Father.—As I wrote fully to yourself, mamma, and uncle, from Valparaiso so lately, there is but little to communicate. We left Valparaiso on the 4th inst., and ran in for two days to Papudo, a small bay thirty miles north of it, where the captain had some observations to make. I increased my collections considerably there, and found some very interesting plants. We arrived here on the 17th after a very pleasant voyage. I spent the first three days in dredging in the bay, and examining the island of San Lorenzo, where there is in course of formation very interesting marine deposits of new date. I expect my observations will throw some light on the newer fossiliferous strata, complicated with volcanic action.

" On the 20th I started for Lima, nine miles distant, and have just returned. The ' City of Palaces ' well deserves the name, for although its ancient grandeur be somewhat faded, and the grass be growing in its streets, it remains a splendid monument of the former greatness of *Los vijos Castilianos.* Here the architecture, the habits, and the blood of the old Spanish hidalgo still linger. The numerous splendid churches, the quaint painting, and fantastic carving of the interior of the houses, the numerous priests of every grade and order, the assassin looking Peruvians, the muffled women, combine to render Lima the most novel and interesting sight that an Englishman can see on·this coast.

" I went yesterday to see a *bull fight.* It was the first of the season, and as I might never have the opportunity of seeing the far famed spectacle again, I thought it a pity to miss it ; but the sight was too repugnant to humanity to make me ever wish to see it again. For your amusement, I shall do my best to describe it.

" The amphitheatre is very large, and surrounded by several tiers of boxes like a circus, capable of holding eight to ten thousand people, and they were quite full ! The President of Peru, and his staff, occupied the seat of honour.

" The combatants of the bull are eighteen in number ; nine on foot, and nine on horseback. Four of the horsemen are armed with short strong lances, and four of the footmen with strong two-edged swords, and red flags. The other ten foot and horsemen have no weapons but red cloaks. Well ! the door is opened, and in rushes the furious bull ; a number of small rockets are discharged at him, and there is a figure of a man opposing him, which he instantly dashes his horns into, thereby exploding the fireworks with which it is filled. The maddened animal now rushes at some of the footmen, who, flourishing their red cloaks, drew him towards the side of the bull ring. Some prodigious feats of courage and activity were performed by some of these people, who did not scruple to engage the furious beast in the middle of the ring when he charged them, throwing the red cloak over his horns, when he retreated, and was met again on his second charge as before. Some of them, meanwhile, are still further maddening the bull, by throwing small pliable lances into him. He now generally leaves the footmen, and charges his mounted antagonists. Those with red cloaks attack him, and, as he is charging them, throw these over his head ; the lancers also attacking him, and endeavouring to strike him through the heart. One man I saw strike his lance in behind the shoulders, and actually drive it into the ground. The bull of course fell dead. Generally, however, he gets terribly mangled by flesh wounds, till faint with exertion and loss of blood. The *matadors*, or swordsmen, attack him with their swords, holding out the red flags with the sword concealed under it. The bull charges full at them. Starting aside, the *matador* buries his sword in the poor animal's side, who now falls, and the *matador* drives the weapon into his spine, killing him at once. Then money, garlands of flowers, and what not, are thrown, chiefly by the women, to the conquering actors in the brutal scene, and the slaughtered bull is carried off by gaily caparisoned horses, amidst fireworks, military music, and a thousand plaudits. Sometimes the bull does not shew good fight, and rather shuns the horses, apparently depressed by the noise and fireworks; the head *matador* then engages him. One bull shewed tremendous fight, actually gutting six horses; their humane (?) riders spurring them at the bull, though their bowels were trailing after them. This bull could be brought down no-how, but by one of the *matadors* striking from behind, and ham-stringing him; and yet he shambled round the circus on his two fore legs, and killed a horse after this, and it was with great difficulty that the head *matador* could get near enough to give him the fatal stroke. Eighteen bulls were killed. I could not help often wishing that some of the humane tormentors of these noble animals had got the stroke, when some of their irrational allies, the horses, suffered. I left the ring half-sick, and thanking God, that there are but few places where humanity is at a sufficiently low ebb to allow of such things being universal and favourite pastime. They are to be seen in Lima every Monday for six months, and form an important item in the government revenue.

" This Peru is a blessed country indeed! A revolution generally every six months. A general manages to get into the good graces of the soldiery, heads an insurrection, captures, and shoots the President. In a very short time his own popularity ceases, and he is in turn seized, and shot. They had an excellent fortress at Callao, but the president dismantled it, as he had no man he could trust to command it. Travelling is well nigh impossible. Even the nine miles of road between the two cities of Lima and Callao cannot be travelled on foot, and nothing is more common than for the coaches running between the two places to be stopped and robbed. A lasso comes whirring from behind a tree ; the driver is *noosed*, and half-a-dozen long muskets are pointed into the carriage windows, with, ' your money or your life !' These robbers are generally soldiers, and the president dare not punish them. Every man must take the law into his own hands, and murder and assassination are, in consequence, every day occurrences. No one thinks of going across street unarmed. Englishmen only are little molested. I asked the driver the reason why a coach was not attacked if it were known that there were three or four English in it. ' *Son diabolos!*' he said, ' the English are devils ! they shoot, or will be shot, sooner than give up their money, but we poor Peruvians would be sent to the galleys for life if we killed a soldier, and without even a trial.' Such is Peru ! These are the descendants of Pizarro, and of Cortes ! The curse of the blood of the Incas has descended on them, and no nation can be much deeper in slavery and crime of the blackest description.

" We leave this place to-morrow (Christmas Eve) ;

did I ever need a remembrancer of home, the season would recal it. It seems strange to talk of Christmas in burning Peru; still we hear them speaking of Christmas turkeys, &c., just as if we were among the snows of England. God bless, and send you all a merry Christmas! I may never meet you again at that festive season, but I well know I will not be forgotten when you meet, and my spirit will overleap the distance, and again form one of you. Sun and storm will have beaten over me before I can expect again to see you, but the heart will remain the same.

"We touch at Guayaquil, and then proceed to the Gallipagos, from thence straight to Panama. I cannot express how anxious I have become for letters; I pray God daily, the news may be good. We expect to be there in February. From thence of course you will again hear fully from me. I need not send my dearest fervent love to my beloved mamma, brothers and sisters, uncle and aunt, all know they have that. I would write the others, but as it is likely my letters from Panama may reach England overland, quite as soon as this or earlier, and as I have nothing to say but what I have given you in this it would seem needless. God bless you all, ever prays your truly affectionate son,

" T. E."

" Excuse blunders, the hour is late, and I am hurried."

" *25th December.*—I found there was no chance of

this letter reaching you under six months, sending it round Cape Horn. I am, accordingly, taking it with me to forward *via* Panama from Guayaquil, or Panama itself. This is Christmas day, and need I say how my thoughts are with you. We are literally roasting; thermometer at ninety degrees; dull, dreary, and stagnant is every thing around. An attempt to drink 'absent friends' after dinner, stuck in our throats, and the clumsy mirth of the forecastle jarred on our ears. Home comes across us yet more vividly on a day like this, and we feel there needs much to weigh in the balance against so long an exile."

The following letter to a fellow student, a young clergyman, is given entire, as a lively *resume* of all the preceding, and also as a touching circumstance that it never met the eye it was destined to gladden; for before it reached Britain, both writer and correspondent had met in, let us hope and believe, "the better land."

"Fonda Ingtera, Quillota, Chili,
"At the foot of the Cordillera of the Andes,
"21st November 1845.

"Yes, verily, oh! dearly beloved, most orthodox Brichimis,—thy quondam associate and brother botanist,—the late illustrious Andersonian Professor of Botany,—he with whom thou hast scrambled along the Findhorn, and waded in Loch S——; whom thou hast, by looks at least, if not by words, upbraided for his levity, now sits in a lovely valley of vineyards, under a broiling sun; the snowy peaks of the Andes in his view; his paper cram full of plants; his sketch-book of drawings, and his stockings of fleas! Oh, *tempora!* oh, *mores!* thou canst not imagine the beauty of the Chilian plants, or the diabolical biting of Chilian fleas!

" I shall now give you a short sketch of my proceedings, as I dare say you will have no objections to hear how your flighty friend gets on in the southern hemisphere.

" We left Plymouth on the 26th June, having been there ten days. I spent the time very pleasantly, chiefly from the kindness of the Reverend W. S. Hore, with whom I had some delightful excursions, and who has a dozen (more or less) very pretty sisters. This was too pleasant to last, and we speedily got into blue water, spent a day at Teneriffe, all parched up and barren, and then took our solitary way across the Atlantic, viewing the usual wonders of the tropics; shaving at the line; sharks, flying fish, and frigate birds; then into that most splendid bay of Rio-de-Janeiro, and there, for ten days, I revelled amongst tropical vegetation, which as far exceeds my anticipations, as it does now my powers of description. After that, cold and bleak was the weather we soon got into, and in a month the Falkland Isles were approached. There it was snowing and blowing; dead of winter; no plants in flower; a small, miserable settlement, &c. And then a dull, dreary two months; oh, the pleasures of rounding Cape Horn! gales, rain, and cold, fierce hurricanes, and enormous icebergs. Our live stock all died, and we had nothing to eat save Her Majesty's allowance, commonly termed ' salt horse.' With what delight did we hail the blue skies and placid waters of the well named Pacific. We looked into the bays of Valdivia, and La Concepcion, to see if the admiral was there. We got fuel at the latter place, and arrived here this day eight days. Sick of tossing and tumbling, I obtained leave to go inland; hired three horses, (one for myself, one for my guide, and the other for my paper and other necessaries), and bolted.

" It would be tedious to tell you of the plants; not a flora in the world like Chili! I botanize all day, partly walking, partly riding. The capacious *vascula* are filled. We have shot two brace of small partridges, and with rice we carry in our saddle bags, my olive skinned guide is dishing them up in a small iron pan, while I am drying my plants. Then we wrap ourselves in the sheep skins that form our saddles, and the blue clear Chilian sky for our canopy, we sleep well, and dream of home. I confess this wild wandering life has many charms for me, but, as poor Peter Peebles justly remarks, ' there are unco drawbacks.'

" The length of time spent on the tame uninteresting sea, the jading sense of haste when in port, the absence of many luxuries, and the want of congenial society rank pre-eminent, and combine to take off somewhat from the charms of such a life as mine. Still when one is let loose among these grand forests or giant mountains, even for ever so short a time, where every sight and sound is novel and intensely interesting, these indeed are moments which amply repay previous months of discomfort. Well! I wish you were along with me. I often sigh for some one to chatter with in my own way about botany."

" On passage from Guayaquil to the Gallapagos,
" 3rd December 1845.

" After a week of the rambling life above mentioned, dearly beloved, and quondam associate, my three reams of botanical paper were full, my leave expired, and I returned to Valparaiso, which we left shortly afterwards. The flora of Chili delighted me much. I enjoyed my short stay exceedingly, and was very sorry to leave it.

" Our next resting place was Callao, the port of Lima, which is a splendid old Spanish town, where yet linger the blood, the manners, and language of the ancient Spanish hidalgos,—those mail-clad followers of Cortes, and of Pizarro, who carried death and desolation among the naked aborigines of a mighty continent.

" I saw grand mass, and a bull fight, and did nothing else for the four days we were there. We left on Christmas Eve, and spent at sea a dull broiling

Christmas-day. We then ran in for an hour or two to a miserable burnt up little place called Payta, and also for a day lay off the island of Santa Clara, gulf of Guayaquil; and now we are on our way to the Gallapagos, where we shall be for a month, and then proceed to Panama, where we shall get (what we have not had since we left England) letters from home. I believe we shall be thereabouts till April, then to the Columbia River. For three or four years we shall be surveying the coast from Guayaquil to the Oregon, and, I dare say, shall return home by New Zealand, the Moluccas, Singapore, &c., round the world.

" Now, old boy ! so much for a full, true, and particular account of my wanderings and ponderings hitherto. I am very comfortable, and have plenty of room, and all other facilities. I sometimes wish I could see old Scotland, and old friends, for a little now and then, but that can't be for many days. Good bye old fellow ! God bless you.—Your affectionate friend,

" T. E."

There was besides the last, another letter that was never delivered. It was to Professor Forbes, A long time elapsed ere the desk in which it was found reached Britain; much longer still, before the sorrowing family in Shetland found courage to examine those last melancholy but precious relics, and by that time

Edward Forbes too had sunk into an early and lamented grave.*

The letter alluded to is dated 24th December. It consists almost entirely of scientific details, describing the result of dredging in Callao Bay, and referring to full particulars sent from Valparaiso. It was left unfinished, no doubt to have additions before being sent from Panama.

> " H. M. S. Herald,
> " Off the Gallapagos Isles,
> " 7th January 1846.

" My dear Brother.—In less than a month now we expect to be at Panama, where of course there will be a large budget of letters from home awaiting me. I am at this distance of time extremely anxious to hear of you all, but trust in God the news may be good, and then all will be well. We are just now standing off and on the Gallapagos Islands, and in the morning expect to get in. We shall only be a week or two there. They look bleak and parched up, which, considering that they are just on the equator, is rather surprising

---

* This may be the proper place to mention, that the voluminous correspondence of young Edmondston with his beloved and valued friend Forbes, was some years ago unfortunately destroyed, and with it, it is believed, his journal and sketches, for after research at the Admiralty, and elsewhere, they have not been discovered.

at first. The weather is most intensely hot, and as this is the rainy season, we are having frequent rains, so it is far from being comfortable. I would gladly exchange it for the cold and snow you are doubtless having now. Yet I do not suffer so much from the heat as some of our officers do, who have been accustomed to it all their lives, I suppose because I have always plenty to do, and little time to think of anything but the work immediately on hand. I have now become quite accustomed to the habits and routine of a ship, although it took some time to get over shore habits, which are so exceedingly different from those one must become trained to on making a ship one's home. Want of room is the great nuisance at sea, though I am now very well off in this respect, as far as a place to work in is concerned, having got a large cabin on the poop fitted up expressly for a museum. Yet a cabin six feet by eight, in which you must stow bed, chest of drawers, wash-stand, &c., is rather confined space, especially in a hot climate, when there can be no greater luxury than plenty of room and air. You would be a good deal amused at what trifling circumstances are considered luxuries after a long sea cruise,—such as, being able to look out of one's window, having plenty of water to wash with, &c. Our mode of life is very monotonous, as may be supposed,—breakfast at eight; the drum beats to quarters at ten, when all hands must attend on the quarter-deck; from that time till three

I am at my work ; dinner at three. At six, to quarters again ; about seven we all generally assemble on tho poop, to smoke a cigar, and walk about till ten, then turn in. This is the routine on week days. On Sundays we all muster in undress uniforms, coats, and swords ; the marines are exercised ; the captain always dines with us on Sundays, and then there is of course a solemn turn out.

" So much for my life at sea. When we are in harbour it is very different ; all then is hurry and bustle. At day-break I set off till about ten or eleven, when the heat becomes too intense, then seek the most shady place in a wood, and sleep an hour or two. I have then generally two or three hours work in tho evening, and a boat comes for me at dark. This will be my life, if God spares me, for the next three or four years, and it is far from being an unpleasant one, though the alternations of exertion and comparative in-activity are more violent than could be wished. The constant succession of new places and objects, brings with it a never failing charm ; while the thought, that by congenial occupation now, one is perhaps laying a foundation for after reputation and independence, is not the least agreeable part.

" I have, since we left, come over so many miles, and seen so many different places, that the time seems twice as long as it really is. I need not describe to you any of the places where we have touched, as I have done so in my letters to papa, &c., which you would see. Of course the great interest to me lies in the various natural productions, and when one is rambling in the woods, little can be seen of the manners of the inhabitants.

" I wish you had been with me during my rambles on the skirts of the Chilian Andes. You recollect our childish wonder at the far famed condor. These fellows abound in the mountains of South America; they measure generally eight or ten feet between the wings. It was not until after many trials that I succeeded in getting a shot. One day, in the grey of the morning, I was descending a steep pass in the mountains, when my guide drew my attention to seven of them sitting on a ledge far above us. I dismounted, and climbed up till I got within eighty yards, and then with my rifle brought down a beautiful fellow. He was shot through the neck. They are black, with a white back, and red head. I also shot a guanaco, or wild llama, which is between the size of a sheep and a Shetland cow. Another kind of game, *rather* smaller, is plentiful, viz., humming birds. I got many of these, generally taking them like moths in my insect net, and I kept three alive for some time on moist sugar. All the birds here are truly magnificent. Orioles are the most plentiful in Chili; they are mostly blue, yellow or scarlet, and black. There are also many most elegant egrets and herons, besides multitudes of other birds. I think the most lovely bird I ever saw is common in Callao harbour. It is a snow white tern, scarcely larger than a sparrow, and seems new. At the same place swarm, in thousands, immense brown pelicans, with pouches that can hold a dozen salmon.

" I saw a bull fight at Lima ; a beastly spectacle, which I would never go a second time to see.

" ' Yule Day ' is now drawing very near ; an unnoticed time with us, though to me it recals very pleasing associations. If you are all, as I trust in God you may be, well, I suppose the *whip-coll* and shortbread will, as usual, be forthcoming in the parlour of Buness, and you will think on the far absent member of your little circle, as he often thinks of you all. Well ! parting and absence, my dear Biot, are amongst the ills of this transitory existence. May we all, by the grace of Him who can grant it, aspire after that state where they shall be unknown. It is now near ten o'clock, at which time the sergeant of marines goes round to see that all lights are out, and being (alas !) amenable to military law, I must conclude. My kindest love to you all. My prayers and blessings be with you ever. Remember me most kindly to good Mr Macintosh, to whom I will write one of these days. My love to aunt Mary, and our cousins of Broomhill. —Your truly affectionate brother,   T. E."

" H. M. S. Herald.

" On passage to the Gallapagos,

January 1846.

" My dearest Uncle.—I wrote you fully from Valparaiso, and forwarded a long letter to papa from Paita to Panama, which, I suppose, will reach home in about two months. We are now on our passage to the Gallapagos Islands, which, I suppose, we will reach in about a week. We shall be twenty days there, and then proceed to Panama, when our after movements will greatly depend on the orders which will be waiting us there; but I believe it is pretty certain that we shall continue about the gulf of Panama till the end of April, and then depart for the Columbia River, spend the summer there, and return to winter about San Francisco, or some other place in Old California.

" I enjoyed myself much during the few days the ship staid at Callao. I went with some of my messmates to Lima; introduced myself to an old botanical merchant there, who knows Hooker, &c., and with him I was very comfortable.

" Lima may be considered the outskirts of civilization, as far as our cruise is concerned, for all the places down on the coast are, I believe, miserable in the extreme. It is a splendid town, a fast decaying, but magnificent relic of the old Spaniards,—those mail-clad conquerors, who once were the masters of well nigh all this coast, and who have left their manners and their language to attest their past dominion.

" I wish you could, with me, have seen Lima ! It is the most completely foreign town you could imagine ; cram full of churches, convents and priests. Every now and then you are arrested by the deep toll of a bell, and see the whole of the passengers uncover, and kneel on one knee in the street. This is the homage paid by all—catholics and heretics—to the requiem bell, and the effect to a stranger is very singular. I could not help fancying how extraordinary it would be, if the tide that pours through Cheapside were to be, by the passing sound of a bell, as suddenly arrested and brought down on their *marrow-bones.* The women wear a dress unknown in any other city. It is a black silk shawl, fastened round the waist, and coming over the head and face, where it is held by the left hand ; thus only one eye is visible ; though you would not think it, it is a most elegant dress. I went on Sunday to hear grand mass celebrated in the cathedral of San Carlos. It is an enormous building ; so large, that people appear mere beetles at the other end of it. It is most elaborately carved and decorated, and all the panels filled with fine fresco paintings. The high vaulted roofs are hung with banners and drapery of various kinds, and the whole building is lighted by thousands of wax candles, some of them twenty feet high. The deep tones of the organ, the chanting of the prayers, the magnificent gold-embroidered dresses of the priests, and the multitude of kneeling people, formed, *as a picture*, the finest thing I ever saw ; though I certainly cannot participate in the feelings of those, who say these things are accessories to the spirit of devotion. To me it seems quite the reverse, and the wilder and simpler the temple, the nearer I think myself to the God of nature, who will be worshipped in a 'house not made with hands.'

" The houses in Lima are mostly old, elaborately carved, and fantastically painted externally,—all with balconies, where, in the evening, may be seen the dark-eyed senors and senoras in their rich dresses, lolling, and smoking choice havannahs. I have managed to pick up Spanish pretty well. I can read any book in it, and speak and understand it very well. It is a very easy and transcendantly beautiful language. Of all things in the earth to raise one to the seventh heaven of romance, Spanish poetry is the best; and a richer treat than to wander through the streets of Lima in the evening, and catch the strain of some old Castilian song, telling, as they generally do, of the warlike deeds of the conquerors of Peru and Mexico, cannot be imagined. It is a wicked, a romantic city, and for a time *will* drive the dull realities of life out of one's head.

" We left this ' city of palaces ' on Christmas Eve. Such a Christmas as we spent ! It was a day not of cheerful communion with dear friends, but of bitter thoughts that they were so far away ; and one who is exiled for a long time from them soon feels, that what he perhaps lightly thought of before, was his greatest joy, and that nothing can make up for the want of the society of those he loves. So it was with us, and our Christmas passed heavily in consequence. Some were bending their thoughts towards England, and its comparatively fertile shores, but my thoughts were farther away on a little storm beaten, barren bit of bog and rock, which, poor though it be, bears the magic name of my *home.*

" The weather just now is terribly hot ; thermometer frequently above one hundred degrees in the poop cabin. You can have no idea of the lassitude and indisposition to exertion which such a temperature creates ! On shore it is bad enough, but at sea, where there is no change in regulation diet, &c., according to weather, it is still worse. We shall be out of it, however, in a month or two, and get northwards to a more congenial climate. - - - - Nothing can exceed the captain's kindness. He has built me on the poop a large and commodious cabin for my workshop, as I found I could not get very well on in the chart room. Here I have shelves for my plants, books, and spirit jars, and every possible convenience of room, air, and light,—four large windows,—the place is as large as an ordinary bed-room, and that on board ship seems a perfect wilderness. - - - - - -

> " Post-office Bay,
> " Charles Island, Gallapagos,
> " 14th January 1846.

" From the name one would fancy letters might be sent from hence, but here as elsewhere, it seems, *quasi lucus non ab lucendo*, for neither post-office nor inhabitant is any where in sight. We arrived here four days ago, and expect to sail to-night, but I have made a noble collection, well nigh every thing being new here. This is the only island of the group where there are any inhabitants, about forty exiles from *La Republica del Ecuador* (the Republic of the Equator, or Guayaquil and Quito). We are about six miles off, subsisting on bananas, pumpkins, and wild pigs. The island is volcanic, and covered with a dense thorny brushwood almost impassable. At the expense of tearing some duck, and flesh too, I have got many good plants though. Sea birds and seals abound. I shot ten of the latter the day before yesterday. They are the Urigne seals, and have small external ears. I went in a gig to shoot birds, and on rounding a small point, found myself quite surrounded by seals gaping and gazing at the boat. I had a little rifle in the boat, and soon turned up one or two. One immense female came sternly on towards the boat open mouthed. I fired a doze of shot in her face, and though wounded and bleeding she again returned to the charge. I had then my rifle loaded, and at ten yards sent a bullet down her throat. We towed this one, the largest, on board. She measured thirteen feet, nine inches long. The other nine that I bagged were smaller, none exceeding seven feet. *But truggs! dey wir the most bootiful fish I ever did see!* I thought of Burrafirth, and Wetherholm, Bartel, and all the accompaniments of your seal hunting. More curious still, as shewing the extraordinary tameness of these animals here,—I was bathing yesterday on a sandy beach, and seeing a dark looking object run at me, made for the shore in no little trepidation, for sharks swarm here. Before I well felt the ground, a small seal came alongside of me, rubbed his head against my legs, and accompanied me to the shore. Though my gun was lying loaded, and I took aim two or three times, and could have blown his head to shivers, I could not have heart to do it, he looked so tame and gentle, or, as a Spaniard who was by said, *tan manso* (so quiet.) All the birds are equally tame, a gun being almost superfluous, for nearly all may be killed by a stick or a hat. We go to two or three other of the islands, and then to Panama."

When the last two of these letters were written, and he ' *lingered loth to quit the pen,*' how little probably did he imagine they were to be the last he should indite to the home for which he expressed such fervent attachment.

Of the result of all the eager hopes and anticipations with which it will be observed he approached the Gallapagos,—a field for his examination so interesting and unique,—no record remains, except a few lines at the close of the last letter to his uncle, which indeed was left unfinished. Without doubt, particulars, copious and interesting, would as usual have been narrated to father or mother on the voyage to Panama. Alas! alas! the ready graphic pen, the warm heart, the busy brain, were in that short interval stilled for ever! Yet why regret that the powerful intellect, the quenchless thirst for knowledge, were removed to the boundless field of infinity,—that the fervent affections and glowing aspirations were transplanted to a more congenial clime? While in the performance of his duty, without time for a murmur, or a farewell, or an instant even to become sensible of the stroke or the pang of death, he was stricken in his life's first prime, we hope and believe, only to serve his God, and drink in the elevating wisdom he loved and aspired after, in a higher, and much nobler sphere!

The following are two accounts of the accident— one from an eye witness, and another from one of the officers left on board the ship—written at the time it took place :—

The first is by Lieut. John B. Anderson, at that time

one of the midshipmen of the " Herald," and a witness of the occurrence,—

" It was on the evening of the 23rd January 1846, that H. M. S. Herald dropped anchor in Sua Bay, on the coast of Peru, close to the river Esmeraldos. Sua Bay is distinguished by two cliffs, or bluff promontories, enclosing a sandy beach; in the centre of the bay stands a palm-thatched house, erected on poles, in the centre of a row of cocoa nut trees. On the right of the bay is an extensive water course running into the sea, and on its bank, close to the water, stood a laden orange tree. The sandy beach stretches pretty far into the land, which is covered by an almost impenetrable forest and under-wood.

" On the morning after our arrival, the captain landed, and fixed the observatory tent on the left hand bluff, while another boat landed Mr Thomas Edmond-ston, the naturalist, accompanied by Mr Whiffin, captain's clerk, Mr W. Billings, assistant-surgeon, and myself, with several others. Mr Edmondston carried a silver-mounted rifle, presented to him by Prince Albert, while I carried for him a large tin case for specimens, and a butterfly net. On landing, we pulled some oranges, which we found were bitter, and so left them.

" We then proceeded to the house, where we found a solitary old Indian women, who made us a few cigars, and on the arrival of another Indian, we obtained some young cocoa nuts, for which he climbed the tree. We then struck into the wood, and soon lost our way, and continued wandering till about four o'clock in the afternoon, firing occasionally to attract attention. The barking of a dog close at hand directed us at length to a clearing in the woods, used for a tobacco plantation, and close to a noble river (perhaps the Esmeraldos), which we had not before seen. Then we saw some Indian huts, and men distilling *aquadiente* (a native rum), with a rude apparatus from the sugar cane. We here obtained refreshments with *chee chee*, made from the juice of the pine apple, and Mr Whiffin shot a bird at an immense distance, that was perched on the summit of a gigantic tree at the edge of the clearing.

" Mr Edmondston then took the rifle, (Mr Whiffin's); placed a green cocoa nut on the ground, and firing at it, at about one hundred yards, divided it in the centre. He then examined the piece, which was a buffalo rifle, carrying twelve to the pound, and expressed a desire to have it.

We then obtained a guide, who took us by a small track to the beach, where we found the two boats waiting. One of the men took the guns and specimens, &c., off to the boat, and laid them in the stern-sheets, and as the water was shallow, and the surf rising, the men tucked up their trousers, and came to carry us off. Mr Whiffin was first, and Mr Edmondston was carried on the back of Thomas Stocker, coxswain

of the whaler; myself, and Mr Hutchinson,* midshipman, following.

" During the act of going off, one of the people in
the whale boat entangled the lock of the large rifle
above mentioned in the foot of his trousers, and in
lifting the hammer it exploded. The ball first passed
through Mr Whiffin's arm, and struck Mr Edmondston
in the right temple, coming out behind the ear. He
had just remarked, ' Hutchinson, I wish I had your long
legs,' when he fell back off Stocker's shoulders, and
went under the water. Some few breathless moments
elapsed before it was discovered what had happened,
and he was lifted quite dead. The sad intelligence
was shouted to the officers still on the beach, and every
one simultaneously discharged their pieces.

" The ball had whistled close to the observatory tent,
and they shouted out about it.

" The boats proceeded on board, and the remains of
the beloved and lamented young gentleman were placed
under a screen on the half-deck, covered with the
union jack.

" The carpenters were employed all night making
the coffin, and a rough head-board, and cross.

" Next day the remains were conveyed on shore,

---

* Late Commander John Hutchinson, who was lost in H. M.
S. " Orpheus," off the coast of New Zealand.

the whole of the ship's boats with ensigns half-mast high attending, and he was laid a little way from the beach, at the back of the right hand bluff. The funeral service of the Church of England was read by Captain, now Rear-Admiral, Kellett, C.B.

" The Herald soon after weighed for the northward."

Extract from " A Midshipman's Diary," by Commander Chimmo, R.N. Published by J. D. Potter, London: 1862.

" It seldom or ever happens that, throughout a long and arduous cruise in unknown places, and along unexplored shores, there is not some misfortune to damp and depress the spirits of all those connected with it, and throw a gloom of melancholy around, which time and change of scene alone can efface ; and it was now our sad lot to experience this.

" All the boats had been away in this new, interesting, and inviting country, taking many of the officers, here shooting, there fishing, some collecting specimens in geology, botany, and conchology ; others reaping richer productions.

" The day had been fine, but it was now threatening ; clouds and lightning were to be seen sea-ward, and a surf had already risen on the beach. Towards evening all had assembled on the shore to return to the ship, and there was difficulty in rushing into the boats without getting wet. During this, the report of a gun was heard; a rush to one boat followed; all pulled hastily on board, and our feelings may be a little imagined, when our most amiable, most beloved, admired, and accomplished shipmate, was handed up the side a lifeless corpse! He was laid out on a grating, the body still warm, and the union jack thrown gently over him. He had been getting into the boat, the fowling-pieces and rifles were laid below, when some one, rushing through the surf, and jumping into the boat, placed his foot on the lock of one of the rifles, and it exploded; the ball passing through his temple, he fell over without a groan. Death was instantaneous. Many near him escaped by a miracle. This sudden and deplorable accident struck us all with horror. Thus died a most amiable and beloved messmate, a kind and willing shipmate, a young and intelligent man, who was an ornament to his profession.

" That was a mournful and dismal night. It was my middle watch. The rain poured in torrents, the thunder pealed forth its deafening sounds; the lightning flashed its terrifying streaks all around, displaying to us a scene at once terrible, awful, and truly melancholy.

" His remains were carried next day to their final place of rest, where we paid the last tokens of respect, leaving a small sheet of copper nailed on a board, bearing an inscription, simple and touching. It did not require much consideration to depart from a place that had so suddenly deprived us of a talented and much esteemed friend."

Thus, by a lamentable accident, in the early prime of his days,—for he had but completed his twentieth year,—full of health and enthusiasm, of noble aspirations and honourable ambition, died this young Shetlander,—a youth of rare promise, whom nature had gifted with splendid talents, and with a warm, loving, and reverent heart. In the course of an inscrutable Providence,—all whose ways we yet humbly acknowledge to be wise and good,—the light of his young life was quenched. Natural science lost one of her most ardent votaries, surviving relatives the pride of their house and name, and a large circle of friends a brother naturalist, whose future career they were wont confidently to prophesy would prove at once distinguished and useful. And thus the Shadow fell over the Sunshine.

-----*0*-----

WITH the following beautiful lines, by Alaric A. Watts, so pathetically and singularly appropriate to Thomas Edmondston, we close this record of his life :—

HE left his home with a bounding heart,
　For the world was all before him;
And felt it scarce a pain to part,
　Such sun-bright dreams came o'er him:
He turned him to visions of future years,
　The rainbow's hues were 'round them;
And a father's bodings, a mother's tears,
　Might not weigh with the hopes that crowned
　　　them.

That mother's cheek is far paler now,
　Than when she last caress'd him;
There's an added gloom on that father's brow,
　Since the hour when last he bless'd him:
Oh! that all human hopes should prove
　Like the flowers that will fade to-morrow,
And the cankering fears of anxious love
　Ever end in truth and sorrow!

He left his home with a swelling sail,
　Of fame and fortune dreaming,—
With a spirit as free as the vernal gale,
　Or the pennant above him streaming:
He hath reached his gaol;—by a distant wave,
　'Neath a sultry sun they laid him;
And strangers bent above his grave,
　When the last sad rites were paid him.

He should have died in his own loved land,
  With friends and kindred near him ;
Not have withered thus on a foreign strand,
  With no cherished friend to cheer him.
But what recks it now ? Is his sleep less sound,
  Where the breezes wild have swept him,
Than if home's green turf his grave had bound,
  Or the hearts he loved had wept him ?

Then why repine ? Can he feel the rays
  That pestilent sun sheds o'er him ;
Or share the grief that must cloud the days
  Of the friends that now deplore him ?
No ; his bark's at anchor, its sails are furled,
  It hath 'scaped the storms deep chiding ;
And safe from the buffeting waves of the world,
  In a haven of peace is riding.

www.ingramcontent.com/pod-product-compliance
Lightning Source LLC
Chambersburg PA
CBHW031147120726
47905CB00006B/1849